PRAISE FOR THE
STEEL BROTHERS SAGA

"Hold onto the reins:
this red-hot Steel story is one wild ride."
~ A Love So True

"A spellbinding read from a
New York Times *bestselling author!"*
~ BookBub

"I'm in complete awe of this author. She has gone and
delivered an epic, all-consuming, addicting, insanely
intense story that's had me holding my breath, my
heart pounding and my mind reeling."
~ The Sassy Nerd

"Absolutely UNPUTDOWNABLE!"
~ Bookalicious Babes

SMOLDER

SMOLDER

STEEL BROTHERS SAGA
BOOK TWENTY-TWO
HELEN HARDT

WATERHOUSE PRESS

For my father

CHAPTER ONE

Rory

I've always loved kissing.

My favorite part of a new relationship is the first kiss. Nothing compares to that first taste of another person, the passion and excitement it brings.

That first kiss is when I can tell whether I'm really into someone. I'm twenty-eight years old, and I've done a lot of kissing of both women and men, but still… Kissing always mesmerizes me.

Especially that first damned kiss.

I can still get wet from that first kiss. That's how I know something more is brewing, that the physical chemistry is there even if the emotion isn't yet.

I don't like to generalize, but men are usually more aggressive kissers than women are. Must be a testosterone thing. I enjoy the primal passion of a kiss from a man as well as the soft gentleness of a kiss from a woman.

But a kiss from Brock Steel?

Seriously in a category all its own.

I didn't plan on making out with Brock behind the band's van at Talon Steel's welcome home party. I'm damned lucky my brother didn't catch us. He's already on edge now that Callie is engaged to Donny Steel, his high school rival.

At thirty-two, he ought to leave high school rivalries behind him, but men are different from women.

No one knows that better than I do. Perhaps that's why I love them both. I love masculinity, and I love femininity. I love everything in between. The similarities and the differences.

As much as I love masculine men, I also love feminine women. I appreciate what's different between the sexes. I'm not attracted to overly masculine women or overly feminine men.

What sets them apart is beautiful to me.

I accepted my bisexuality long ago, and it makes sense for me. I honestly don't know whether I'll end up with a man or a woman as my life mate.

But there's one thing I *do* know.

I want to be a mother.

And my biological clock is ticking away.

I can always adopt. Or perhaps I'll get involved with a younger woman who doesn't have the biological clock problem. Truly though? I'm ready now. I don't want to be one of those women having babies in her late thirties and early forties. I want to be young and energetic as I raise my child.

So what's this got to do with Brock Steel being an amazing kisser?

I'm almost afraid to put it into thought.

Maybe if I say it to Callie, I'll be able to accept that I'm actually thinking it.

Last time I saw her, she was headed into the house with Donny. They've been in there for a while.

I know what that means. They're somewhere having a quickie. Why not? They just got engaged. Plus, with both of them living at their parents' houses, they probably haven't had a lot of alone time lately.

I know my sister. She marches to the beat of her own drummer. She won't have an issue with a quickie while a big party is going on outside.

And Donny? As one of the original Three Rake-a-teers, he won't either.

Still, I head to the deck. Maybe I can find her.

Bingo. In the kitchen… She throws a half-eaten piece of cake into the garbage. Unusual for her. Callie hates waste, but then again, neither of us has had much of an appetite lately, with all that's going on. Pat Lamone has seen to that.

I walk through the French doors and into the kitchen. "Callie! There you are. I need to talk to you."

My sister raises her eyebrows and glances at her fiancé.

"Go ahead," he says. "I'll be out in a minute."

Callie nods and follows me back out onto the deck. I grab her arm and pull her over to a secluded part of the yard.

"Cal," I say, "I have an idea, and don't say anything until you hear me out."

CHAPTER TWO

Brock

An hour earlier…

She's tall, with gorgeous dark-brown hair and big milk-chocolate-brown eyes fringed in long black lashes.

Rory Pike.

She's singing with her brother, Jesse, and the band tonight, so she's dressed like a rocker. Skinny black jeans, leather boots with silver adornments, and a tight lacy T-shirt that accentuates those tits that could kill a man.

I've been with a lot of women, but I swear to God, Rory Pike is the hottest thing walking. She always has been.

Her sisters, Callie and Maddie, are also beautiful, but Rory? She's something special for sure. She lights up a room. Hell, the whole freaking yard. Every eye is on her when she's on stage. She's like a magnet for men and for women.

I should leave her alone. I should listen to Donny. She did just break up with someone—a gorgeous woman, no less.

Can I compete with Raine Cunningham? She's also a hottie, but she's all girls all the time from what I hear…though I admit a threesome crossed my mind more than once while they were together.

David Simpson, my cousin from Uncle Bryce and Aunt

4

Marjorie, stands beside me.

"It's never going to happen, bro," Dave says.

I feign innocence. "What's never going to happen?"

"You and Rory Pike."

"She likes men."

"That's not what I'm talking about. She's out of your league."

I have to stop myself from erupting in laughter. "Out of *my* league?"

"Prom queen, homecoming queen... Not to mention all the men here—and quite a few women—have their eyes on her."

"Have you forgotten who you're talking to? I seem to remember beating you out for prom king our year."

"By one vote."

"One vote is all it takes."

"This isn't high school anymore, cuz. Most of her serious relationships have been with women, from what I hear."

"Do I look like I'm planning for a serious relationship?"

Dave laughs. "That's my point. Everyone knows *you're* not looking for a serious relationship. But Rory Pike is older. Closing in on thirty. She most likely *is* looking for something beyond a quick fuck at your place. That's why she's out of your league."

"So that's what you meant. I knew you couldn't mean I'm not good-looking enough for her."

Dave rolls his eyes. "You are the absolute worst."

"Yeah? I never denied it, man. I'm going for it."

"Not if I get to her first." Dave smiles.

My cousin looks exactly like his mother—with his chiseled face and dark-brown hair—except he's got his father's blue eyes. Me? I'm a dead ringer for my father, Jonah Steel. Nearly black hair and dark-brown eyes. Dave and I have been fighting over women since we were big enough to toddle up to the swings on the playground.

We even shared a woman once back in college. Yeah, a threesome. It was hot, but we never did it again. Too weird seeing each other naked. But damn, the woman had a great time. Two men focused solely on her. Her moans alone were worth the effort.

I'm sure as hell not going to share Rory Pike with anyone— especially not my male model cousin. He's too fucking pretty. Me? I'm more ruggedly handsome—according to women, anyway. Chicks like that. At least that's what they say.

Of course they like pretty boys like Dave too.

Which is why I'm not letting him near Rory Pike.

Last I saw Rory, she was headed behind the stage. The band is probably getting ready to do a set.

Not only is Rory a looker, but she also has the voice of an angel. She's classically trained, but damn, the girl can rock as well as Joan Jett herself.

I'll have to get past her brother, Jesse, and the rest of the band, which includes her cousin as well. Jesse and Cage might not look too kindly on me hitting on Rory. Jesse already lost one sister to a Steel boy tonight when Donny got engaged to Callie.

Yeah, I should stay away. Definitely.

Or . . . definitely not.

Rory Pike is here, Rory Pike is available, Rory Pike is the hottest thing walking, and I'm horny as hell for her.

I walk behind the stage. Jesse and Cage aren't around, which is a good thing. The drummer, Dragon Locke, is messing with some electrical cords.

"Hey, Dragon."

"Hey, Brock."

"Where's Rory?"

"She went out to the van to get some stuff."

"Yeah? Where are you all parked?"

"Out front."

"Perfect. Thanks."

The front of the house. No one will be at the front of the house because everyone's back here enjoying the party. Pretty much the whole town is here to welcome my uncle Talon home from the hospital.

His shooting is always on my mind—along with the fact that my father may have been the intended target. I'm trying like hell not to let it consume me. At least not tonight. And Rory Pike could well be the soothing salve I need to get my mind off our family trouble.

I skate the perimeter of the house, head out front, and sure enough... There she is.

Rory Pike.

Her gorgeous ass in those skintight black jeans is sticking out from the back of the van.

Jesse and Cage are nowhere to be seen. I couldn't have asked for a better setup. The time is ripe.

"Hi there," I say.

Rory looks over her shoulder. "Oh. Hi, Brock."

"Can I help you with anything?"

"No, I'm good. I'm looking for an extra cord."

"What for?"

"One of the cords to our amplifier system seems to be missing. I'm not sure what happened."

"We could probably find one inside the house."

She sticks her head again in the back of the truck and paws through a box. Then she pulls out a cord. "No need. I found one."

Shit. That means I won't get her alone in the house.

"Excuse me." She fumbles with her phone. "I have to get this back."

"You calling someone?"

"Yeah. Jesse and Cage are on their way into town to try to find a cord. I need to let them know it's time to come back."

Perfect. Jesse and Cage are off the premises. I can come on to Rory without her massive brother and cousin hanging around.

"I can take it for you," I say.

Rory smiles. "That's not necessary, but you can walk with me if you want."

"How far away are Cage and Jesse?"

"I don't know. They left about fifteen minutes ago."

So they'll be fifteen minutes. Nice. A lot can happen in fifteen minutes. I've been known to rock a woman's world several times in fifteen minutes. Just call me the orgasm king.

Rory's lips are so red. Red and parted and saying *kiss me*. Her hair—thick, dark, and beautiful—floats around her shoulders and curves over her gigantic breasts. Her high cheekbones are pink with a natural blush, and those eyes . . .

"I could get lost in your eyes," I say.

My words surprise even me. Sure, I was thinking them, but I didn't expect to say them out loud.

She widens her eyes, making them even bigger, deeper, more intense.

"You're beautiful, Rory."

"Where is this coming from, Brock?"

"What? Me saying you're beautiful? Is that a surprise to you?"

"Coming from you it is."

"What's that supposed to mean? You think I don't have eyes?"

"You know what I mean. You don't say stuff like that."

"What makes you think I don't tell women they're beautiful?"

"That's not what I mean. I just know who you are. You're one of the Three Rake-a-teers."

"So's my cousin, and I think he just got engaged to your sister tonight."

She parts her lips slightly farther. God, I could slip my tongue right between them.

She doesn't seem to have an answer for that.

Good. Point one for me. Fifteen minutes until her brother and her cousin get back. I reach forward, stroke her soft cheek.

Damn. Her skin... It's like crushed silk. My groin tightens. Just from touching her.

This isn't like me. This isn't like me at all.

She doesn't back away, so I go for it.

I kiss her.

When her lips remain parted, I take that as an invitation. I slide my tongue between them.

A soft moan escapes her throat, vibrates into me, and I find her tongue with my own.

She's kissing me back, and boy, can this woman kiss.

I wrap my arms around her as she slides her own around my neck. She threads her fingers through my hair, and I slide one of my hands over her gorgeous ass.

My God, I could kiss her forever. She tastes of honey and peppermint, and I'm hard. Hard enough that I could drop my pants and glide into her right now.

Not enough time for that, though.

We kiss. Hard and raw and passionate.

Until—

She pushes me away, our mouths releasing with a smack.

She wipes her lips.

"You okay?" I ask.

"We shouldn't be doing this."

"Why not? You're unattached. I'm unattached."

"That's not what I mean. Jesse and Cage . . ." She gestures.

I turn around. Sure enough, Jesse's beater Mustang swivels up the drive.

"Meet me later," I say.

"I have to sing a few numbers. We're already late getting started for our first set because of the missing cord, which I should've gotten to Dragon by now."

I grab her hand. "Come on. We'll take it together. That way you don't have to explain what you're doing here with me."

"You read my mind." She smiles a dazzling smile.

And damn . . .

I'm afraid I might be a goner.

The clincher is that, for the last several moments, I haven't given a thought to the predicament my family is in.

CHAPTER THREE

Rory

I can't believe I'm actually going to vocalize my thought. I hastily look around, making sure Callie and I are alone. Everyone in town is at this party, but the yard is so vast that there are plenty of private enclaves.

"I'm aging here, Ror," Callie says.

My sister's cheeks are flushed, and her hair is... Yeah, they were having a quickie.

"Anything you want to tell me?" I ask.

"I'm sure you've already guessed."

"Yeah. It's pretty obvious."

"We did something... new."

I lift my eyebrows. Usually I can read Callie like a book. For example, I knew she let Donny spank her when we were in Denver. And I have a feeling...

"But it's... intensely personal."

"We tell each other everything, Cal. I mean, I already told you I made out with Brock."

"This goes way beyond making out."

Got it. Spanking isn't the only thing Callie let Donny do to her ass. But I'm not going to push it. "All right. I'll let you keep your little secret for now. Are you ready to hear mine?"

"Yeah. Spill it."

I swallow, gather my courage. Am I really going to say this out loud? "I was thinking... I really want to have a baby."

"I know that, Ror. That's hardly a secret. You'll be a great mom."

"But I don't want to wait any longer."

"Are you sure? With the financial problems that—" She stops abruptly.

"What?"

She shakes her head, laughing softly. "The financial problems of our family. I can help, Rory. I'm marrying Donny Steel. I can help our family."

I suck in a breath. "Oh my God, Callie. That's not why you're marrying him, is it?"

"Of course not! I love him, and he loves me. *That's* why I'm marrying him. I haven't taken any of his money. Not to deal with our financial issues or with Pat Lamone, although he's offered."

"Of course. I'm so sorry. I'm not sure where that came from."

"It's okay. Honestly, it didn't occur to me until after he asked me to marry him. It never occurred to me that I could help our family with his money."

"Once you're married, some of it might belong to you."

"Donny and I haven't talked about it, but I won't have any claim to the vast Steel fortune. I'm sure he'll share his portion with me. And if it could help Mom and Dad..."

"You're forgetting one thing, Cal."

"What's that?"

"Mom and Dad probably won't take the money."

She smiles. "I know. I'll have to insist."

"That's not going to help."

She nods. "Where the hell does Pat Lamone get off calling us gold diggers? We've never dug for gold in our lives."

"Because he knows we were going after the Steel reward all those years ago."

"That doesn't mean anything. Everyone wanted that reward."

"Yeah," I say, "but we were the ones who really tried to get it."

"Well, he stopped us." She sighs. "I don't want to think about this. This is my happy night."

"Me neither. In fact . . ."

"Right. You wanted to tell me something. What is it?"

I bite my lower lip. "If I put this into words, it means it's really a thought I'm having."

"That's right. So what is it?"

"Brock . . . He's young and great-looking and comes from amazing stock."

"That's not news, Ror." She chuckles.

"I know. But do you think . . . Would it be crazy . . . ?"

"Rory, you're going to have to actually finish one of your sentences at some point."

I inhale and let it out slowly. Time to get to the point. "What if I ask him to father a baby for me?"

Callie's jaw drops. Any farther, and I'd have to pick it up off the ground for her.

She doesn't say anything for several seconds that seem to draw out into minutes.

Finally, "What?"

"I'm pretty sure you heard me. That's why your jaw's lying on the ground."

"Rory, that's crazy."

"Is it though? I want a kid so badly I can taste it, Callie. I'm not getting any younger."

"You're twenty-eight. You're hardly an old maid yet."

"I know. But there are risks after thirty-five."

"You're seven years away from thirty-five."

"I get that. It's just . . . I want to do this while I'm young. I've thought about it a lot, especially since Raine and I broke up. I don't want to wait, Cal. I want to have children while I'm still young enough to enjoy them. I don't want to be one of those moms who doesn't live to see her grandchildren grow up."

Callie doesn't respond.

"So . . ." I prompt.

"I don't know. Brock Steel? No way is he going to want to be a father. First of all, he's young. Second of all, he's Brock Steel. He's a womanizer."

"You're marrying a womanizer, Cal."

"That's different. Donny's a lot older than Brock."

"It's not like I'm going to ask him to actually *be* a father. I'm asking for a sperm donation."

"So you want him to come in a cup and then you'll inseminate yourself?"

"No, I was actually thinking . . ."

"You want to do it with him?"

"It's the most tried-and-true method, Callie. It's more likely to take if you do it the natural way."

Plus, it's been a while since I've been with a man. A good old-fashioned fuck sounds great. I'm tingling just thinking about it.

And Brock Steel? I mean, he looks like he could get a woman knocked up with mere eye contact.

HELEN HARDT

Can I say all this to Callie? So far she hasn't responded.

"I can take one of those tests," I continue. "I can find out exactly when I'm ovulating, and then we do it."

"And you think he'll be okay with this."

"The doing it part? Yeah."

"Of course he'll be okay with the doing it part. He's Brock Steel. And you're Rory Pike. Man, the two of you would make a gorgeous kid."

"Right? He's the perfect specimen."

"I wouldn't use the term *specimen* when you ask him for this."

"Why not? I think he'll take that as a compliment."

"I'm not sure he will."

Maybe my sister is right. Brock Steel may have grown up a bit since his college Rake-a-teer days. "Fine. I won't use the term *specimen*. But he's perfect. He's young and healthy and gorgeous. He's smart. All the Steels are. This is el primo genetic material I'm talking about."

"Are you sure that's how you want to do this, Ror? Don't you want to wait until you fall in love?"

"I've been in love. Things didn't work out for me. Everyone wants me to pick a side, and I can't do that. I like women. I like men. I have to be me."

"Yeah. I know. But you *will* find someone who gets that. Maybe you need to find another bisexual person."

"I can't wait around forever for that to happen. I'm not getting on one of those stupid dating sites."

She nods at that one. We've talked about it. Neither of us likes that idea, even though it's how most of our generation meets.

"Still, you're asking a lot of him."

"I'm only asking for a donation. He doesn't have to be involved at all."

"But maybe he'll want to be. Don't you want the Steel money on your side?"

"No. I mean, sure, it would be a nice fringe benefit, but I can do this on my own. This is important to me, Callie. It's something I've wanted forever."

"I know."

"Don't you think about it?" I ask.

"Honestly? I never thought beyond my career goals. At least not until I met Donny."

"Do you want kids now?"

"Believe it or not, I think I do. But I also want a law school education and a career."

"You can have both."

"I know. But I want to at least wait until I've finished law school before I have children."

"You're two years younger than I am. That can certainly happen for you."

"You keep thinking that your age is the problem."

"My age *is* part of the problem, Callie. Because kids are my goal. I've always wanted to be a mom. You haven't. You're thinking about it because you're in love now. You've found your life mate, so kids are on the radar for you. You're realizing that you *do* want them because you're in love with a man and you can finally see a family. But I'm different. I've always wanted them. Whether I'm in love or not, I know my destiny is to be a mom."

"I know that. I know you've always wanted to be a mother, but you also wanted to be an operatic mezzo-soprano. Would you have put your parenting plans on hold if you had made it in opera?"

I cast my gaze to the ground, to the toes of my black leather and chrome-spiked boots. "Low blow," I say.

"I'm sorry. You're right. But it's a valid question. If you had made it as a performer, would you still be wanting a child now?"

"I don't know. I *didn't* make it as a performer. So really, why does that matter?"

I hate thinking about all those auditions. All those callbacks that never amounted to anything. I was never New York good. Only Colorado good.

Okay, maybe I fell somewhere between New York and Colorado. I wouldn't have gotten callbacks otherwise. But I just couldn't make it. Sure, I won some small roles in local opera companies. A few local musical theater companies. You can't make a living doing that, which is what led me into teaching. I'm good at it, and singing with Jesse's band is fun, but I'm not a rocker at heart.

The truth is, I'm no longer an operatic performer at heart either.

I'm a mom. That's what I want to be.

"This isn't a fly-by-night thought," I tell my sister. "I've done the math. I realize I'll have to keep teaching. I also realize I'll be living in a small apartment because I don't want to be the woman who lives with her parents and raises her kid. But I want this, Callie. I want it so much."

"Then you probably should go to a sperm bank," she says. "Don't bring Brock into this. You hardly know him."

"I know him well enough to know he'll probably consider this a compliment."

"That's just it. He's Brock Steel. He considers everything a compliment."

I sigh. "Well, it was just a thought."

"So I talked you out of it?"

"I didn't say that."

"What can I say to talk you out of it, then?"

"I'm not sure you can."

"Tomorrow. We'll hang tomorrow, and we'll figure something out."

I sigh. "Fine. But don't worry. I'm not going to do anything."

Not yet, anyway.

CHAPTER FOUR

Brock

As much as I want another interlude with Rory, I don't get one at the party. She and the band play another set, and then she spends most of her time talking to Callie, until Donny drags Callie away.

Dave and I head into town to Murphy's Bar, where Jesse, Cage, and the band are playing pool and are flanked by Rory's sister Maddie along with my cousins Breanna, Gina, Angie, and Sage. Otherwise known as the awesome foursome—the youngest of our clan, they're all the same age and are seniors in college.

Dave and I take a seat at the bar as I look around.

"How about Maddie Pike?" Dave says.

"Too young."

"You're closer in age to her than you are to Rory."

He's not wrong. Maddie is three years younger than I am, while Rory is four years older.

"Maddie is nearly as gorgeous as Rory. She's got the same hair, the same eyes, the same bodacious tatas."

I shake my head. "Did you really just say bodacious tatas?"

"Guilty. I think they're pretty damned bodacious."

"Are you using word-of-the-week toilet paper or something?"

"Don't tell me that a learned fellow like yourself doesn't know what bodacious means."

"Oh, I know what it means. I'm just not sure I've ever heard you use it."

"It seems very apt for the Pike sisters' racks."

Again, he's not wrong.

"So what do you think?" Dave asks.

"About what?"

"About Maddie Pike?"

"I think she's got her sights set on Dragon."

"Jesse won't let Dragon near her."

"And you think he'll let one of *us* near her?"

"Good point. Still ... Doesn't hurt to try."

"Be my guest."

"Don't mind if I do." Dave hops off the stool and heads toward the back where the pool tables are.

"What will it be, Brock?"

I turn toward the bar. Brendan Murphy, his long orange hair pulled back in his signature low ponytail, stands there, a white bar towel in one hand.

"Give me a Cap Rock martini."

"Another chip off the old block," Brendan says.

"Hey, it's damned good stuff."

"You know it. Coming up."

I turn back toward the pool tables. Dave has already sidled up to Maddie Pike and is helping her with her form. Which is hilarious because Dave sucks at pool.

But Maddie is batting her big brown eyes at him, totally letting him fiddle with her cue stick.

Funny. If I weren't still thinking about Rory's lips against mine, I might be quarreling with Dave over her youngest sister.

Brendan brings my drink. "Here you go."

"Thanks, man. Put it on my tab."

"Already done." He turns.

"Hey, Brendan?"

"Yeah?" He turns and meets my gaze.

"Any news on who trashed your place?"

"Not yet. I've been checking in with Hardy every hour on the hour. Nobody seems to have a clue."

"Hey, just so you know . . . Dale and Donny have filled me in on what you found under your floorboards."

Brendan looks to his left and then to his right. "I don't want to talk about that stuff here."

"That's cool. I just wanted you to know that we're on it."

"Hey, man, all I want to know is who the hell trashed my place. Then I want your family's lien off my property."

I nod. "I understand. I hope you trust that none of us have a clue what's going on."

"I'd *like* to trust that."

"You can. We were just as surprised as anyone."

"Even with all the rumors?"

"What rumors?"

"That the Steels own this damned town."

"Yeah, we've all heard the rumors. None of us ever thought it was true."

"I never thought it was true either. But then I found this lien."

"One lien doesn't mean ownership of the town."

He nods. "Excuse me. I need to take an order." He walks out from behind the bar to a table where two guys I haven't seen before sit down.

One lien doesn't mean ownership of the town. I play my

own words back in my mind. Brendan only knows about the lien affecting his property.

He *doesn't* know about the research that Donny and Callie did that proved our family has liens on almost every property in town.

I'm not going to be the one to break that to Brendan. At least not tonight.

I glance again at Dave flirting with Maddie, and I take a drink of my martini. Then I set it down as my phone vibrates on the wooden bar.

"Hey, Donny," I say into the phone.

"Brock, hey. Where are you, man?"

"I'm at Murphy's with Dave."

"Yeah, okay. Listen. I need to go to Grand Junction tomorrow. Something to do with my dad's case. You in?"

"Don't you want to ask Dale?"

"I did. He's finishing up the move to the new place."

"Did I seriously just hear you correctly? This has something to do with your dad, and Dale *doesn't* want to go?"

"Oh, he wants to go. But he had to make a choice, and his new wife trumps just about everything. Plus, I think my big brother is finally trusting me to handle things."

"What do you need me for, then?"

"I don't want to go alone."

"Are you meeting someone big and scary?" I chuckle.

"For God's sake, knock it off. It's a nurse who worked on my dad's case. But I think we should appear in numbers. Callie can't go because she promised Rory she'd hang out with her tomorrow."

"This means we can't go back to the land near the Wyoming border."

"It means we put it off another day, anyway."

Yeah. Putting off looking for rotting corpses on Steel land? I can handle that. "Sure," I tell him. "Count me in."

I end the call and set my phone back down on the counter.

A hottie approaches me, brown hair, pretty blue eyes, and a seductive smile. "Hey," she says.

"Hey yourself."

"Buy a girl a drink?"

"Sure. What'll you have?"

"What you're drinking looks nice."

Nice? A Cap Rock martini is not *nice*. It's smooth and herbal and full of alcohol. "You think you can handle what I'm drinking?"

"I think I can handle three of what you're drinking. And you."

She's coming on strong. Women who come on to me seem to have two types. There's the *I'm going to come on strong and dare you to turn me down* type, and then there's the *I'm going to flirt softly and let you make the first move* type.

I like both types, to be honest. And tonight? I'm horny as hell after kissing Rory and grabbing her ass, so the *come on strong* type is just what I'm looking for.

"What's your name?" I ask.

"Sadie."

"Are you new around here? Not sure I've seen you before."

She closes her eyes demurely and then opens them. It wasn't a natural blink. It was forced, and it was meant to show me her long eyelashes.

Yeah, I know the type.

"I just moved here from Denver. I'm staying with my friend. Nora. She's a waitress."

"Nora. Right."

The name sounds slightly familiar. I think she was at our last party, totally hitting on my cousin Henry. I don't recall seeing her at the party tonight, but I don't recall seeing this woman either.

I signal to Brendan. "I'll have another, and the same for the lady, please."

"You got it." Brendan gets busy behind the bar.

"What's your name, cowboy?" she asks.

"Brock."

"Brock. You look like a Brock."

"Brock Steel," I say.

Her eyes widen slightly, but then she gets control over them. "So you're one of the Steels."

Right. Like she didn't know that when she approached me. Like I said, I know the type.

"Yes, I'm one of the Steels."

"Is it true you guys own this town?"

"Don't believe everything you hear, Sadie."

Brendan pushes our drinks toward us.

"My tab," I say.

"Already done." Brendan begins mixing another drink.

"So what is this, exactly?" Sadie asks. "Looks like a martini."

"Give the woman a gold star. It's not just a martini, but the best damned martini this side of the Mississippi. It's made with Cap Rock gin, an organic gin made here in Colorado, and very dry vermouth that my uncle makes at his winery."

She brings the martini glass to her lips and takes a small sip. Again with the wide eyes, and again she tries to make it look like she had no reaction. "Tasty."

"Not too strong for you?"

"Cowboy, nothing is too strong for me."

I smile.

Rory Pike may have left me horny, but Sadie is just the prescription I need.

CHAPTER FIVE

Rory

It's after midnight, and I can't sleep. I head through the Jack and Jill bathroom and into Callie's room. She's still awake as well.

"Feel like a drink?" I ask.

"Not really."

She's still in her clothes—which for Callie consists of skinny jeans and a button-up blouse that I can't wear.

"You sure? I'm buying. To celebrate your engagement."

She sighs. "Why the hell not? It's not like either of us can sleep."

"Just what I was thinking. You want to head over to Murphy's?"

"Yeah. Donny's helping his mom clean up, and then tomorrow he's got something going on in Grand Junction."

"You're not going with him?"

"You asked me to spend the day with you, remember?"

"Yeah. Right. Except that was your idea. You're going to work on talking me out of the whole Brock Steel thing."

She chuckles. "Yeah."

"Let's go."

We make our way to the driveway and get into my car. "You want me to drive?" Callie asks. "I'm not planning to drink."

"Doesn't matter. You can drive home if you need to. I won't drink a lot."

"I feel like we need to always be on alert with Pat Lamone out there. And those photos . . ."

"We may *have* the photos. We've got the thumb drive from that box we found."

"We can't depend on that, Ror." She shakes her head. "You know, if you weren't a few days over eighteen, I'd actually want him to publish the damned photos. Heck, he doesn't even need to publish them. Just possession of nude photos of minors can get him on child porn charges."

"Well, he's in possession of yours. We can still get him."

"No. I can't take that chance. If he knows you were over eighteen, he could still publish yours and not risk any fallout. Except for a lawsuit from us, which we can't afford."

"Once you marry Donny, I guess *you* could afford it."

"Wait . . . Are you saying you want me to get him charged? Because I'm not sure we can. They're not in his possession. They're in *ours*."

"But we didn't take them. We can tell Hardy what happened."

"We can't. Not without any evidence that he took them and buried them. I'm just not sure it will work."

"Well, you're the legal expert." My heart falls a bit. It would almost be worth it to have my naked body all over the internet to get Pat Lamone put away for child porn.

We stay silent for the rest of the ride, until Callie finds a parking spot about a block away from Murphy's.

We walk inside, and—

Brock Steel is sitting at the bar with a woman I don't recognize. She has dark hair and blue eyes, and she's flat-chested.

I can't help a little sliver of gratitude at that.

I may not be able to wear button-down shirts like Callie, but every eye is on me when I walk into a bar.

And, of course, the only two available seats at the bar are right next to Brock and his lady.

Callie smirks at me. Yeah, I get it. It's her way of telling me I'm seeing Brock in his natural habitat.

Am I surprised? No. I know who Brock Steel is. After all, I'm the one who coined the term Rake-a-teer. The Three Rake-a-teers—Donny Steel, Brock Steel, and Dave Simpson.

Correction—they're now the *two* Rake-a-teers, since Callie snagged Donny and made an honest man out of him.

I suppose it's too much to hope that I could make an honest man out of Brock Steel.

I shake my head slightly. No time to have thoughts like that. Brock is a sperm donor, nothing more. Make that a *potential* sperm donor. I'm not interested in a relationship with him.

No. Not at all. That slight sliver of jealousy at seeing him with no-boobs? That's nothing. It's purely physical because I made out with him earlier, because I'm thinking about asking him to father my child.

Yeah. That's all it is.

I scan the rest of the bar quickly. Jesse and his bandmates are in the back playing pool. They don't look like they've just beaten anyone to a pulp, thank God. I rush toward him, grab his arm as he's about to move his cue, and pull him away from the crowd.

"What was that for, Rory? I had the right angle and everything."

"I want to make sure you didn't go after Lamone."

"No, I didn't. Cooler heads have prevailed. For tonight at least."

"Good. Please, Jess. Just stay out of it."

"I will."

"What stopped you?"

"I couldn't… I just couldn't tell Cage and the others about what went down. That the bastard has those photos. You and Callie are my sisters."

"Right. Though I'm sure you could have made something up."

"I thought about it. I won't lie."

"I'm glad you didn't. I don't want you getting arrested for this. Anything happens to Lamone, and this whole thing will blow up in our faces."

"I know. It's just…" He squeezes his fist around his cue stick, his knuckles whitening. "I hate that motherfucker. I hate him with everything in me."

"Believe me. So do I."

Jesse glances toward the bar. "Callie's gesturing to you."

I nod. "Got it. And Jess?"

"Yeah?"

"Thanks."

"For what? Not kicking Lamone's ass?"

"Yeah. And also for wanting to." I squeeze his arm and then head to the bar, just as Brendan sidles over to take our drink order.

"Just a Diet Coke for me, Brendan," Callie says. "What do you want, Ror?"

"I think I'll have a beer. Fat Tire."

"You got it, ladies."

I pull out my credit card and hand it to Brendan. "Start a tab for us."

"Will do." He takes my credit card, slides it through his machine, and then hands it back to me. "Drinks'll be right up."

"I assume all is okay with Jess?" Callie says.

I nod. "He let it go. For now, anyway."

"Maybe I should go back and say hi."

"Hi to whom?" I say nonchalantly. "Maddie? She's back there hanging all over Dave and Dragon Locke."

"And Jesse is shooting darts out of his eyes."

"Yeah, I guess we don't need to worry about our baby sis." I slide my glance, as nonchalantly as I can, to the woman sitting on my other side.

She's quite attractive in an unassuming, no-chest kind of way.

"He saw us walk in," Callie whispers. "He couldn't take his eyes off you."

"Why should I care?" I shrug.

"Right."

Brendan slides our drinks in front of us, and I take a deep sip of my beer, letting it warm my throat.

"Hey, Rory."

Brock Steel's voice glides over me like warm chocolate. All the Steel men have deep voices, but Brock's is sex on a stick.

Sex on a chocolate-and-caramel stick. With sprinkles.

He's leaning forward, the brown-haired woman still sitting between us.

I take another sip of my beer and then lean forward myself to meet his gaze. "Brock."

"This is Sadie," Brock says. "Sadie... Sorry. I don't know your last name."

Sadie smiles—a great big one, showcasing perfectly straight pearly whites. "Sadie McCall."

"Sadie McCall," Brock says. "This is Rory Pike."

Sadie holds out her hand. "Charmed."

"Nice to meet you." I shake her hand. "This is my sister Callie."

Callie stands to shake Sadie's hand, but then she takes a seat back on her stool.

Now what?

"Any of you ladies feel like a game of pool?" Brock asks.

Sadie quickly downs what appears to be the rest of a martini and jumps off her stool. "Me. I'd love a game."

Good enough. Let them go play. I don't care. I came here with my sister, to celebrate her engagement. Not to commiserate over the shitstorm that has roared into our lives. And certainly not to erupt into jealousy over Brock Steel and a new girl.

Callie should be happy. Over the moon. Her orange sapphire ring sparkles on her left hand. She's engaged. Not just engaged to anyone, but to a Steel.

Once we figure out this whole Pat Lamone situation, Callie will be set for life. Happiness, security, true completion.

No. I'm not envious. Not at all.

"Do you think she could've jumped out of her seat any faster?" Callie asks.

"Who is she? I've never seen her."

"Me neither." Callie takes a sip of her soda. "So are you rethinking your position on the whole baby thing?"

"Why should I?"

"Because look at him. He's all over that new girl."

"They're playing pool," I say. "He's hardly all over her. Besides, why should I care?"

"Hey, I never said you should care. Except you should.

Don't you care about the kind of man the father of your child is?"

"I care about his genetics. His personality isn't part of that."

"How do you know?"

"Because it just isn't."

"Maybe it isn't, but maybe it is. I took a few science courses in my day."

I roll my eyes. "I didn't. Except for what was required in college. Then I forgot every bit of it once I passed the final."

"So maybe personality is a part of genetics," Callie says. "We just don't really know, do we?"

"Why are you trying so hard to talk me out of this?"

"Because, Rory, this is serious. This is you talking about having a child that's half you and half Brock Steel."

I say nothing. I want a baby so badly. But Callie is probably right. Brock Steel? I figure it will take him about another half hour until he finds a way to get Sadie whatever her name is into bed.

He's definitely a man whore. Nothing I didn't already know.

I polish off the rest of my beer and pretend not to stare at Brock.

And I try not to think about the fact that I wish I were the object of his attention instead of Sadie.

CHAPTER SIX

Brock

Why did Rory Pike have to show up here tonight? I was doing just fine with Sadie. She's pretty—flat-chested but pretty. And she's interested. Really interested. Totally up for a one-nighter.

But damn. She's worse at pool than Dave is.

In reality, Dave isn't all that bad, but the Steels are notoriously good. Dave's just not as good as the rest of us. But this woman? Sadie doesn't even know how to hold a cue stick. Why the hell did she offer to play pool with me?

I know the answer to my own question, of course. She's hoping to get into my bed. Which is where we were headed before Rory Pike walked in.

Now, the best Sadie's going to get might be a kiss good night, and I'm honestly rethinking that as well. I'm kind of getting turned off by her complete ineptitude with the pool cue. Not that you have to be a champion pool player to get into my bed, but you can't hop off a barstool and be ridiculously excited to play when you don't have the first clue what you're doing.

I've done my part. I introduced Sadie to my cousins, to Maddie, to Jesse and the band. To Rory and Callie. To everyone else who's walked into the bar and headed back toward the pool tables.

I've attempted to teach her how to handle a pool cue with no luck at all.

I bought her two drinks.

Now, I'm done.

"It's after two o'clock," I tell her, "and I have to go to Grand Junction tomorrow with my cousin. I'm afraid I'm going to call it a night."

"I understand. Let's get the hell out of here," she says.

"You need a ride home?"

"Yes. I would love a ride home."

Yeah, she's not getting my point, but she will when I drop her off and leave.

"Where are you staying?"

"I'm staying with Nora, but she happens to be visiting a friend tonight, so I have the place all to myself."

Great. Just great. An hour ago, this would've been good news.

I glance toward the door just as Callie and Rory are leaving. Definitely nothing keeping me here now.

"It's just down the block," Sadie continues. "Above Lorenzo's."

"I'll walk you home," I say, feigning a yawn. "Then I've got to go home and get some sleep."

She grabs my hand and intertwines our fingers together. "Are you sure? I'd really love to get to know you better."

"Maybe some other time."

Her lips curve downward into a pout. "Promise?"

I can't promise anything at this point. Not until I screw Rory Pike and get her out of my system. And I have a sinking feeling that getting Rory Pike in my bed won't be easy.

She's not like other women. I'm not talking about her bisexuality, or the fact that she's the most gorgeous woman on the planet, or anything else about her looks or personality.

She has something more. Something special radiates from her. Something that's starting to ignite inside me.

I'm not sure I like the feeling.

I went into this thinking I could seduce her, catch her on the rebound from Raine, have my way with her, and give us both a night to remember.

Now?

I'm not sure one night with Rory Pike will suffice.

What I *do* know? I'm going to find out whether one night will suffice, and I'm going to find out before I tempt any other woman into my bed.

"We'll see," is all I say to Sadie.

She bites her bottom lip. "If it's all right with you, then, I think I'll stay here for a while."

"It's absolutely all right with me." I sigh and then give her a quick peck on the cheek. "Nice meeting you, Sadie."

"You too, Brock." She winks. "We could've had fun tonight."

"I'm sure." I say a quick goodbye to my cousins, making sure none of them needs a ride home, and then I leave.

Only to return quickly to find Brendan at the far end of the bar. "Did Rory and Callie already pay for their drinks?"

"Yeah, Rory put them on her card."

"Do me a favor. Add their drinks to my tab and give them credit."

"Come on, Steel."

"Just do it, Brendan. And add yourself a healthy tip."

"Okay." He gives me a semi-smile with a sigh. "Thanks."

"Don't mention it."

I pay my tab at Murphy's every month without fail. I'm not a huge drinker—not like some of my cousins—but Murphy's gets a fair amount of business from all the Steels.

As I head home, I find myself driving by the Pike place even though it's out of the way.

The house is dark, though Rory and Callie are probably still up. It's two thirty a.m., but they only left the bar a little before I did, and Jesse and Maddie are still at Murphy's.

Rory's in that house somewhere. She's been living at her parents' place since she and Raine broke up.

Damn.

This isn't like me. Brock Steel doesn't drive by women's houses in the middle of the night.

It's a crush. Just a crush. A crush on the most beautiful woman in Snow Creek.

Who *wouldn't* have a crush on Rory Pike?

I'm not sure how long I sit in my car, engine still running, staring at the dark Pike house.

I'm not sure when I put my foot on the pedal and drive home.

The only thing I'm sure of is that taking a cold shower and jacking off isn't going to help me tonight.

CHAPTER SEVEN

Rory

Zach, my new rescue dog, wakes me up promptly at six thirty. I actually managed to log a few hours of sleep. A beer at one in the morning probably helped.

I pad out of my bedroom, let the frisky pup out, and then I start a pot of coffee. Mom isn't up yet, which is unusual, but she and Dad were out late at the Steel party.

They must be over the moon about Callie's engagement. One daughter taken care of—by a Steel, no less. Callie will never have to worry about money, and now she'll be able to go to law school as planned.

I sit down at the kitchen table, my stomach growling. Hungry? At six thirty a.m.?

My body is rebelling. I haven't been eating well since the whole Pat Lamone thing was dredged back up. Everything tastes kind of like sawdust. Not even as flavorful as sawdust, to be honest. Still, I have to keep my body going. Callie and I both do. I rise and open the fridge. Bacon, eggs, toast. None of it sounds good.

So I head to the cookie jar.

Chocolate chip cookies. Not the most nutritional food for breakfast, but they actually sound good. I pull two of Mom's giant cookies out of the jar, place them on a napkin, and bring them back to the table.

I take a bite, letting the soft and buttery goodness explode on my tongue.

Has there ever been a problem in the world that a chocolate chip cookie couldn't solve?

I used to think there wasn't.

Until Pat Lamone and Brittany Sheraton came back to town.

"Hey." Callie follows a scampering Dusty—her rescue—into the kitchen. After she lets her dog out to join mine, she sits down next to me. "Cookies?"

"Yeah. The only thing that doesn't taste like complete shit to me."

"I hear you." She grabs my second cookie and takes a bite.

"Hey!"

"Sorry." She rises, walks to the counter, brings back the cookie jar, and sets it in front of me. "Here you go."

I can't help a slight chuckle. "Looks about right." I take another cookie out of the jar as I polish off my first.

"Thinking about Brock?"

I am, but I hesitate to admit it. I don't want to look as self-absorbed as I feel. "No. Just about our situation."

"Yeah. Me too." She holds her left hand in front of her, and the track lighting in the kitchen bounces rainbow spikes off her orange sapphire engagement ring. "I'm on top of the world. Part of me is anyway."

"You should be," I say. "Don't let Pat Lamone ruin this for you."

"You're right."

"So... What did you think of Sadie?"

"She really didn't make an impression on me."

I take a bite of my second cookie more harshly than I mean to, and for a split second, it's Sadie's head that I'm ripping off. "Brock probably screwed her last night."

"Probably."

Nice. My sister doesn't even try to assuage what could be my fears. True, she doesn't know what I'm feeling. Heck, I'm not even sure what I'm feeling.

"I'm still considering... You know."

"I know you are, Ror. Just because I tell you not to do something doesn't mean you're not going to do it. It probably means the opposite."

"I respect your opinion, Cal," I say.

"I know that. But you're Rory Pike. You're going to do your own thing no matter what anyone tells you. Even me."

Callie's not wrong. "I just want a kid badly."

"I know. There's no way I'm going to talk you out of it. I won't even try."

I scoff. "Yeah, you will."

She laughs. "Yeah, I will. But seriously. I think there might be a better choice than Brock Steel."

"You might be right. We don't have a sperm bank here in Snow Creek though."

"Sure we do. Go have a one-nighter with someone."

I lift my eyebrows. This isn't Callie speaking. More like the anti-Callie. "Seriously?"

"I'm kidding, Ror. Man, what's with you? Or both of us, for that matter? This whole Pat Lamone thing has really messed us up."

"No kidding. And for the record, I happen to think Brock Steel is of high genetic quality. Better than I'd get at any sperm bank."

"I know you do. You're probably right. The Steels are hardy stock for sure. But it's a big step for him. He's only twenty-four. I don't want you to get your hopes up just to have them dashed. We both know Brock is only looking for one thing from you, and it's not fatherhood."

I shove another bite of cookie into my mouth. Sawdust again, with a chocolate edge. "You're right. I guess I will check out sperm banks. Do you think there's one in Grand Junction?"

"Probably. Let's research it today."

"Sounds good." I rise.

"Where you going?"

"Pour some coffee, will you? I'm getting my laptop."

"It's not even seven o'clock."

"So what? I'm going to research sperm." A few moments later, I return with my laptop and fire up. "What do I type into the search engine? Sperm bank?"

"That's as good a place as any to start," Callie says.

Good enough. *Sperm bank Grand Junction Colorado.*

"I'll be damned. There *are* a few." I tap on the first option. "Check this out. They've got their profiles online."

Callie scoots her chair closer to me so we can both see the screen.

"I can choose hair color, eye color, height, weight. My God, there are photos. Intelligence quotient. Hobbies, likes, and dislikes."

"It's a smorgasbord." Callie takes a sip of coffee and then another bite of cookie.

"I like brown hair and brown eyes. I mean, that's what I have. That would virtually guarantee that our kid would have brown hair and brown eyes."

"Not necessarily. Brown hair and brown eyes are both

dominant traits. Most people with brown hair and brown eyes carry the genes for the recessive traits as well, so you could end up having a blond-haired and blue-eyed child, even with a brown-haired and brown-eyed guy."

"For God's sake, Callie. Can you turn your brain off for one minute?"

"Hey, I'm just telling you. If you want to have a child who has brown hair and brown eyes, there's absolutely no way to guarantee it. On the other hand, if you had blond hair and blue eyes, and you chose a blond-haired and blue-eyed guy, your kid would have blond hair and blue eyes. Except it might have green eyes, since green are more recessive than blue."

I roll my eyes. "Whatever. I don't really care what color hair and eyes my child has."

"But you just said—"

"I know what I said. All I care about is that I have a happy and healthy child."

"Good. All these guys have been well vetted. Any of them will give you just as beautiful a kid as Brock Steel would."

I nod. My sister's right, as she usually is. I get so sick of her being right all the time. It's totally annoying.

"Unless..." she continues.

"Unless what?"

"Unless... Your interest in Brock Steel is more than just genetics related."

"Come on, Cal. You know me better than that."

Callie doesn't reply.

And I find myself wondering...

What about Brock Steel?

Certainly not relationship material. His interest in Sadie last night proved that, not that I had any grand delusions about him.

But damn ... I wanted to be the object of his attention last night. I was nearly ready to bare my breasts to the whole bar to get him moving toward me.

Clearly, I'm just horny. Horny for a man in particular since it's been so long, and Brock Steel is all man.

And he can kiss. Fuck it all, the man can kiss.

And I do love kissing.

But no.

Brock Steel is not for me. Not in any way other than a potential sperm donor.

No matter what ridiculous feelings I'm having.

CHAPTER EIGHT

Brock

I was right. Jacking off during the wee hours of the morning didn't help. Rory Pike plagued my dreams, and I woke up in a fucking cold sweat.

And now?

I'm sitting at a coffee shop in Grand Junction with Donny, waiting to meet some nurse who may have poisoned my uncle in the hospital.

As much as I want Rory Pike, all I'm thinking about now is that old barn.

To be more specific—the sickeningly sweet smell in the old barn.

I can't say I'm unhappy that Donny called the trip off today so we could meet this nurse who has information about Uncle Talon's case. He wanted both Dale and me to come along, but Dale's finishing up the move to his new place, so it's just me.

I have a bad feeling about this.

A really bad feeling as Donny and I sit at an out-of-the-way coffee shop in the city.

"That's her," Donny says. "It's got to be."

I look toward the doorway where a woman wearing dark glasses and a scarf around her head enters. She's also wearing scrubs, which is kind of a giveaway... although I suppose people other than doctors and nurses wear scrubs.

Donny nods toward her, and she approaches the table.

"Ms. Murray? Janine?" Donny says.

She nods.

Donny stands and holds out the chair between us. "I'm Donny Steel, and this is my cousin Brock Steel."

I rise as well. "A pleasure."

Ms. Murray simply sits.

Then . . . silence for a few moments.

A few very long moments.

Will she actually use her vocal cords at some point during this meeting?

"I suppose it's easiest to just begin." I force out a smile.

She looks at me and then at Donny. Then at me again.

"I want you to know," she finally says, "I would never intentionally harm a patient."

The word *intentionally* isn't lost on me.

And that sick feeling I've had since the evening at the barn intensifies.

"That's not exactly true, is it?" From Donny.

Which surprises the hell out of me. He's going right in for the kill.

I get it. I do. This is his father. I'd be doing the same for my own father.

What surprises me is that Donny isn't normally like me or my father or Dale. He's usually a little more subtle.

Apparently not today.

Our companion turns pink. I want to tell Donny to go easy on her, even though she apparently doesn't deserve it. We're not going to get anything out of her if he freaks her out to the point where she stands and walks away.

When neither of them says anything, I speak. "Just start at the beginning."

The nurse nods again. "I got a phone call through the nurses' station. They scared me. They said they would hurt my baby."

Donny remains stoic. "You have a baby?"

"Yes. Maria. She's six months old."

This can't be leading to anything good.

"Go ahead, Ms. Murray," I say.

"Honestly, I don't know how this happened. My mother stays with Maria during the day. But the person on the other end of the line said to call him from a secure line at a certain time. We do have secure lines at the hospital, so I had no choice. I wrote down the information."

"All right. When did you call him back?" Donny asks.

"I found a line open during my break. I told my supervisor I had to make a personal phone call and that my cell phone was dead. So in private, I made the call. They said..."

"What did they say?" I ask, trying not to sound too threatening.

And believe me, I have to try. I'm starting to get very pissed off. I'm sitting across from the person who poisoned my uncle. Sure, she didn't mean to. Sure, she was probably forced to. Doesn't change the fact that she did it.

Usually, Donny will play good cop to my bad cop. But he seems to be in a bad cop mood, so it's up to me.

"I was told..." She clasps her hand to her mouth. "I can't believe they somehow did this," she chokes out.

"It's okay." Again I force my voice to remain calm. "Take as long as you need to."

As long as it's within the next few seconds.

"The person on the other end of the line, he said—"

"So it was a man?" Donny says.

"I think so. Or a woman with a low voice. But it wasn't *really* low like yours. But it could definitely have been a man's voice."

"Okay," I say. "Go on."

"This person—they said I would find something in Maria's diaper. In her diaper!"

Donny and I both drop our jaws.

I try to process what I've just heard as a Ping-Pong ball ricochets around in my heart. Whoever this degenerate is stuffed something in a baby's diaper?

An innocent baby?

I'm not sure why I'm surprised, given what I just recently found out about Dale and Donny's past before they came to the ranch. Whoever we're dealing with doesn't mind using kids.

That nausea that I'm keeping at bay? I'm not sure how much longer I can. Already I sense acid gurgling up my esophagus.

Donny clears his throat. "How did he . . . ?"

"I don't know. My mother never takes her eyes off Maria. Perhaps she got a phone call or something. I never asked her because I was afraid to say anything to anyone."

"What did you find in your baby's diaper?" Donny asks.

"It was a note. And a vial of something. The note said I should put the contents of the vial into Talon Steel's food."

"The atropine," I say.

"I didn't know what it was. But I was afraid not to. They said they'd hurt my baby, and obviously they got to her. Somehow they put that in her diaper. My God, what if it had broken? My baby could have been poisoned. Or cut by the glass of the vial."

"Didn't they wrap the vial in anything?" I ask.

"Yes, in some gauzy fabric. And then the note was wrapped around it. But still . . ."

"The note was wrapped around the gauze? Or around the vial?"

"Around the vial," she says. "Then gauze around that, and then plastic wrap around the gauze."

Of course. Because if the baby soiled herself, the note and vial needed to be safe.

My God, who the hell are we dealing with?

Someone who thinks things through, and someone who has no qualms about using innocent children.

In other words, a total psychopath.

"So you found the substance." Donny makes notes on his phone. "And you didn't know what it was."

"Honestly, I didn't even think about what it could be. I was worried about my baby."

"We understand that," I say.

"Do you? Do you really understand? Somehow they got to my baby. She's six months old!" Ms. Murray darts her gaze around the coffee shop. She spoke too loudly, and now she's afraid.

"I know this is hard for you," Donny says, finally reverting to his calming and soothing persona. "Brock and I are both so sorry that these heinous people involved your child."

This gets to me.

I love my uncle. Truly, I do.

But he's a sixty-year-old man.

Whoever these people are, they have no problem using an infant.

This just got a whole lot more sinister. *Psychopath* is too weak of a word.

"All right," I say. "Please, just tell us the rest. But first of all, is Maria all right?"

Ms. Murray nods and hiccups. "Yes, she's okay. I couldn't tell my mother what happened, but I did tell her not to go anywhere and to keep the doors locked at all times."

"I'm so sorry," Donny says. "I can't imagine what it must be like to be afraid for your child in your own home."

"It's awful. And I have to work. If I don't work, I can't take care of Maria. And my mother."

"Does your mother live with you?"

Ms. Murray shakes her head. "She has an apartment a couple miles away."

"And do you live in an apartment or a house?" I ask.

"It's a small house. It once belonged to my father. He and my mom are divorced. And now he's . . ."

"Go on," Donny says.

"He passed away a few years ago. He would have loved Maria."

She's digressing. I'm impatient, but I hold my tongue. This is a frightened mother. If we force her to go more quickly, she may run.

Luckily, she starts speaking again. "I didn't know what to do. They already got to my baby somehow. I don't know how they got past Mom. But they did. So I did the only thing I could do. I put the contents of the vial in Mr. Steel's food, and then I called them back and said it was done."

"Do you still have the number?" I ask.

She pushes a piece of paper toward me. "This is it."

"And have they contacted you again?" From Donny.

She shakes her head. "You're not going to have me arrested, are you?"

"No, we're not going to have you arrested," Donny says. "But we are going to need your cooperation."

"There's nothing more I can do. I never saw the guy."

"Would you recognize the voice if you heard it again?" I ask.

"I don't know. I might."

"We may ask you to listen to some voices," I say. "Also, we're going to have to take a look at your house."

Ms. Murray drops her jaw open.

"You want to be safe, don't you?" Donny says. "These people got into your home somehow, got something into your baby's diaper. An innocent child who can't recognize them out of a lineup. Who can't even say what happened to her."

Ms. Murray gasps. "Oh my God. You don't think they did anything... to her."

"No," Donny says quickly.

I force my expression to remain stoic. How can Donny say that after what happened to him in his childhood? But I get it. He doesn't know for sure, but he doesn't want to alarm the mother any more than she already is.

"But it might be a good idea to have Maria looked at by a pediatrician," Donny continues.

Ms. Murray gasps again.

"There's no need to be alarmed," I say. "But it's always good to be sure. If Maria seems fine to you, if you didn't notice any marks on her, they probably didn't do anything other than change her diaper and put the substance inside."

Ms. Murray nods and sniffles, and then she grabs a tissue out of her handbag and unceremoniously blows her nose. Tears well in her eyes. To be honest, I'm surprised she made it this far without sobbing.

"Listen, Ms. Murray—Janine," Donny says. "I am going to find out who did this. I am going to find out who tried to poison my father. I have unlimited resources and a brother who's stronger and meaner than I am. We will not let this lie. We will find out who's behind this, and we will make sure they pay. Especially someone so horrible that they would use an innocent six-month-old baby."

Ms. Murray nods, hiccupping again.

"Here's something I don't get," I say, thinking out loud. "You work in a hospital. You have access to all the drugs. Why would they put drugs in your baby's diaper? Why wouldn't they just force you to get the drugs yourself at the hospital and then poison the patient?"

Donny's eyes widen.

"What?" I ask him.

"Ms. Murray," Donny says. "Do you know if atropine is used for any veterinary purpose?"

"For animals?" She shakes her head. "I'm not sure. Probably."

I grab my phone and do a quick search. "Says here that it's used for pupil dilation in dogs. Also as a preanesthetic to reduce salivation."

"Damn," Donny says, raking his fingers through his hair.

"Why does this matter?"

"Because . . . I think I may know who's behind this. Or who's at least a person of interest."

"Who?" I demand.

"Let's just say that things are converging."

I nod. In other words, he'll talk to me about it later.

Ms. Murray starts talking then. "I don't know how I could've forgotten this. We learned about all the drugs in nursing school, and even about how they're used in nonhumans. You're right. Atropine is sometimes used as a preanesthetic for dogs to keep them from salivating. Why didn't I think of that?"

"Because you were concerned about your baby," Donny says, again using his comforting tone. "But you're confirming that a veterinarian would probably have atropine. Or easy access to it."

"I can't say for sure. I mean, I've never worked with a veterinarian. I have a cat. I go to a veterinarian."

Now she's rambling. "Don," I say, "we need to talk."

He nods. "We do. Did you want to ask Ms. Murray anything else?"

I stand. "Not right now."

"We have your information, and we will be in contact with you. In the meantime, I want you to call this security company." Donny hands her a card.

"Monarch security. Why?"

"Tell them Donny Steel referred you. Tell them to get your place set up with twenty-four-hour security and to bill it to me."

"Oh, I couldn't."

"These are bad people, Ms. Murray," I say. "They threatened your infant child. Please do as we ask."

She nods, gulping.

"Can we give you a lift home?" I ask.

"No. I have my car. My mom is with Maria."

"I'm going to have one of our investigators check out your house," Donny says. "We might be able to tell how the perpetrator got in."

Ms. Murray gulps again. "Okay."

"Brock and I will be in touch. We'll walk you to your car."

Ms. Murray stands. Her pallor is gray, her lips thin. Her blond hair is beginning to fall out of the scarf on her head.

She's frightened. And rightly so.

After Ms. Murray is safely on her way, I turn to my cousin. "Anything you want to let me in on?"

CHAPTER NINE

Rory

After my three morning students on Monday, I have the afternoon free. I could go by the courthouse and see if Callie wants to have lunch, but I figure she'll be doing more research and probably having lunch with Donny.

I sigh. My small studio is above what used to be Raine's beauty salon. It's a simple studio apartment, one of two apartments above the salon.

Willow White, Ashley Steel's mother, bought the business from Raine, and she's downstairs now, working at getting the salon ready for her reopening.

I still have some stuff down there that I need to move out and take back home. Or at least move it up to the studio. I also have stuff in the apartment across the hall. Just a few boxes that I haven't bothered moving yet. Now is as good a time as any since I have the afternoon free.

I leave my studio and walk a few steps to the door to the apartment, pull out my key, and try to open the door.

Except my key no longer works.

Willow must've had the locks changed.

Okay, then. This is embarrassing. Didn't she realize I still have stuff up here? She's getting her salon stuff moved in, but as far as I knew, she wasn't actually moving into the apartment for another day or two.

I walk down the stairwell in the back of the building that leads to the rear entrance to the salon. The door is locked, so I walk around to the front. That door is open, and it jingles as I enter.

Willow wipes the sweat off her forehead and looks up. "Afternoon, Rory. Can I help you with something?"

"Yeah. I'm sorry to bother you, but I still have a few boxes in the apartment. I thought I'd get them out of your way, but I need the key."

"Oh, sure." She wipes her forehead again. "I'm exhausted and sweaty from moving things in. Please excuse my appearance."

"You look fine. Very refreshed."

I'm not being completely honest, but Willow doesn't look bad. She's quite pretty, even with her blond hair pulled back in a bandana and no makeup. She's a natural beauty, almost as pretty as her daughter, Ashley, though Ashley has full, pouty lips that she clearly got from her father, whoever he might be.

Willow laughs. "You're a good liar. You, of course, look beautiful as always."

I drop my gaze to my jeans and flip-flops. Normally I dress a little better for my lessons, but I didn't have it in me this morning.

Willow grabs a key out of her purse and hands it to me. "Here you go. Just bring it back when you're done."

"Will do."

I head back up, and then carry the boxes—most of which are books, heavy books—down to my car. I love to read. So does Callie. Raine isn't a big reader. Some of these books have been in their boxes since we moved in together. That won't happen again. I'll purchase a bookshelf—or build one myself—and set them up in my bedroom.

Better yet—I need to find a place to live. Money is pretty scarce, and my family needs me, but a twenty-eight-year-old woman should *not* be living with her parents.

I considered asking Callie to find a place with me in town, but now that she's engaged, that doesn't make a lot of sense. If she moves in with anyone, it will be with Donny.

Once the boxes of books are secure in my car, I head back into the salon and hand the key back to Willow.

"I still have some boxes in the back of the salon too," I say. "I'm sorry I left them here for so long."

"Don't be silly. It's only been a couple of days."

Right. Only a couple of days...but more than enough time for her to change the locks.

I'm being petty. Willow is a lovely person as far as I can tell. Time to go back to being nice Rory. How have I let Pat Lamone and his BS affect me so negatively?

"Is there anything I can help you with?"

"Oh, no, I'm pretty much done here. Just unpacking all my stuff. Everything's in such good condition. Raine left the place perfect for a new venture."

"Yeah, this other thing kind of came up suddenly. Her friend from Denver offered her a partnership at his new downtown spa and salon."

"It sounds like a great opportunity," Willow agrees. "And it certainly worked out well for me. I wasn't sure if there was enough business in Snow Creek for two hairstylists."

"Raine did it all. Not just hairstyling, but she did nails and facials and all that other stuff."

"I only do hair. I wonder. Maybe I should hire someone

to do the other stuff."

"It's hard to say. I'm not sure you have enough business to have a full-time person doing just nails and facials."

"Yeah," she says. "Plus, most nail techs aren't aestheticians. Raine must've done it all."

"Yeah, she has the full cosmetologist's license and aesthetician's license. Another reason why her friend was able to offer her a partnership in the salon and spa. The only thing she doesn't do is massage therapy."

Willow opens her eyes wide. "Massage therapy. Boy, it's been forever since I've had a good massage. They were above my pay grade back in LA. I wonder…"

"I don't know. I'm not sure there's that much of a call for a massage therapist in Snow Creek."

Though I could use one at the moment. My back spasms at the mere mention of a massage. Damn, I'm tense.

"You're probably right. I guess I have to get used to small-town living. I'll tell you, after living in LA for so long, coming to a small town is like living on a different planet."

"How so? I mean, I know it's different, but I've never lived in a big city. The closest was Grand Junction when I went to college."

"The people here are so different. So friendly. Not that the people in LA aren't friendly. They're a lot friendlier than on the East Coast. New Yorkers? Give me LA any day. New Yorkers are just downright rude."

"I wouldn't know."

A lie, but I can't talk to Willow—or anyone—about New York. It's too much like a knife to my gut. All those callbacks, and not once did I get a contract in New York.

Never New York good. Only Colorado good.

"I was only there once," Willow says, "when I went to a stylists' conference a couple years ago. I'll tell you, they walk so briskly down the streets, you're lucky not to get bulldozed over."

She's right. I wish her easy demeanor were catching. I like Willow White, despite the whole lock-changing thing. I probably would have changed the locks right away myself.

"So what else is different about Snow Creek?" I ask her.

"The biggest difference is that nothing is open on the weekends. That is the strangest thing."

"A lot of them are open on Saturdays. But you're right, not Sundays. That's family day around here."

"I noticed there are only two churches in Snow Creek, and both of them are very small."

"Yeah. There's the churchgoing crowd and the non-churchgoing crowd. But we all seem to get along pretty well."

"Yeah. I have to say, small-town life is certainly worth getting used to. Everyone's been very welcoming."

"Snow Creek's that kind of town. Most people who come here never leave."

"I certainly don't plan to. Ashley and Dale are here, of course, plus . . . I just needed something different, you know?"

"I know. I'm so sorry for your loss."

"I'm slowly healing. Dennis and I . . . Well, we just didn't have a chance. We had only known each other for about six months when we got married, and then . . . Who knew we were fated to only have a twenty-four-hour marriage?"

"I know. It's not fair."

She sighs. "Life rarely is fair, Rory. I should know."

I'm not sure what she's referring to, but I do understand. "I hear you. Me too."

"I'm really sorry about the fire that destroyed your family's property," she says.

"Thank you."

More pity. Of course, I just gave her sympathy over her late husband. I like this woman, but I sure as heck don't want to spend the afternoon in a mutual pity party. Time to get out of here.

"I'll just get my boxes in the back," I say.

"Of course. Nice to see you."

I head to the salon storage area. Not much of this was ever mine, but I did loan Raine some artwork for the salon. Just a few small paintings, which she boxed up when she moved her stuff out. At the time, I couldn't bear to come in and take them.

Even now, I'm not sure I want them. They'll be a reminder of Raine and our failed relationship. One more person who couldn't deal with my bisexuality.

Funny, though. I don't miss her that much. Near the end, all we seemed to do was argue—mostly about me looking at a man. Strange that she didn't mind me checking out other women. Maybe because she did it too. If we were truly happy, would either of us be checking others out? I mean, people don't stop being attractive just because you're in love. True?

I have no answers. Twenty-eight, and I'm still as confused about relationships as I was at eighteen.

It's probably best for me to be myself by myself for a while. Kissing Brock Steel was fun—amazing, actually—but I'm sure not ready for anything else.

Which means... I'm probably not ready to ask him to have sex with me so that I can conceive a child.

Of course, I don't have to tell him that's the purpose of it. All I have to do is seduce him when I know I'm ovulating.

But that's dishonest. I'm not that woman. I'll *never* be that woman.

And then I know what I'm going to do this afternoon.

I grab the box of my artwork and walk to the front of the salon. "I think that's all of it," I tell Willow. "Thanks a lot for letting me keep the studio. We need to decide on some reasonable rent."

"Don't worry about that, Rory. I don't plan on charging you rent."

"I'm certainly willing to pay my way."

"Look," she says. "I've been through hard times. I know what it's like, and it would've really helped me out if someone had just given me a little bit of a break."

"I'm afraid you're mistaken, Willow. We're not destitute."

"I know that. But I am now in a position to help someone else—pay it forward, you know?—and I'd like to do it if you let me."

I can't lie. It *would* help me out. "That's very generous of you. Thank you. But I'm afraid I just can't accept. We Pikes pay our own way. Always."

"I understand." She smiles. "How does two hundred a month sound?"

"It sounds like you're giving me a hell of a deal."

"Am I? I guess I don't know what I'm doing when it comes to things like this. I never imagined myself as a landlord. What do you think would be fair?"

"Five hundred," I say, lowballing her just a bit. "I think five hundred is what the studio is worth on a monthly basis."

"We'll make it three hundred, then," she says, "and I won't take no for an answer. If you don't want to rent it for three hundred, I'm sure I can find someone who will." She smiles.

I can't help a chuckle. "You drive a hard bargain. Three hundred it is. And thank you, Willow."

"Like I said, it's my time to pay it forward. You will as well, when it's your time."

I smile weakly. She's right, of course. I'll be happy to pay it forward someday. I'm just not sure the day will ever come when I'll be in that position.

I leave to carry the last box to the car.

I like Willow.

Perhaps we can be friends.

Having good friends is never easy when you're considered the most beautiful woman in town. Add the bisexuality to it, and I'm kind of a pariah. Any difference, no matter how subtle, that goes against the grain is wildly noticeable in a small town.

Willow's from LA. Beautiful women who like girls are everywhere on the West Coast.

I stop, put my box down, and waltz back through the door of the salon.

"Did you forget something?" Willow asks.

"I did. Would you like to hang out sometime? Maybe get a drink or dinner?"

"Sure. Sounds fun."

"Maybe . . . tonight. I'll get Callie to join us." I want to make sure Willow doesn't think I'm hitting on her. I like her a lot, but I'm not attracted to her in that way.

"I'd love to get to know both of you better. After all, we're family now. Or we will be once Callie marries Donny." Willow pulls out a card and hands it to me. "I just had these made."

The card is cute. *Willow's Th-HAIR-apy*. And it's pink, which is a strange choice. She'll be doing men's hair too, but hey, the line between the genders has been blurring for some time.

"My cell phone's on there," she says. "Tonight will be tough for me since I've still got so much to do here, and I need to get settled in the apartment. But any time after that is good. Give me a call."

"I will. See you soon, Willow."

I leave the salon once more, pick up my box, and walk around the back to where my car is parked.

And who's standing right next to my car?

Brock.

His slightly wavy hair is unruly, and he's wearing a long-sleeved T-shirt that stretches tight over his muscled chest and arms. Jeans and cowboy boots complete the picture, the jeans hugging his hips and thighs.

He walks toward me quickly and takes the box. "Let me get that for you."

"Thank you." My cheeks warm, and I'm sure I'm embarrassingly pink. "What are you doing here?"

"I think I need voice lessons." He smiles.

"That'll be the day." I roll my eyes.

"Actually... The family always said I could sing. Maybe you can tell me if they're right."

"Brock, you did not come here for voice lessons."

"Maybe I did, or maybe I didn't. Why don't we discuss it over lunch?"

I open my mouth to tell him no when my stomach lets out a huge growl.

Thanks, tummy. Nice betrayal.

Except it's not really betrayal. The thought of having lunch with Brock? I don't hate it. In fact, I like it. I really like it.

Which is not a good thing.

I'm not looking for a relationship. I'm looking for a sperm donor.

And if I *were* looking for a relationship, I certainly wouldn't find it with the biggest womanizer in Snow Creek. No matter how much my body is tingling at his nearness.

"I'll take that as a yes."

"You'll take what as a yes?"

"Your stomach. Your stomach already told me yes. Now I just need to hear yes from your beautiful lips."

Absently I bite my lower lip.

Brock sucks in a breath.

He's attracted to me. I already know this, given our little kissing session the other night.

After he secures the box in my trunk and closes it, he moves toward me until only about a foot separates us. "I haven't been able to stop thinking about you."

This time *I* suck in a breath.

I'm not sure what to say, so I don't say anything.

A few seconds later, "So about that lunch?" He lifts his eyebrows.

Lunch. Lunch is lunch. Sometimes lunch is just lunch. What is lunch, anyway?

God, my thoughts aren't making any sense. This does not bode well.

"Lunch it is. Where do you want to go?"

"We could walk over to Ava's."

"Sounds great." Ava Steel's bakery has the best sandwiches in Snow Creek, it's close, and it will be quick. Perfect recipe for a lunch I'm not sure I should be having with a man I'm not sure I should be having it with.

Ava's is only a few buildings down. I inhale the pungent yeasty aroma. Ava Steel makes better bread than anyone I know. No one tops her—not even my mother, and her sourdough is something legends are made of.

Ava sells bread, pastries, and sandwiches. The only drink she sells is bottled water from the Rocky Mountain Springs. No coffee, because she didn't want to compete with Rita's Café, which is also our local coffee shop.

Ava is different from the rest of the Steels. She bought this place on her own. Callie told me. She didn't use any Steel money, she runs it by herself, and she pays her staff from the profits. She lives above the bakery.

She's pretty amazing. Even if she does dye her hair pink. Raine mixed a special color just for her. I have to say, it works for Ava. Her natural hair is light brown, and her eyes are a searing blue that she got from her mother, Ruby Steel.

She's gorgeous. But she was never homecoming queen. The only Steel woman not to make it her year. Well, that's not exactly true. Gina, Angie, and Sage weren't queen either, but they were homecoming attendants. Brianna Steel was the queen their year. They couldn't all be queen, and four Steel women graduated that year, along with my sister Maddie, who was the fourth attendant.

The real reason Ava Steel wasn't the homecoming queen is because she refused to compete.

She's definitely her own person.

"Hey, Maya," Brock says as we enter the bakery. "Is my cousin around?"

Maya wipes her hands on her apron. "In the back. You want me to get her?"

"Only if she's not too busy."

"Not a problem. What can I get you two?"

"I'll have the Brock, of course."

I smile. All Ava's sandwiches are named after family members.

"How about you, Rory?"

"I think I'll have the Jade."

The sandwich named after Donny's mother is a grilled cheese with tomato, one of my personal favorites.

"Make that on sourdough, please," I add.

"You got it. I'll get you some waters, too."

"Thanks." Brock leads me to a vacant table.

"So what are you up to today?" he asks. "You have any lessons this afternoon?"

"No, I'm done for the day." I check my watch quickly. It's already after one o'clock. "How did you know where I was?"

"Your car was parked in the back, so I went up to the studio, but you weren't there. No one was waiting out in the hallway for their kid for a lesson, so I came back down and then I saw you through the window of the salon. I figured I'd stand by your car and wait for you."

"What if I was getting my hair done?"

"Nice try. Willow hasn't opened yet."

"Maybe she opened for me. Privately."

He smiles, shakes his head, and then reaches across the table and grabs one of my hands.

Something smolders within me at his touch.

It's scary.

And also . . . not so scary.

"I was wondering," he says. "Would you like to go out with me sometime?"

"Isn't that what we're doing now?"

He laughs then. A Steel laugh. One of those laughs that just jumps up from the belly and rings out like joyous bells. "This is lunch. This is not the Brock Steel experience."

I can't help a soft chuckle. "There's a Brock Steel experience?"

"Rory, for you? There's definitely a Brock Steel experience."

My cheeks are warming, and I'm not sure I appreciate what my body is doing. It's rebelling against me. It's showing Brock Steel how attractive I find him.

Then I laugh. I really laugh. From embarrassment? Nerves? Who knows?

"You find that funny?"

"No. I mean, yeah. I do find it kind of funny. But I get it. You're Brock Steel. All the Steels are magnificent looking, and you're at the top of the heap. Of course there's a Brock Steel experience."

He quirks his lips upward. My God, he's sexy.

"Top of the heap, huh? You should understand what that's like."

Man, this guy has an ego the size of Texas. "I should understand that?"

"Rory Pike is the most beautiful woman in Snow Creek. Everyone knows it. And it's not just your gorgeous face and hair. But that body..." He shakes his head, licks his lips.

Yeah, and this is the guy I want to father my child? Granted, he'd be beautiful. He'd also be maddeningly annoying.

"So you get it," he continues. "When two attractive people like us meet, fireworks explode in the sky."

"First of all, we met a long time ago."

"Yeah, but you were always with someone, and so was I."

This time I let out a huge laugh. "Since when have you ever been with anyone, Brock? You flit from one woman to the next like they're shots of tequila laid out on the bar."

"Let me be honest with you," he says.

"You mean you haven't been honest up to now?"

He shoves an unruly tress of hair behind his ear. "You don't even give a guy a chance, do you, Rory? But you know what?"

"I notice you didn't deny my women-like-shots-of-tequila comment."

"Why should I? I'm an honest guy. I like women."

"So do I," I can't help adding.

"Yeah. You do. But you also like men."

"Guilty." I take a sip of the water that Maya just set in front of me.

"I have to tell you," he says. "There's some shit going down in my family."

"Mine too," I say.

He lifts his eyebrows. "There is?"

"Hasn't Donny filled you in?"

"I'm afraid not."

"Callie probably asked him not to."

"Then he definitely wouldn't. My cousin is a man of his word. We all are."

His tone is sincere. Very sincere. And I get it. Brock Steel may be a total womanizer, but he's also a good man.

And I like him. I like him a lot.

So I smile. I give him the full Rory Pike dazzling smile treatment. Because you know what? Being here with him makes me feel good. Yeah, his ego's the size of Texas and Oklahoma combined. And yes, he has probably laid everything except the brick path that leads to my house. But damn, I like him. And you know what else? I like kissing him. I really would like to do it again.

"Brock?"

"Yeah?"

"I would love to go out with you sometime."

CHAPTER TEN

Brock

I try to keep the goofy smile off my face. Since when do I get all giddy when a woman says she'll go out with me? This is totally not me.

"Great," I say. "How about tonight?"

"Tonight's Monday, Brock."

"What? You don't eat on Mondays?"

"No. I just ... I guess I assumed you meant sometime on the weekend."

"Why should we wait for the weekend?"

"Don't you work during the week?"

"I work seven days a week, Rory. I'm a rancher. If I waited until I had a day off to do anything fun, I'd *never* get to do anything fun."

She looks down at the table. "Sorry."

"Don't be. Be glad you don't have to work weekends."

"I'd gladly work weekends if I were doing what I originally wanted to."

"Don't count yourself out."

"The world counted me out a long time ago. I'm good. I'm just not that good."

"I'm not sure I understand."

"Okay. You played football, like all the Steel boys. Let's

just say I was never Division I. On a good day, I might've been Division II, but really I'm Division III."

"I've heard you sing."

"So has everyone in Snow Creek."

"Well, I, for one, think you're fantastic."

Her cheeks pink a little.

"I appreciate you saying that. I do. I've made peace with my career."

"Somehow I'm not sure you're telling the truth, Rory."

She looks at me then. Meets my gaze. Man, her big brown eyes are beautiful.

"Actually, I have. Sure, I have twinges of envy for those who made it when I didn't. And I know I'm good. I'm just not good *enough*."

"Only in your own head."

"Actually... In the heads of all the opera companies who heard me audition after I finished my master's."

I'm not sure what to say. So she didn't make it. Who cares? She's a success here in town. Everyone knows and loves her.

"What about your brother? You sing with him."

"He's a rocker. You've heard him. He's hugely talented as well, but he's never made it big."

"Didn't he have plans to go on tour?"

"Yeah. It was a small tour around some elite venues in California where top agents hang out. The band was psyched, but Jesse couldn't go because of the fire. And Dragonlock may be named after Dragon, but Jesse's the voice of the band. The rest of them aren't lead material."

"I'm sorry about that."

"It was a tiny tour, Brock. Sure, agents would have seen them, but if no one bit, they would've been lucky to break even."

"I'm not talking about the tour. I'm talking about the fire."

She looks down at her empty glass. "You guys lost stuff too."

"Yeah, but your family lost almost everything. If there's anything we can do ..."

She shakes her head vehemently. "Please don't go there. I can't take your pity."

I smile at her. "You're a lot like your sister. Donny says Callie wouldn't take anything either."

"Well, we are proud people." She rolls her eyes. "Despite what some others say."

I raise my eyebrows. "Despite what some others say? What's that supposed to mean?"

"Crap. I shouldn't have said that."

"What's going on?"

She sighs. "Apparently ... someone here in town thinks the Pikes are gold diggers."

"Who?"

"I don't want to talk about it."

"Does this have anything to do with—"

"Leave it, Brock. Please."

Maya delivers our sandwiches, which offers us a quick respite. Rory picks up one half of hers, takes a bite, and then—

"Crap, that's hot!" She takes a quick sip of her water.

"Yeah, grilled cheese will do that to you."

She continues drinking.

"You okay?"

"I'm fine. I just seared off a layer of skin on my tongue, but what the hell?"

I smile. "I wouldn't want anything to happen to your tongue. I happen to love your tongue."

Her cheeks redden. And my dick hardens.

"Our first date will be better," I say.

"You mean this isn't our first date?"

"No, this is lunch. The first date is dinner. The Brock Steel experience."

That gets a chuckle out of her. "So tell me … What exactly *is* the Brock Steel experience?"

"That, my gorgeous lady, is something that can't be described. You have to experience it."

She chuckles again. "All right. Tonight it is, then. Is there anything I should do to prepare for the Brock Steel experience?"

Yeah, make sure you have birth control and sexy lingerie handy.

I don't say this of course.

"All you need to do is show up," I say. "Just leave the rest to me."

CHAPTER ELEVEN

Rory

Callie flops on my bed as I'm getting dressed for the *Brock Steel experience.*

"Something interesting happened at work today."

"Yeah?"

"Hardy Solomon brought over a case right before we closed up for the day."

By the tone of her voice, I already know this isn't good news.

"Spill it," I say.

"Seems four guys were lurking around Mrs. Mayer's house, where Pat Lamone is renting a room. They smashed the mailbox and broke a few windows."

I gasp. "Is Mrs. Mayer okay?"

"Yeah. She's in Denver visiting her daughter. But Pat is naming Jesse, Cage, Dragon, and Jake as the four men."

I wrinkle my forehead. "Jesse didn't do this. It's a high school prank. He wouldn't do something so ridiculous."

"Agreed, but that didn't stop Lamone from fingering Jesse and the rest of his band. I don't believe it for a minute, but I haven't been able to get hold of Jesse to get his alibi. Do you know where he is?"

"He probably has a gig or something."

"They'd have told you if they had a gig. They'd probably want you to sing."

"I don't always sing with them. Only when I'm available."

"And you're not available tonight?"

"I'm going out."

"With whom?"

I smile wryly. "One guess."

"Are you serious? Brock?"

"Yes. And he promises me the"—air quote—"*Brock Steel experience.*"

"Oh my God."

"Yeah. I have no idea what to expect. Okay, I have every idea what to expect."

"He'll try to get you into bed."

"That's right." I hold back a smile.

Callie clears her throat. "Anyway, back to Lamone. Donny and I think Pat probably did all the damage himself and made up the four guys thing. I mean, it's a little too convenient, right? Mrs. Mayer's out of town, and four guys who look like Jesse and his friends—who are all over thirty years old, mind you, not really the mailbox-smashing type—just happen to be out carousing and decide to vandalize a sweet widow's house?"

"Lamone is such an ass. Why would he even try to get Jesse involved?"

"To hurt us, and unfortunately, Jesse is already involved. He's been involved since he saw those pictures of us. And he's mad as hell. Can you blame him?"

Yeah, my brother seeing me naked and spread-eagled in an old photo that Pat Lamone took of me when I was unconscious wasn't on my bucket list.

"No, I don't blame him. But he didn't do this. He'd never

harm Mrs. Mayer."

"Hardy's looking for him."

I rub my temples, trying to ease the headache that seems determined to erupt the same night I'm supposed to have the Brock Steel experience. "God, Callie, is there no end to this? Why is he looking for Jesse?"

"Since Lamone filed a report and named the band members, Hardy has to investigate. Donny and I are working on it. There's so much else going on with his family, though."

"Yeah, Brock mentioned that."

Callie gasps. "How much did he tell you?"

"Nothing. That's it. Just that there's some shit going on with his family."

Callie nods. Clearly she knows more than she's telling me, and right now, that's okay. I can't handle more than Pat Lamone and this impending Brock Steel experience at the moment.

"Let me know if you find Jesse."

"I will. In the meantime, enjoy the Brock Steel experience." Callie exits my room through our shared bathroom.

I have no idea what the Brock Steel experience entails. All I know is that it includes dinner, but I don't know where. Are we going to eat here in Snow Creek? Or are we going to drive into Grand Junction for a more formal dinner?

To be ready for anything, I choose skinny black pants and a stretchy white sweater. Simple black pumps that go with any occasion and gold hoop earrings. Red lipstick, blush, a touch of mascara, and my long hair down in waves over my back.

By the time I'm ready, Brock has already arrived. I walk out, trying my best to look demure, and find him sitting in the living room talking to my mother.

"There you are, Rory." My mother smiles.

"Hi." Embarrassment swirls through me as my voice cracks a little.

Brock rises. "Good evening, Rory. You look gorgeous, as usual." He walks toward me and gives me a chaste kiss on the cheek.

"Thank you," I murmur.

"You two have a good night. It was nice to see you, Brock." Mom heads out of the living room toward the kitchen.

"I see you charmed the apron off my mother," I say.

"Lovely lady, I can charm anyone."

I resist the eye roll. It's the truth, after all. Heck, Brock Steel is even charming me. I'm totally falling for his politeness, his gentility, and of course his gorgeous looks. Not a good look on me.

"I wasn't sure how to dress for the Brock Steel experience," I say.

"You chose well."

"Where are we going?"

"I thought we would drive into Grand Junction and go to the Fortnight."

"Snow Creek food not good enough for the Brock Steel experience?"

"I love Snow Creek food. But Rory Pike deserves the best."

My cheeks warm as we leave the house and walk to his car at the end of the drive. A Tesla, no less. Navy blue. I'd have expected something a little flashier from Brock Steel—a red Alfa Romeo maybe—but as he opens the door for me and I slide into the passenger seat, my perspective changes.

This is Brock Steel in automobile form. I inhale. The damned car even smells like him.

After he sits down in the driver's seat, he turns to me and slides one finger down the apple of my cheek, leaving smoldering embers on my flesh.

"I'm very happy about tonight," he says.

"Tonight hasn't started yet."

"I'm very happy it's about to start." He brushes his lips gently over mine.

I'm pretty sure my skin is on fire from his kiss, which was nearly as chaste as the one in the living room. I'm not sure how to respond, so I don't. He starts the engine, and we're off.

Conversation is surprisingly easy with Brock. We manage to talk about his work and mine without it turning to all the crap we're both going through. Works for me. I'm not sure how much I should say to him regarding Lamone and my past. I need to talk to Callie first.

Besides, for one night, I'd like to forget about Pat Lamone. Forget that he's trying to pin some fake vandalism charge on my brother. Perhaps Brock wants to forget about his own family drama as well.

Still the gentleman, Brock parks, leaves the car, and opens the door for me. He takes my hand, and we walk into the Fortnight.

"Good evening, Mr. Steel." The maître d' smiles.

"Good evening."

"Your table is ready." He hands two menus to a hostess in a long black skirt who leads us through the dining room to a secluded private table.

She hands me a menu first and then one to Brock. "Your server will be with you soon."

I take a quick look. No prices are listed. I lift my eyebrows.

"What?" Brock asks.

"It's just ... This menu doesn't have any prices on it."

"Yeah. I asked them to print special menus for us."

"Why?"

"Because I don't want price to be an issue with you. I want you to order what you want, regardless of the cost."

"Except that doesn't really work," I tell him. "I know Wagyu beef is a heck of a lot more expensive than chicken piccata."

He laughs. "Smart girl."

"You don't have to be smart to know that."

"Rory Pike, for the most beautiful girl in Snow Creek, you have the worst time taking a compliment."

"What makes you say that?"

"I compliment your intelligence by calling you smart. You tell me everyone knows what you know. This afternoon at lunch, I told you how wonderful I thought your voice was. You proceeded to tell me how you never made it in opera. I tell you you're gorgeous. At least you don't have a comeback for that one."

Heat flows into me. I'm sure I'm blushing. I look down absently. Yeah, my chest is pink. What do I say to that? Do I say I know I'm beautiful? That makes me sound conceited. Do I throw it back in his face? That just proves his point that I can't take a compliment.

"Have I rendered you speechless?" His dark eyes twinkle.

"I've been told since I was a kid how pretty I am," I say. "I guess I learned not to throw that one back. But then Callie came along, and you know how smart she is. Just brilliant. A different kind of mind from Jesse's and mine. She is logical and analytical where Jess and I are creative and emotional. He and I heard from the day she started talking how smart she was. So I guess I just learned to think of myself as second best when it comes to intelligence. And then, when I didn't make it in opera, second best when it comes to talent as well."

It's a stark admission, and I don't make it lightly. And I find myself wondering why I made it to Brock Steel, a man I hardly know.

"So you were typecast," he says. "You were the pretty one and Callie was the smart one."

"Yeah, pretty much."

"I get that."

"Do you?"

"Yeah. My brother, Brad, is the smart one."

"Really?"

"That surprises you?"

"Well, yeah. All the Steels are so brilliant and so gorgeous. I guess I find it hard to believe any of you are the"—air quote—"*smart ones.*"

"Brad runs a nonprofit corporation. He's a genius in business. Me? I'm a rancher. I raise beef."

"You make a heck of a lot of money raising beef," I say. "Surely that takes some smarts."

"Of course it does. I think there are different kinds of smarts."

"So why does Brad get credit for being smarter than you are?"

"Because of the type of intelligence he possesses. He's got a business mind. He helps Dad on the business side of the operation, and he runs the Steel Foundation with Henry. He's a workaholic, frankly."

"All the Steels have great work ethics."

"There's a difference between work ethic and being a workaholic. Brad does nothing but work. Me? I believe in balance. I help Dad run the ranching side, and when I'm working, I'm all in. But I take time for fun while Brad lives and breathes work. He'll probably take over as CEO when Dad steps down."

"He'll leave the foundation?"

"Yeah. Henry is primed to run the foundation on his own."

"So you get it."

"I do. That doesn't mean I believe it. The world can think Brad is smarter than I am, but I know the truth. We're equally intelligent, just in different ways."

"So you think Callie and I are equally intelligent?"

"I'd stake my fortune on it."

I smile. I can't help it. Brock Steel makes me smile. Brock Steel makes me feel good about myself. I hope in some small way I do the same for him. Though he already has an ego the size of the universe.

"So tell me," he says. "If you're the pretty one and Callie is the smart one, what does that make Jesse and Maddie?"

"Jesse was a star athlete, as you know. Plus he's the oldest and the only boy, which already gives him a leg up. Maddie, she's the vivacious one. The one with all the personality."

"I'm pretty sure I remember you being vivacious in your day. Ms. Homecoming Queen, Ms. Star of Every School Play and Musical."

"There's a difference. I'm an actress. I was *acting* vivacious."

"Well, if I'm honest, you *are* beautiful. The most beautiful in your family. But Callie and Maddie are also beautiful, and Jesse is very good-looking."

"Something you want to tell me?" I lift my eyebrows.

"No. You're the only bisexual person at this table. That doesn't mean I don't know a good-looking man when I see one."

Nice. I'm impressed. This is a man who's completely comfortable in his own skin. Why shouldn't he be? He's male perfection.

I smile. "I'm only teasing."

"I figured."

The ease of the conversation surprises me once more. I'm telling this man things I don't normally talk about, especially on a first—or is this the second?—date.

I want to share everything about myself.

Yes, it's scary, but it also feels good. Really good. It feels almost . . . *right*.

What the heck? *Let's go all in.*

CHAPTER TWELVE

Brock

"You can ask me about it," she says.

"About what?"

"My bisexuality. I know you're curious. Most people are."

Understatement of the year. I'm curious as hell about everything Rory Pike, but I never dreamed she'd tell me anything about her orientation. "I am. But... it's a personal thing."

"True. But it doesn't feel all that personal to me. It's just part of who I am. It's as natural to me as my brown hair."

I clear my throat and adjust my junk discreetly. At least I hope it's discreetly. "That's really interesting. When did you discover your ... you know?"

"My bisexuality? You can say the word, Brock."

"Yeah. Right. Your bisexuality." *For God's sake, stop acting like a horny teenager.*

"Looking back, I think I always knew. Back in middle school, when everyone was having their first crush, I found myself thinking about boys *and* girls in the same way. I wanted to kiss the cutest boy in the class, and I also wanted to kiss the cutest girl in the class."

"Really?"

"Yeah. Of course I couldn't tell anyone about it, especially not at that age. I didn't actually come out until after high school, but you probably know that."

"In college, then?"

"Yeah. College is a great place for experimentation." She laughs.

"What's so funny?"

"Just thinking about my first few times. It's amazing the sheer number of straight girls I was able to seduce."

My groin tightens. The thought of Rory and all the cute straight girls on campus... She's not playing fair. And I'm being immature. Or at least my body is.

"But it lost its excitement after a while," she says. "None of those girls were interested in a relationship with me. For obvious reasons. They weren't actually gay or bi."

"So would you say you were with more women than men in college?" *Damn, Brock, shut up!*

"I wouldn't say that. The stuff with straight girls was mostly fooling around. We kissed, maybe did some second-base action. They weren't willing to go all the way."

"God, Rory." I can't help it. I'm hard as a damned rock.

"What?"

"Do you have any fucking idea how turned on I am right now?"

She laughs, thank God. I haven't disgusted her with my immature horniness.

"I know what girl-girl does to a red-hot-blooded straight man," she says, her gorgeous eyes twinkling.

God, is she doing this on purpose?

"Yeah, girl-girl. Boy-girl. Or just Rory Pike. You are the hottest thing walking, babe. And I'm far from the only one who thinks that."

"Why is it that you're the only one I want thinking that right now?" she says coyly.

Damn. She's out of her shell now. No wonder she seduced all the straight girls in college. This woman has mad skills to go with her beauty. My cock grows even harder. Rory's teasing, of course. I hear it in the tone of her voice. But fuck, her words . . .

"Then I'd say I'm on the right track," I finally reply.

Her cheeks blush a glorious soft pink. She opens her mouth to say something, but our server appears.

"Good evening, Mr. Steel, and . . ."

"Ms. Pike," I say.

"Ms. Pike. Wonderful. I'm Lori, and I'll be your server. What can I get you to drink this evening?"

"Rory?" I ask.

"I think I'll just have sparkling mineral water, thank you."

"Cap Rock martini for me," I say.

"Thank you. Did you want to order any appetizers?"

I glance at Rory.

"I don't think so," she says.

"You sure? The steak tartare is excellent. A hundred percent Steel beef."

"I don't eat raw meat. Most of the time." She lifts one eyebrow.

Just slightly, but I notice. I notice everything about Rory. More teasing. God, I'm going to explode.

"One order of steak tartare for me, then," I say to Lori. "And bring some crispy brussels sprouts for the lady."

Rory wrinkles her nose. "Brussels sprouts. Really?"

"That's what you're getting unless you tell me what you actually want."

Yeah, two can play this game. Though the raw meat

comment almost undid me.

She glances down at her menu. "Fine. I'll have the oysters on the half shell."

"Awesome," Lori says. "Did you want West Coast or East Coast?"

"East Coast, I think."

"Perfect. I'll get everything started, and I'll be back with your drinks in a few minutes." Lori whisks away.

"Thought you don't eat raw meat." I smile. Sort of.

"Oysters aren't meat. They're seafood. And they're a delicacy. I'm happy to eat any delicacy." She bites her lower lip.

Damn, damn, damn. She's trying to kill me right here at the Fortnight.

I gaze at her. Right into her beautiful eyes, until she finally looks away.

Okay. Now what? I'm truly interested in learning more about her bisexuality, and not just because it's hot. I'm actually interested. I'm interested in everything about her.

"Tell me more about this self-discovery of yours. About your sexual orientation."

"I'm more than my sexual orientation, Brock."

"Don't you think I know that? You're also more than just your gorgeous face and awesome rack."

Her eyes widen.

Okay, maybe that was too far.

But then she smiles. "Thank you for noticing. And I actually get it—why you're interested. Why everyone's interested. As a bisexual, I'm in a minority, so people in the majority—like you—don't quite understand. I can't really explain how it all works, except to say that it's normal for me."

"Meaning...?"

"Meaning you're a straight man. What's normal for you is to be attracted to women and only women. So just imagine that being bisexual—being attracted to both sexes—feels that way to me. Completely normal."

"I'm not sure anyone's explained it in such a succinct way before," I say.

"I'm not sure anyone's ever explained it to you at all before."

I laugh. "Touché. You're right about that."

"You don't have any friends that are a different sexual orientation?"

"No, I do. One of my buddies from college is gay. But it's not something we talk about. I guess it's a guy thing."

"Maybe. Maybe you're just more comfortable asking me, a woman."

"You know? You're probably right. You're easy to talk to."

"So are you," she says, "and it surprises the heck out of me."

"Rory, why does that surprise you? Surely you don't think I'm nothing more than a pretty face."

That gets her. She looks down. "I don't. Not anymore, anyway."

"See? You and I have that in common. We're judged on our looks alone. But I'm interested in more than your looks."

The truth of my words surprises me more than a little. Since when am I interested in something deeper?

"So you're interested in my bisexuality, then," she says.

"That among other things. I'm interested in everything about you. I hope I've made that clear. But sure, I'm interested in your orientation. I think everyone is interested in something that's different."

"Probably. Although I don't go around asking straight people when they realized they were straight."

I laugh again. "Rory, you are something else."

She smiles demurely. I mean, really demurely. This woman is well practiced in the art of the smile. "Thank you for noticing."

"Babe, anyone would have to be blind not to notice you."

She scoffs softly. "I mean, thank you for noticing that there's more to me than the surface."

"There's more to *everyone* than just the surface," I say.

"I know that. But you're Brock Steel. A Rake-a-teer."

Am I supposed to apologize? "Guilty. I like women. I like taking women to bed. I like taking beautiful women to bed. But it's a lot more satisfying when they have something between their ears as well."

"Really? Even for a one-nighter?"

"Of course. Lovemaking is an art. The smart ones know what they're doing. Or if they don't, they're willing to learn. The others tend to just lie there."

This gets a laugh out of her. A really happy laugh. A laugh that makes me want to say something hilarious just to hear that sound for the rest of my life.

Boy, that thought jars me. The rest of my life? I'm twenty-four. A Rake-a-teer, as Rory says. I can't be thinking about the rest of my life with Rory Pike or anyone else.

Definitely time to change the subject.

I pick up my menu. "So what looks good?"

"Not raw beef, that's for sure. Maybe the scallops."

"You're going to pass up Steel beef for scallops?"

"Sue me. I love seafood." She licks her lips. "I love delicacies."

Man, oh man . . .

"You may have your heart's desire tonight. It's all part of—"

"The Brock Steel experience," she finishes with me.

Fuck me. I'm beginning to crush hard on Rory Pike. Really hard. I can't wait to get her into bed later tonight.

CHAPTER THIRTEEN

Rory

By the time we're done with dinner, my body is smoldering. The back-and-forth banter has me hotter than I've been in a long time. I can barely make it to Brock's car on my jelly legs.

"Where to now?" I ask.

"I thought maybe a little dancing at the Plaza."

I must drop my jaw, because he lifts my chin, and my lips close.

"Surprised?"

"I figured you'd say something like 'back to my place, babe.'"

He lets out a laugh.

"You know, the Brock Steel experience and all."

"I won't deny that a roll in my bed is a very important part of the Brock Steel experience, but I'm not all about sex, Rory, no matter what you've heard."

Way to make me feel like a heel. Crap. "Sorry."

"No need to apologize. Now . . . about that dancing at the Plaza?"

"There's a Plaza in Grand Junction?"

"Well, no. It's the dancing lounge at the Carlton. But it will do."

"I haven't been dancing in . . . I mean, not counting when

I dance at the parties at your house."

"You mean Uncle Talon's house."

"Well, yeah. The big Steel ranch house. Why doesn't your father live there? Isn't he the oldest?"

"He is, but my grandfather was still alive when my father ventured out on his own. He lived in the guesthouse for a little while, but then he had his own home built. Uncle Talon went off to the military after college, and Aunt Marjorie was still in school. Uncle Ryan moved into the guesthouse after college and stayed there for quite a long time. Until he got married. When Uncle Talon got back from the military, and after our father died, he moved into the main house with Aunt Marjorie while she finished college. Then he just never left, so when he and Aunt Jade got married, they kept the big house because my father already had his own."

"And your dad was okay with that?"

"Have you seen my dad's house?"

"No."

"That's because all the big parties are at the main house. I'll show you my dad's house sometime. You'll see that he lost nothing by not taking the main house."

"I see. I guess we got a little off track. But my point is, no. Raine wasn't a big dancer, so I haven't been dancing in forever. Except for that little bit I do at your parties, and that's very little because I'm usually singing with the band."

"Do I have a treat for you, then. It's big-band night at the Carlton, so we're going to do some actual dancing."

"Actual dancing?"

"Well, I'm no Fred Astaire, but I think we'll have fun."

The trip to the Carlton takes only a few minutes. The valet opens the door for me, and Brock hands him the keys and then leads me into the Carlton through the lobby and toward the bar. This hotel is Grand Junction's finest. Which explains why I've never stayed here. In fact, I've never been in this bar.

A band is playing. Glenn Miller. The musicians are all tuxedo-clad, a far cry from what Jesse and his bandmates wear when they perform.

Part of me saddens as the tuxedos jar a memory. I met many tuxedoed men during all my auditions. I dressed in the female version of a tuxedo—a cocktail dress—and I sang my heart out for company after company.

I could barely afford the required clothes. Mom and Dad were great about helping me, and I did pay them back. But not with money I made performing, as I originally intended. With money I made teaching.

Those who can, do. Those who can't, teach …

How I hate that adage.

A few couples are on the dance floor, swing dancing.

How does Brock know? How did he know I would enjoy this music?

Ambivalence slides through me. I love anything classical, and though this music doesn't fit the actual definition of classical music, it is classic in its own way. The big bands of the forties sure knew how to make music.

Yet seeing the musicians dressed as they are … Just too much baggage there.

"Would you like a drink?" Brock asks.

"You know? I didn't drink at dinner, so I think I would."

"What would you like?"

"Honestly? I'm not sure. What's a good after-dinner drink?"

"Irish coffee is always a safe bet. Or any kind of brandy or cognac. Or really... Whatever you want. I don't stand on ceremony."

"What are you having?" I ask.

"I'm not an alcohol snob like my dad or Dale. But I do enjoy a nice cognac."

"Make it two, then."

Truth be told, I'm not sure I've ever tasted cognac. We snag two seats at the bar, and Brock orders our drinks. A few minutes later, two large-bowled goblets sit in front of us.

The stem is short, and I don't know how to pick it up. Brock lifts his, cradling the bowl in his hand.

Easy enough. I do the same.

He swirls the brown liquid in the glass and then sniffs it. I've seen people do this to wine, but never cognac.

So I copy him, taking care not to slosh the liquid out of the cup.

He takes a sip. So I take a sip.

It's smoky, strong, kind of woodsy. But it's smooth. It glides down my throat, and I don't have the urge to choke on it. That happens to me sometimes with hard liquor.

"What do you think?"

"It's good. What kind of cognac is it?"

"Rémy Martin. Do you like it?"

"So far."

"Good." He takes another sip and then smiles and sets his glass down on the bar. "Would you like to dance?"

"I don't know any of the steps."

"And you think I do?" He chuckles.

I set my drink down on top of a cocktail napkin. "In that case, sure. Let's dance."

He leads me to the dance floor. Only two other couples are dancing, one of whom seems to know all kinds of intricate steps. The other just moves together, holding each other.

I place my left hand on Brock's shoulder, my right hand in his left.

"I like this," he says.

"Dancing?"

"You. In my arms."

I say nothing, though I like it as well. We fit together. We're both tall, first of all, but he's tall enough that I can wear heels and not feel like an Amazon. My three-and-a-half-inch pumps still put me slightly below his eye level.

When the music gets slower, I find myself leaning into him.

His chest is so hard. Rock hard. I've always wondered how the Steels stay in such great shape because I never see them at the gym. Snow Creek only has one gym. Of course, they probably all have fitness centers in their houses.

For a moment, I let myself enjoy being held.

This is what I miss when I'm with a woman. The hardness. The differences between our bodies. My last two relationships have been with women. Now? I find myself hungering for the hardness of a man.

I just never thought it would be *this* man.

Really, I'm only looking for a sperm donor. Hot sex can be a great precursor to pregnancy. If I orgasm, there's a better chance of conception.

Mental note: get an ovulation kit.

Is there a chance I'm going to end up in bed with Brock Steel tonight? He already said bed is part of the Brock Steel experience. All I'd have to do is give him one slight hint, and we could be rolling in the hay.

But is that what I want?

Or do I want to get to know him better?

Already I know the answer to my question, and it scares the hell out of me.

I want both.

CHAPTER FOURTEEN

Brock

I can't think straight with her tits pressed against me like this. Maybe this wasn't such a great idea. I began this evening hoping to get her into my bed.

Now? I still want to get her into my bed, but I find myself really liking her. There's a lot more to Rory Pike than a hot body and a beautiful face. Somehow I want her to understand that as well.

I guess we never had that problem in our family. We were all valued as individuals, not based on one simple trait.

Not that I think that's what the Pikes have done. Rory the beauty. Callie the brain. Maddie the personality.

I know the Pikes. They're good people. They wouldn't do that to their kids. But I suppose it's possible the same thing happened with Brad and me to a lesser extent. I kind of overstated it when I told Rory about it. Neither of us was ever made to feel that we were "less than" because we excelled better at something than the other did. I told Rory that Brad was always considered the smart one, and that's true. But we are all loved equally for our uniqueness.

That's something all our parents did right.

Unfortunately, I'm finding they did a lot of things wrong too. Like keeping family history from us. Family history that's raising its head now.

But I don't want to think about that. Soon enough I'm going to have to go with Dale and Donny back to that property up north. I'm going to have to find out if there are decaying human bodies in that old barn.

Nope, not going there. Not tonight. I want to enjoy this evening, see where it goes organically. I told Rory I'd give her the Brock Steel experience, but now? I don't want to use my patented moves on Rory Pike. I want to let her take the lead.

I can't help but chuckle.

Rory pulls away from me slightly. "Something funny?"

"No. I was just thinking of something else."

"What?"

"It's nothing." I pull her back toward me. "Your hair smells amazing."

"I use a honey lavender infused shampoo, professional grade. I guess I won't be able to get it anymore now that Raine is out of my life."

"I'll figure out how to get it for you."

This time *she* chuckles. "You still think you can buy everything, don't you?"

"I didn't mean it that way."

I truly didn't. But it's true. I don't think sometimes. Do I think I can find that shampoo for her and get it? Absolutely. Probably within a few seconds on my phone.

Growing up a Steel does have its benefits.

Rory doesn't reply. I hope she believes me. I was only trying to please her. And strangely enough, I really want to please her.

Finally she says, "I'm sure I can find it somewhere on the internet. These days you can find anything, even things that only licensed professionals are supposed to buy."

"If you can find it, please do," I say. "Your hair... It's so soft and smooth, and the fragrance is... I don't know. I've never smelled anything like it."

"You probably have if you've ever gone out with a woman who went to Raine's salon."

Since Raine was the only hairstylist in Snow Creek for the last couple of years, Rory is undoubtedly right. But this is the first time I've noticed it.

And that's because of who it's attached to.

When the song ends, the band takes a fifteen-minute break, so I take Rory back to the bar, where she takes another drink of her cognac.

"This is growing on me," she says.

"Good. I'm glad you like it."

"Would it surprise you to know I've never tasted cognac before?"

"Should it?"

"You know as well as I do that my family doesn't have the kind of money yours does."

"That doesn't mean you've never had cognac."

"We're not your kind of family. Plus, Callie and I don't drink very much. We never have."

"Nothing wrong with that." I take another sip. This is a nice cognac, but it's not the best. The best cognac is Armagnac from France. I didn't want to freak Rory out by ordering that. It's pretty expensive.

"What are you thinking about?" I ask.

She has a serene look on her face. Her eyes seem focused on something far away, perhaps in her mind. "It wouldn't interest you."

"Why would you say that? Of course it would interest me."

She sighs. "I'm just thinking about... my life. About how part of me still yearns for the spotlight. When I hear big-band music like this and I see the musicians dressed so formally, I remember the audition process. Recitals. I miss it."

"Have you thought about doing a recital?"

She laughs then. "In Snow Creek? Who would come?"

"Probably the whole city, Rory. It would be something new and exciting."

"I don't know. With everything else going on in my life. In your life."

"What's my life got to do with it? In fact, what if I bankrolled the whole thing?"

Her eyes go wide then. "No. A thousand times no."

"Come on, Rory. This isn't a handout. This is me providing our city with a cultural event. And let me tell you, cultural events are lacking here in Snow Creek."

"Brock..."

"Honestly, I think this is an amazing idea."

Truth. Absolute truth. Rory could get her recital, and our city could get a cultural event, something we've never had before. And why am I suddenly interested in cultural events?

Because it would please Rory. My God...

"I'm loving this idea," I continue. "What do we need?"

"Well, first of all, we need an event location. We don't have an auditorium in Snow Creek."

"We have a cinema."

Rory pauses a moment, cocks her head. "You know, that could actually work."

"Of course it could work. A lot of cinemas rent out their space for conferences and workshops. Why not a recital?"

She twists her lips, her head still tilted.

"What else?"

"I'll need an accompanist. On piano."

"Surely someone in Snow Creek plays piano."

"No. I would need a professional accompanist. One who knows all the classical and musical theater pieces."

"Okay, we'll bring someone in from Grand Junction."

"And . . ."

"Yeah?"

"I need a dress. A cocktail dress."

"Easy enough. Not in Snow Creek, of course, but here in the city you can find anything. What about music?"

"I have plenty of sheet music, including the piano accompaniment. That won't be a problem."

"Let's do this, then."

She shakes her head, smiling. "You're crazy."

"I've been called that before."

"No one in Snow Creek is going to be interested in this."

"Why do you say that?"

"Because no one in any big city was interested in me, Brock."

"Hey, I was just in middle school at the time, but I seem to recall you starring in every high school musical to a packed house."

"That's because all the people who came had kids in the chorus or in the play."

"So? I think this can work, Rory. I wouldn't suggest it if I didn't think it could."

Her face shines with radiance. Her beautiful full lips curve upward. And her eyes—those big brown eyes that could melt the snow caps on Pike's Peak—look happy. She wants this.

And I want to give it to her.

"Let me do this for you," I say.

"Why? Why would you want to put something like this together? Just for me?"

"Because of the look on your face right now."

Her rosy cheeks pink further. I reach forward, trail my finger over one. Then I touch the long strands of her hair. So beautifully brown and soft.

God, I want to kiss her. I want to kiss her more than I've ever wanted to kiss a woman in my life.

And rather than frightening the hell out of me, the thought makes me feel . . . right.

Just right.

"*The Three Bears*," I murmur.

"Three bears? What are you talking about?"

"Just right," I say. "I feel just right."

She smiles, and I trail my index finger over her glossy bottom lip.

And I'm determined, right then, that I'm not going to take her into my bed tonight. No. I'm going to savor this.

Savor every moment.

And also, I'm going to produce a recital for her. Brock Steel, producer. I don't have a clue what I'm doing, but I can get help from her brother, Jesse, on sound. Plus, the cinema has a built-in sound system. I can find an accompanist in Grand Junction. We'll need to put together rehearsals, and we'll need to work on scheduling.

Thanksgiving is coming in a couple of weeks. Perhaps that could be the theme.

Or maybe we wait and make it a holiday recital, for Christmas. After all, Thanksgiving is Uncle Ryan and Aunt

Ruby's anniversary. We'll be having a big party.

Ideas flow through my head, exciting me.

Totally crazy. Never in my life have I been interested in entertainment production of any kind, but at this moment, it's all I can think about.

"You're beautiful," I say. "And I'm not just talking about what's on the outside."

Rory takes the last sip of her cognac and meets my gaze, her brown eyes smoldering. "How'd you like to get out of here?"

I smile. She's inviting me to take her to bed. I'm not shocked. Our chemistry so far has been off the charts.

And of course a certain part of me is really fond of the idea.

But . . .

It's not the right time. Even though I want it more than anything, it's not the right time. Which is so strange, because it's always the right time to have sex as far as I'm concerned. Especially sex with the most beautiful woman on the planet.

I take her hand, rub my thumbs into the softness of her palm, nod to the bartender to close out our tab, and then I lead her out of the bar, out of the hotel, to my car.

We don't talk much as we drive back toward Snow Creek. To my own surprise as well as hers, I make the turn toward the Pike Ranch.

"Brock?" she says.

"Yes?"

"Don't you want to . . ."

"More than I want to breathe."

"You know my parents are home. Maybe Jesse and Callie too."

I nod. "I know."

"Don't you live in your family's guesthouse?"

"I do."

"Then shouldn't we—"

I stop in her driveway. Then I turn, cup one of her cheeks. "Not like this," I say.

"Not like what, exactly?"

I kiss her then. Slide my lips over hers, let our tongues touch briefly. My cock is at attention—it has been since her meat comment early in the evening—and I'm ready to go everywhere—over her nipples, her beautiful skin, between her legs to taste her most secret treasures.

She leans into me, tries to deepen the kiss.

I pull back.

She lifts her eyebrows. "Seriously?"

"Maybe this evening didn't mean as much to you as it meant to me," I say.

She doesn't reply. Just lifts her eyebrows a bit farther.

"I don't want to be your rebound guy."

"Who said anything about a rebound?"

"You just got out of a relationship. I don't want to be the rebound sex."

"Oh... Okay." She turns and throws her back against the passenger seat.

Great. I pissed her off.

"I'd like to fuck you into tomorrow right now."

"Why don't you, then?"

"I think I just told you."

"What if I'm only looking for a rebound guy?"

Man. Boner killer. But I'm sticking to my guns. "Then you've got the wrong man."

"The entire town would say I've got exactly the *right* man."

"The entire town would be wrong, then. This time."

She sighs. Then she opens the passenger door and hops out.

"Wait." I hop out of my own side. "Let me walk you to the door."

"What's the point?"

She whisks away, walking alone to the door.

I turn toward her to keep up. Sure, I may be a womanizer, but I'm also a gentleman. I have *always* walked a woman to the door. Usually *my* door, but hey ... Things change.

I kiss her cheek. "I had a great time."

"Yeah. Me too."

"You think about that recital. I want to do that for you."

She nods. "Thanks for dinner. And the dancing."

"Anytime." This time I kiss her lips, making a concerted effort not to use any tongue. "I'll call you."

She mumbles something I can't make out.

"What?"

"Never mind." She opens her door and disappears behind it.

CHAPTER FIFTEEN

Rory

"You've got to be kidding," Callie says as she wipes sleep out of her eyes.

"Totally not kidding. He did *not* try to get me into bed."

"Were you out with Brock Steel? Or his evil twin? Scratch that. His polite twin."

"Brock Steel, or someone who looks exactly like him."

"Yeah, like I said. The polite twin."

"Maybe because it's a work night."

"I'm pretty sure that's never stopped any of the Rake-a-teers before. It sure never stopped Donny."

I shake my head. "It was strange. We were really clicking. At least I thought we were. So I asked him if he wanted to get out of there."

"And what did he say?"

"He brought me here."

Callie raises an eyebrow.

"Not to sound full of myself or anything, but I'm not used to being turned down. By men or women."

"And certainly not by Brock Steel," Callie adds.

"No kidding. If there was ever a sure thing, he is it."

"What else happened? What did he say when he dropped you off?"

"He said he'd call me."

"Well, that's a good thing, right?"

"Maybe. I don't know. He said he didn't want to be my rebound guy. What the heck is wrong with being a rebound guy? What the heck is wrong with some hot rebound sex? Most guys would be all over it."

"Yeah ... and Brock would be at the front of the line."

"Right?"

Callie pauses, tilting her head a bit. "What else did he say?"

"You're not going to believe this. He wants to produce a recital for me."

"A recital?"

"Yes. I want him to father my child, and he wants to throw me a recital."

Callie laughs then. A sleepy laugh. "Did I just hear you right?"

"Yes, he wants to throw me a recital."

"No. Did you actually ask him to father your child?"

"Of course not. I briefly considered it, but then I didn't."

"Thank God."

"Yes, I know your feelings on the matter."

"My feelings on the matter aside, it almost sounds like ..."

"What?"

"It sounds like he might want to make something work with you."

"That's ridiculous. He's a Rake-a-teer."

"Yes. But so is my fiancé."

"True, but your fiancé is thirty-two as opposed to Brock's twenty-four. There's a difference."

"Maybe. But I don't know, Ror. I'm as surprised as you are

by Brock's attitude. Maybe he actually feels something."

The thought sends a tingle through me. Brock? Feels something? The truth is I'm feeling something too. None of which makes any sense. For me maybe. But for Brock?

"How could he feel anything? We barely know each other."

"Still, you never know."

I scoff. "He's playing some kind of game, and I'm not going to be a part of it."

"What kind of game could he be playing?"

"I don't know. Make the bisexual homecoming queen fall in love with him? Laugh about it to his friends? Before he dumps me?"

"That would just be ... mean."

She's right. I'm not sure why I'm thinking that. Brock isn't that guy. I hope. "Yeah, it would."

"Brock Steel is a lot of things, but he's not a mean person. None of the Steels are."

She's got me there. The Steels have been nothing but generous to us.

I sigh. "So what do I do? Date him?"

"That's up to you, I think."

"What about my baby?"

"I don't know. If you want a baby more than anything, and you're not willing to wait to have it the natural way—"

"The natural way? It may not happen the natural way for me, Cal. You know that. I could very well end up with a woman as my life mate."

"Right. I don't know, then. If it's the most important thing to you right now, you should go to the sperm bank."

She's right. Absolutely. "Right. I will go to the sperm bank.

Tomorrow. I only have lessons in the morning. There's just one thing."

"What's that?"

"I want you to go with me."

"I have this little problem," she says. "It's called my job."

"Let's get real, Callie. You're engaged to a Steel. You're going to be starting law school in the winter, as planned. You don't need the job."

"Am I really hearing you, Rory? You want me to just walk out of my job because I'm marrying money?"

I sigh. "I didn't mean it that way, and you know it. But you know as well as I do that Jade Steel created the job for you."

"I do know that, but I also know that Jade is not coming back, so now we have a workload problem. Donny's the only city attorney, and we're used to having two."

"You're not an attorney yet, Cal. You can't fill that void yet."

"Not as an attorney, no. But I can help with the workload."

I sigh again. Why am I being so ridiculous? This isn't me. "You're right. I'm sorry I suggested otherwise. I know you and your work ethic. Heck, I have a work ethic too. At least I used to when I did something worthwhile."

I wish I could take back that last part. Why am I dwelling on my failures? I got over that a long time ago. At least I thought I did.

"You're a teacher, Rory. Everything you do is worthwhile. You're bringing music into the lives of children. What could be more noble than that?"

And for the third time, I sigh. A big one. She's right, of course. Teaching is a noble calling, especially when music is being taken out of public school curricula every day due to budget cuts.

But there's still a part of me that longs to be on the stage.

"Then let Brock throw this recital for you."

I drop my jaw. "Did I say that out loud?"

"No, actually. I could just tell by the wistful look on your face. You were thinking about performing."

"You know me better than I know myself sometimes," I say. "When he suggested the recital . . . I don't know. I mean, I love performing with Jesse in the band, and I do love rock and roll. But my first love has always been the stage. The musical theater stage. The opera stage."

"I know."

"He said . . . He said he wanted to do it because of the look on my face."

"He probably saw the look I'm seeing right now." Callie yawns.

"I'm sorry. I'm keeping you up, and you do have work tomorrow. And so do I. If I don't teach those lessons . . ."

"New musicians aren't made," Callie finishes for me.

"You always have an answer for everything," I say.

"It's part of the beauty that makes me *me*." She yawns again. "Now get the heck out of here so I can get some sleep."

CHAPTER SIXTEEN

Brock

A couple cold showers later, I can finally walk.

My sleep is plagued with Rory Pike's face. Specifically, that serene look when she thought about a recital.

I'm determined to make this happen for her.

I rise at five a.m., my normal time. Such is life on the ranch. I'm my dad's right-hand man and I usually head to the main house to have breakfast with him and Mom.

To my surprise, only my mother is seated at the table, while our housekeeper, Patrice, is frying eggs and bacon.

"Where's Dad?" I ask.

"Business in the city today," Mom says. "He left about a half hour ago."

"What kind of business in the city starts at six in the morning?"

"Got me, but he said it was important."

My mother smiles. Her naturally blond hair is now an ashy white. Neither Brad nor I got her blond hair, but Brad did get her amazing green eyes.

My mom is a gentle soul. A published psychiatrist, she was instrumental—I found out from Dale—in Dale and Donny's recovery when they came to the ranch.

She's retired from private practice now, but she still

HELEN HARDT

helps the family when they need counseling, and she spends most of her time working on publications.

Melanie Carmichael Steel.

Sixty-five years young.

Hardly a wrinkle mars her gorgeous face. Only a few laugh lines and smile lines. She's as beautiful as she was the day I came into the world. She was forty-two when she had me. She didn't think she could have another baby. In fact, she and Dad were looking into adopting when I decided to make myself known.

She always called me her miracle baby. But I look at her now, and I know why she was able to have a baby so late in life. Her genetics are extraordinary. She doesn't look a day over fifty.

"You have a pensive look on your face, honey," she says to me.

"I think it's just fatigue. I got in pretty late last night."

"Oh?"

That's Mom's way of asking me where I was. She knows I'm twenty-four and a grown man, so she won't come right out and ask, but she's inviting me to tell her.

And she knows I always tell her.

She doesn't always like to hear the answer, but I always tell her.

"Had a date. With Rory Pike."

Mom raises her eyebrows. "She's dating men now?"

"She's bisexual."

"I know that. Her last couple of relationships were with women, though."

"So?"

"So ... I don't want you to get hurt, honey."

"When have you known me to ever get hurt?"

"I've told you this before." She smiles. "You will fall eventually, and when you do, it will be hard."

"I'm still too young to fall," I tell her.

"Are you?"

No.

The word pops into my head without me even having to think it. I'm not too young to fall. Not at all. Did I expect to fall for Rory Pike? No. I expected to fuck her and get her out of my system, like I do with everyone else.

I could have fucked her last night. Hell, she offered herself up on a gold platter and seemed very put out when I didn't.

"I don't know," I finally say.

"Are you going to go out with her again?"

"If she accepts."

Mom reaches across the table and pats the top of my hand. "She'll accept."

After last night, I'm not so sure. "I hope so."

"She will." A huge smile spreads over her face.

"What?" I ask.

"I don't know. I was just thinking about what gorgeous kids the two of you would make. All that dark hair and those deep-brown eyes."

"I think you're getting ahead of us, Mom."

"I'm not getting any younger, Brock. I'd love to have some grandchildren, and your brother doesn't seem like he's going to settle down anytime soon."

"He's been dating Marie forever."

"I know. That's the point. If they were going to get married and have children, they would've done it by now."

"He's still pretty young. Twenty-six."

"I know. I figured he'd be the one to give me grandchildren before you. But you never know."

"Mom, I know. There will not be *any* grandchildren anytime soon."

That's for sure. I want to get to know Rory Pike. I want to get her into my bed. I want to produce a recital for her.

But children? That is *far* into my future.

Patrice slides a plate of steaming eggs and bacon in front of me.

Mom points to the toast. "That's sourdough from Ava's bakery."

I nod and take a bite. "I just had lunch there yesterday," I say with my mouth full.

"For God's sake, Brock, swallow first."

I laugh as I swallow. "You're such a mom."

"And if you want to date someone seriously, whether it's Rory Pike or anyone else, you need to stop talking with your mouth full."

I nod again. "When you're right, you're right, Mom."

"I've been waiting for you and David to grow up. It sure took Donny a while, and I'm glad you're not going to wait until you're thirty-two."

"Who says I'm growing up?" I slather peach jam on my second slice of Ava's toast.

"Trust me. A mother knows." She smiles as she rises. "I'm heading to my office. I've got a deadline on my next book, and I need to get writing."

"Got it. Love you, Mom."

"Love you too, Brock."

I sink my teeth into a thick slice of bacon, savoring the smoky meat.

Kids. Mom wants me to have kids.

That is *so* not going to happen.

My phone buzzes in my pocket, and I grab it.

It's Dale.

"Saturday. The north property. Two p.m. Can you make it?"

CHAPTER SEVENTEEN

Rory

Shocker of all shockers.

It's Saturday, and I haven't heard one word from Brock Steel since our date Monday evening.

I'll call you, he said.

Sure. He'll call me.

Christ, I practically threw myself at him, and he turned me down.

So much for what I thought had gone on. He was a guy who wanted to create a recital for me, who told me I was beautiful, who told me he wanted to see that look on my face forever, and then he refused to get into the sack with me.

What the hell does it all mean?

I'm driving into Grand Junction today. I chickened out Tuesday, so I made an appointment to go to a sperm bank today. They're open on weekends, of course, because working women are huge clients of sperm banks.

Obviously, Brock Steel isn't going to donate any of his swimmers, so I have to find another specimen.

Specimen.

That's all this is to me. A specimen. A donor. A tiny bit of DNA that I need so I can have a child.

Callie tried to talk me out of it again last night, after

she got in from her date with Donny. She prefers the sperm bank to the idea of asking Brock to donate, but she wants me to wait until I'm in a relationship.

"Being a single parent is hard, Ror," she said.

She also told me that she and Donny are moving into the guesthouse behind the Steel main house. Dale and Ashley are finally moved into their new place, and Donny's taking the guesthouse for now, while he and Callie build their new house.

I'm happy for her. Truly. But Callie won't be around here for me to talk too much anymore, and I doubt she and Donny will want me hanging around their place.

I'm on my own.

I guess, in some small way, I always have been.

I drive up to the sperm bank.

Then I sit in my car. I'm twenty minutes early. I can just drive on. Go away. I don't even have to cancel my appointment. Heck, I don't even have to go home. I can just drive off and never look back.

It's tempting sometimes.

I could move to a new place, where Rory Pike isn't the homecoming queen, isn't the resident bisexual, isn't the most beautiful woman in the town—the beautiful woman who couldn't make it as a performer.

But Snow Creek is home.

It's still tempting, though.

"For God's sake, Rory, get a fucking grip." I open the car door and get out, my purse slung over my shoulder, and I walk defiantly into the building that houses the sperm bank.

The sperm bank. Or Western Slope Family Planning, as it's called.

Oh. My. God.

"May I help you?" a receptionist asks.

"Aurora Pike. I have an appointment to talk to one of your counselors."

"Certainly. You're a little early." She nods toward the waiting area. "Just have a seat, and someone will be with you as soon as possible."

"Thank you." I turn, again defiantly, and find a chair.

Only one other woman sits in the waiting area.

She looks up at me as I sit down.

"Hi," she says timidly.

"Good morning."

"I'm so nervous," she says.

Do I look like I have *wants to talk to strangers* tattooed on my forehead?

Apparently.

"No reason to be nervous."

"It's such a big step, you know?"

That's what the counselors are here for. To talk to you about all this crap.

"It is," I say.

"I just… No one wants to date me or anything. This is really my… only shot at this."

I take a look at her then. A good long look. She's pleasant-looking—not beautiful, but pretty. A spray of dark freckles graces her nose and cheeks, and she's not wearing makeup that I can see.

She continues. "You're so pretty. Why are you here?"

"It's a long story," is all I say.

She seems to get the idea then. She looks back at the magazine on her lap and says nothing more.

A few minutes later, a woman in a white coat walks out.

"Sandy Thomas?"

The other woman stands. "I'm Sandy."

"Come on back."

I feel oddly abandoned. I didn't really want to tell Sandy my life story, but I was rude. I didn't mean to be. It's just that this is all so personal. I don't have my sister's support, and my parents don't even know I'm here.

That's not really fair to Callie. She'll support me in whatever I decide. She just doesn't think this is the best idea in the world. And part of me agrees with her.

Part of me, though—that part of me that wants a baby, no matter the cost—is ready to do anything to make my dream happen sooner rather than later.

A baby. A baby before I'm too old to enjoy it. A baby while I'm young enough to know I'll be able to see not only my child grow into an adult but also my grandchildren.

That's what I want.

"Aurora Pike?"

"That's me." I stand.

Another counselor in a white coat holds her hand out. "I'm Davida. It's nice to meet you. Come on back."

Davida is a beautiful woman with dark skin and piercing black eyes.

She's also bisexual. Not gay. Bi. I've learned to have a radar about these things, and when I find a bi woman, I instantly take notice. Raine wasn't bi, and that was a big part of our problem. She didn't understand my attraction to men. Davida would understand, and she's not wearing any rings on her left hand.

I'm instantly attracted to her.

Funny, though. I'm not thinking about what it might feel like to kiss her full lips. Or what she might look like naked.

In fact, the only person I really want to see naked right now is Brock Steel.

Doesn't matter. I'm not here to pick up a woman. I'm here to get information on sperm donors.

Davida leads me to an office in the back, and then she walks behind a desk.

"Have a seat, Aurora."

"Rory. Everybody calls me Rory."

"Very good, Rory. Everyone calls me Davey."

I smile. "Nice to meet you."

"So, Rory, what can I do for you today?"

I clear my throat. "I . . . want a baby."

She smiles. "Do you?"

"Of course I do. Why else would I be here?"

"Because you didn't sound too convinced just then. You hesitated a bit."

"I *am* hesitant. Not because I don't want a baby, but because I'm sitting here in the sperm bank talking to someone I don't know, who's going to try to counsel me. I know everything you're going to say before you say it."

She chuckles. "You do?"

"Yes. You're going to ask if I've ever been in a serious relationship. Don't I want to wait? I'm twenty-eight years old, Davey. I'll tell you what I told my sister, who I tell everything to. I'm worried about my biological clock."

She opens her mouth, but I stop her with a hand gesture.

"Yes, I know twenty-eight is not that old. I know huge problems don't begin to happen until the thirties, and that women are having babies well into their forties with no complications these days. I know all of that. But I also know that I want to be around for a lot of my children's life. I want to see them grow up, and I want to see his or her children grow up. Maybe even great-grandchildren. I want all of that. It's what I've always wanted since I was a little girl."

"Actually, Rory," Davey says. "I was going to ask you if you had a look at the donors on the website."

Oh, shit. My cheeks are blistering hot. Clearly I've made a huge fool of myself.

"Oh."

"I'd like to make sure you're familiar with our services before we go into any other questions."

"You mean... You're not going ask me if this is what I really want?"

"Of course I will. When we get to that. But I'm not here to judge you, Rory. I'm here to help you. Believe it or not, most of the men who donate their sperm don't want us to just give it out willy-nilly. They want to make sure that whoever gets inseminated is serious and wants a child. We actually see a lot of married couples."

"Married couples?"

"Of course. Sometimes the man is infertile, so the couple will get a sperm donation from another man who shares physical characteristics with the husband."

"Sure. Of course, that makes sense. I guess I just thought... I don't know what I thought. I'm too much inside my own head right now."

"I totally understand. Would it help if you knew that I'm also a single mother? That I was inseminated by one of our donors?"

"Really?"

"Yes. I'm not married, and I was in a situation kind of like yours, although I'm a bit older. I'm thirty-five now, and I was thirty-three when I gave birth to my daughter."

"How did the experience go for you?"

"I now work here as a counselor, so that's the best answer to your question. It's been an amazing experience. I love being a mother."

"Do you plan on ever being in a relationship?"

"Perhaps. If I meet someone who I love and who I want to spend my life with. But like you, I didn't really want to wait around before I could be a mother."

"So you do understand."

"Of course I do. Now, let's get back to basics. Have you had a chance to look at our website?"

"I have. And I've looked through some of the potential donors."

"What are you looking for in a donor?"

"Good genes, I guess."

"All our donors have that in abundance."

"I guess… I don't mean to sound full of myself or anything, but I would like the child to look like me, so I'm looking for a man who shares my characteristics. Dark hair, dark eyes. Average height."

"Average height for a man is five feet nine inches."

"Then tall. Something over six feet. Wait, I'm sorry. I mean someone. Some*one* over six feet."

"Good. Good for you. You're thinking in terms of people, not sperm."

"I'm trying to."

"That's good. It's important to know that even though our donors have relinquished all parental rights to any of their offspring, they are still people. They may have genetic issues that we don't know about, that our testing didn't show."

"What are you saying? Are you going to make me sign a release form stating that I won't sue you in case my kid has a problem?"

"Actually, that's exactly what I'm going to tell you. But we're getting way ahead of ourselves."

"Why do you say that?"

"Because my job here is to counsel you. To make sure you're actually ready to have a child."

"And you think that's any of your business?"

"Rory, I'm assuming you chose this clinic for a reason. There are others out there who don't require any counseling before insemination. We don't take that approach here."

I rise. "Maybe it's better if I go somewhere else, then."

"Or ... Maybe it's better if you wait on this."

"You don't know me at all."

"You're right. I don't. Which is why I made the suggestion. You don't seem to want to go through our process, and that's certainly your prerogative. There are plenty of clinics out there who will just sell you a vial of sperm. They may sell you an at-home insemination kit as well. We don't do that here. We treat this as a process. We're not satisfied just to inseminate a woman. We want to make sure that the baby we're helping to bring into the world is born into a loving environment, to a parent who's ready for it."

I tamp down the anger that rises. Davey is only doing her job.

"I *am* ready for it. I was born ready for it. I've wanted to be a mother since ... Well, since I can remember."

"And you don't want to wait and see if you meet someone, to share this process with him?"

"My last two serious relationships were with women," I say.

120

"Don't you want to see if you fall in love and share the process with her, then?"

"I'm bisexual, Davey." Apparently her radar isn't as good as mine.

"I see. Then perhaps you'll fall in love with a man, and you can do this process the natural way."

"Don't you think I've been through all of this in my own head? My last girlfriend was a few years younger than I am. If our relationship had lasted, she would've carried our child, not me. I'm getting too old."

"You're not that old. But you know all this. I'm afraid I can't recommend you for insemination at this time."

"You've got a lot of nerve. You can't *recommend* me?"

"If you're familiar with our website, as you said you were, you'd know our process. We don't just sell sperm. Some of our donors want to be involved in their offspring's life. Some of them don't. Have you decided how you'd like this to work? Do you want a donor that is in your child's life? Do you want your child to be able to find their biological father if they wish to?"

I swallow.

"Just as I thought. I'm not trying to be disrespectful, Rory. Truly I'm not. But if you haven't given all these things some thought, you're just not ready for this."

I turn then. I turn without saying thank you. Without saying anything. I walk away from Davey, who isn't nearly as attractive to me now. And I walk away from Western Slope Family Planning.

My next stop is a drugstore. Where I buy an ovulation kit. I'm not sure the pharmacy in Snow Creek even sells ovulation kits, but if they do, I can't be seen buying it there. People will talk.

People always talk.

I tamp down the feeling that Davey is right, that I'm not as ready for this as I think I am.

I want a child, damn it. And I want it with Brock.

He hasn't called me.

So what? Maybe I'll call him.

And damn it, I *will* get him into bed with me.

CHAPTER EIGHTEEN

B r o c k

"I did some research," Dale says, handing Donny and me each a face mask. "This will help with the smell."

"Oh?" I say.

"Yeah. It's made with activated charcoal, which will catch the organic vapors caused by the rotting flesh. It will help us get through this without puking our guts out."

"Right." He's talking about me, of course. I'm the one who retched last time. Dale and Donny are stronger than I am.

They've been through so much more.

We've unloaded the ladders already, along with the tools. Now, all that's left is to enter the barn, take down the ceiling, and—

I place the mask over my nose and mouth.

It doesn't stop the gagging.

I swallow down the nausea. It's time to be strong. Time to be a man, as my father would say.

Time to be a man, son.

How many times has he said those words to Brad and me over the years? He was a good father, but he was strict and hard on us.

"There's no place for weakness on a ranch," he used to say. "No place for weakness and no place for crybabies."

He was speaking more to Brad than to me. Brad was the one who wore his emotions on his sleeve. Brad's personality is more like Mom's, where mine is more like Dad's.

Which is both good and bad.

If my father were here, would he be gagging at the thought of what we were about to do?

I don't know.

I'm wondering whether I know my father at all.

The three of us stand about fifteen feet away from the barn in question. Not one of us makes any attempt to move.

Finally, Dale takes a step forward. "We have to do this, guys. We don't have a choice."

I regard my cousin. His long blond hair is pulled back in a low ponytail, and a Colorado Rockies cap sits on his head. He's dressed in old jeans and cowboy boots, same as Donny and me, but he has a different air about him.

He's determined.

And I must get determined as well.

I take a step forward.

Then Donny does the same.

One by one, we each take one step, wait a few moments, and then take another.

The barn doesn't seem to be getting any closer, until suddenly the door is right at my face. It's cracked open.

"Watch out for dog shit," Donny says.

"That's why I wore these old shitty boots," I reply.

One of my oldest pair of working boots, they've certainly seen their share of shit. Cow shit, mostly, but a little horse shit and dog shit as well.

I slide the door open.

We have flashlights, but the sun is high in the sky, and it

shines through the cracks. Still, we need our lights.

Dale secures a lamp on his head. "Sorry," he says. "I should've gotten one of these for the rest of you."

"No worries," Donny says. "Let's just get this over with."

I don't realize I'm holding my breath until I suck in a gasp. The charcoal mask helps, though I can still smell the sweetness of human decay. I believe that odor will always be with me. Sometimes at night, when I'm alone in my bedroom, I can still smell it.

I look above me, scan my flashlight across the ceiling. Nothing. Nothing to indicate that there might be human bodies up there.

"Now or never," Dale says, positioning a ladder. "Let's get this show on the road."

I force my feet to move. *Go away from it in your head. Don't think about what you're looking for. This is a ceiling just like any other ceiling, and it needs to be removed.*

"Be careful," Donny says. "We don't want any of the... you know, stuff... to fall on our heads."

Great. Just great. I pick up a saw. I can use tools in my sleep. My father and my uncles taught me everything about running a ranch, including carpentry work where necessary. Sure, we hired most of the big jobs out, but all of us were taught how to handle tools, basic carpentry, basic veterinary care, basic care of the orchards.

Everything to run the ranch successfully.

We work hard. We all work damned hard, even though none of us has to.

And sometimes I wonder what it's all for.

What secrets does this barn hold? And why... Why did our fathers keep it all from us?

I escape in my mind. I force myself to think that I'm just doing basic carpentry work around the ranch. Except most of our barns don't have ceilings. Just joists and rafters.

Have I ever removed a ceiling before? No, I haven't, but I know how to.

All this should come naturally to me.

I secure my protective eyewear, flip the switch on the battery-powered saw, and I cringe as the blade cuts through the wood above me.

Dale and I saw, while Donny stands below us, ready to catch anything that might fall.

In a few minutes, Dale and I are ready to remove the first square of boards.

"Do you feel any give?" Donny asks.

"I don't. I don't feel anything. Just the weight of the boards."

Dale and I pull the cut board away carefully, and as we hand it down to Donny, nothing falls on our heads.

"One of us needs to go up," Dale says.

I swallow against the gag in my throat. Steel. I need to have nerves of steel, like my name implies.

"I'll go."

"Here." Dale strips off his headlight and hands it to me.

"Thanks." I strap the light around my own ball cap and climb up.

"Careful," Donny says. "Can it hold your weight?"

I hoist myself up. "So far so good."

"What is it?" Dale asks. "What do you see?"

My jaw drops.

CHAPTER NINETEEN

Rory

I'm home, and thankfully Callie is not. I have our bathroom to myself. I fumble with the ovulation kit, reading the directions quickly.

Luteinizing hormone, otherwise known as LH. Apparently that's the hormone that signals my ovary to release an egg, so when the LH reaches a certain level, I can assume that ovulation will occur in the next twelve to thirty-six hours.

To determine this, I must pee on a stick, just like a pregnancy test.

I should pee between noon and eight p.m., because apparently some women have a surge of LH in the mornings, which can screw with the result.

Check. I'm within the time frame.

I also have to make sure my urine is concentrated, which means I have to avoid peeing for an hour or two before the test.

Check. I haven't peed since before my appointment at the sperm bank.

Here goes nothing.

I'm about midway between cycles, so there's a good chance my LH will be at the required level.

I sit down on the toilet to do my business.

Then I wait.

I wait . . . and I wonder what the hell I'm doing.

What exactly am I going to do if the test is positive? Force Brock to have sex with me tonight?

I can always go to a different sperm bank—one that's content to just sell me sperm.

But there's a reason I went to the clinic I did. I was familiar with their website, and I liked how they did things.

Maybe Davey's right. Maybe I'm not quite ready.

I nearly fall off the toilet seat when the alarm on my phone goes off.

Time to read the test.

I take a look.

My heart races. I've reached the threshold. I *will* ovulate in the next twelve to thirty-six hours.

Which means I need to have sex tonight. Or tomorrow night.

Brock hasn't called me. "I'll call you," he said.

No call.

But you know what? This is the freaking twenty-first century. Nothing is stopping me from calling him.

I laugh out loud at the absurdity of it all. I'm sitting on the toilet, my jeans around my ankles, testing for ovulation, only to find out I'm ripe.

Ripe for the picking.

With no one to pick me.

It doesn't have to be Brock Steel. I just have to have sex with *someone* tonight. Someone male, who won't insist on a condom. Or on pulling out.

I laugh out loud again.

So much I haven't considered.

I'm not on the pill. I haven't had to be, since my last two

serious relationships were with women. Pregnancy wasn't an issue. Plus, I've been tested, as have all my partners, and I'm disease free.

I pose no threat to a man.

But what if… What if the guy poses a threat? I can't go around having unprotected sex and hoping to get pregnant. I could get something other than pregnant, and that would not be good.

One-nighters are out of the question. I won't let a strange man near me without a raincoat. That would just be stupid.

But Brock…

Is it any safer with him? He's a womanizer. The man has had a lot of sex, and I'd be willing to bet he never has sex without a condom.

So how does that help me?

Once more, I laugh out loud.

It doesn't. It doesn't help me at all.

I toss the ovulation stick into the trash and get off the toilet. This is a stupid idea. It was all a stupid idea.

Back in my bedroom, I check my emails.

Funny that I haven't looked at them before now, but I gasp when I see that there's one from Brock.

He checked into the cinema for my recital, and he's booked it for two weeks from now—the week before Thanksgiving.

Two weeks? He wants me to put a recital together in two weeks?

With everything else that's going on?

I sigh.

He didn't call, but he did do this. He cares. Not enough to sleep with me, but he cares.

Then another email catches my eye. It's from Doc Sheraton.

Except it's not from Doc Sheraton—only from his address. And it's sent to both Callie and me.

We know what you've done. Don't think you have all those pictures. We have copies.

Callie storms into my room, holding her phone. "Have you seen this?"

My heart is pounding now, more so than when I took the ovulation test. "Yeah. I just did. Where were you?"

"Outside with Dusty." She shakes her head. "I knew it. I knew he had more copies."

"He's just *saying* he has more copies. Obviously they went to the tree to try to dig up the stuff they left there, found them gone, and assumed we have them. They're probably bluffing."

"What if they're not, Rory? We can get them on child porn charges for my photos, but what about yours?"

What about mine? I should be upset. Really upset. All I can think about is my ovulation test, Brock Steel, and some ridiculous recital I have to put together while all this is happening.

When all I really want is a baby.

But is it fair to bring a baby into this world? When naked pictures of my child's mother may soon be plastered everywhere?

Callie paces around my room and then into the bathroom. Out again, and then back in, and then—

"What the fuck is this, Rory?" In her hand, she holds the ovulation test box.

CHAPTER TWENTY

Brock

I gape at the sight before me.

"What's up there?" Donny yells.

"Nothing," I say, completely flummoxed.

I slide the charcoal mask from my face.

Against my better judgment, I inhale.

The scent. It's here, but it's much fainter than I remember.

Dale hoists himself up next to me. "Oh my God."

"It's gone," I say. "Whatever was here is gone."

"You took your mask off."

"Yeah. The smell. It's here, but it's faint."

Dale removes his own mask and inhales. "Damn. You're right. Whatever was here—if there was anything here—is gone. Which means . . ."

"That someone knows we're onto them. Someone knows, and they're covering their tracks."

"We still have the bones," Dale says. "The ones you and I found."

"Those are old, though. Just bones. They're not from any recent rotting flesh."

"True."

"Guys, what the hell's going on up there?" Donny yells.

"Come on up, Don," Dale says. "We need to check out every crevice."

"Coming." A few seconds later, Donny hoists himself up.

"You sure this place can handle all three of us? Our weight?" Donny asks.

"If my suspicions are correct," Dale says, "this place held a lot more weight than us. And recently."

I nod. "I think you're probably right. Look over there." I point to a place on the wall that's a slightly different color. "Looks like someone got here before us."

"Damn." Dale shakes his head. "We shouldn't have waited so long."

"You're right," I say. "We fucked up."

"You guys both need to give yourselves a break," Donny says. "We're dealing with so much more than just this. Dad's shooting. The nurse who poisoned him."

"True enough," I say, "but we could've had these people. We could've had evidence. And now... Fuck it all."

"We need to get some guys in here," Dale says. "Professionals. People we can trust. Because the three of us just don't know what we're looking for."

"I know what I'm looking for," I say. "Look for blood. Look for anything that says... Hell, I don't know."

"That's my point," Dale says. "I agree with you. Let's look around. Let's shine our lights in every corner of this attic, and maybe we'll get lucky. Maybe whoever took whatever was up here left something. A clue. But I'm betting they didn't."

"Why would you think that?"

"Because if these people are who I think they are, they know what they're doing. They know better than to leave evidence."

"Fuck, Dale," Donny says.

"That human-trafficking ring was brought down," Dale

says. "I know that. But that doesn't mean other shit isn't going on."

"Who do you think is behind this, then?" I ask.

"Human traffickers—at least the ones who took us—train their potential cargo. Not everyone lives through the training, so they need to get rid of those bodies."

"You are *not* telling me what I think you are. You're totally not telling me that you think some human smuggler is hiding dead bodies on Steel property." Sweat drips from my forehead into my eyes. I blink against the sting. It's November, but it's hot up here in this makeshift attic.

"It's just a theory," Donny says. "But we know what these people are capable of."

"There's a kink in your theory," I say. "This is Steel property. It belongs to our family. *Our* family. The Steel family—the family that can buy and sell almost every other family in this country. Surely there are better places to hide your dead bodies."

"There are," Dale says.

"Oh, fuck." I rub my eyes with my gloved fingers, making them sting even more.

"See what I mean?" Dale says.

"Somebody has it out for us. Somebody's trying to incriminate the family." I curl my hands into fists. "But if that's the case, why would they move the evidence? Wouldn't they *want* to incriminate us?"

"Maybe," Donny says. "Maybe not. Or maybe they want to do this on their own terms."

"Who?" I demand. "Who the hell would want to do this on their own terms? And why would it matter? If they want to incriminate us—leave disgusting rotting human flesh evidence on our property—what the hell does it matter what their terms are?"

"I don't know," Dale says. "But this is far more sinister than we originally thought."

"How is this more sinister?" I ask. "Whoever is behind it moved the evidence so we wouldn't find it. Wouldn't that make this *less* sinister?"

"I don't know," Dale says. "I just don't fucking know. But this feels wrong. All wrong."

"Of course it feels wrong. Someone has potentially been storing dead bodies on our property." I flash my light around the dark attic. "What is this building hiding? What are we not seeing?"

And then I see it.

I fucking see it.

CHAPTER TWENTY-ONE

Rory

I roll my eyes at my sister. "I'm pretty sure you can read."

"Seriously? You're going to try to get pregnant?"

"No. I mean . . . maybe."

"Without telling Brock?"

"I don't know. Brock turned me down."

She nods. "You haven't seen him since Monday night, right?"

"Right."

"You said you had a nice time. That he took you to dinner and dancing."

"He did."

Callie sets the box down on top of my dresser. Then she opens my top dresser drawer and shoves the box inside. "You shouldn't leave this sitting out. Sometimes Mom comes in here on a sanitizing rampage and cleans our bathroom."

"Right. I wasn't thinking."

Normally I clean the bathroom. I know it's strange, but I actually enjoy cleaning, especially bathrooms. But Callie is right. Mom has been known to come in and straighten up. I quickly walk into the bathroom, find the stick that I peed on, wrap it in tissue, and shove it to the bottom of my purse. I'll throw it away when I get into town sometime.

"I still can't believe it," I say. "Brock Steel, who will lay anything in a dress, turned me down. Rory Pike. The woman everybody says is the most beautiful woman in Snow Creek. How does that happen?"

"I don't know," Callie says. "It is pretty off-brand for him."

"Right? I'm beginning to question my power of seduction."

"Has anyone *ever* turned you down, Rory?"

"No. Male or female. That's my point." I'm embellishing a little. A few of the straight girls in college didn't bite. Very few.

Callie sighs and sits next to me on my bed. "I know you're freaking out right now, but we need to think about this email we just got."

I sigh. "You're right. What do we do? It's not like they asked us to meet them somewhere or anything."

"I don't know. I need to talk to Donny. Maybe he'll have an idea."

"Yeah. Maybe he will. Right now, though, we don't have any evidence that Pat and Brittany actually have the photos."

"But he says he does."

"Except we don't know it was him. It came from Doc Sheraton's email account."

"Which means it's from Brittany. Brittany and Pat."

"Is it?" I shake my head. "I swear to God, I don't know which end is up anymore, Callie."

"Doc Sheraton is a good guy. In fact..."

"What?" I ask.

"He couldn't keep his eyes off you, Ror."

"You better not be suggesting what I think you're suggesting."

She sighs. "No, I'm not. Never again will I ask you to put yourself in that kind of position."

"Especially after where we ended up the first time."

"I know."

My sister gives me an idea, though. "What if we went into town? Went to see Doc Sheraton and asked him what the heck this email means?"

"We know what it means."

"Sure, *we* know. But it came from his account. Maybe it's time Daddy finds out what his little darling is up to."

"The only one who can get hurt by that is you, Rory. You're the one whose pictures can be displayed. If he displays mine, we've got him on child porn."

"True. But you know what? Maybe I need to just accept the risk. How else are we going to finish this?"

"No. *Hard* no. I'm not going to let you do this."

"Callie, so much more is going on right now."

Her eyes widen again. "How much do you know?"

"I'm just talking about our family. The fire. We're in dire straits, for God's sake."

"Oh. Yeah."

"Why? What are you talking about?"

She opens her mouth. Closes it. Opens again.

"Are you going to talk anytime soon?" I ask.

"Rory," she says, "there's some stuff going down with Donny's family. I'm not sure how much I can tell you. But I will tell you this. It makes what's going on with us and Pat Lamone seem like nothing."

The Steels? The golden Steels? Something's going on with *them*?

Granted, Talon was shot. "Are you talking about Talon?"

"Talon, yes, among other things."

"What other things?"

"I wish I could tell you everything. I have to talk to Donny first. I can't break his trust."

"I understand." My words aren't lies. I *do* understand. But right now, I want to know. "You can also trust *me*, Callie."

"I know that. I trust you and Donny both more than anyone. But this is big, Ror. I can't break his confidence without his permission."

I say nothing for a few tense minutes. Then, "I get it."

"Do you? Because for a minute it didn't seem like you did."

I sigh. "Of course I get it. Just . . . Maybe we do go to town. Find Doc Sheraton."

"It's already afternoon." Callie looks at her watch. "He's only open on Saturday morning."

"Then we go to his house."

"And risk running into Pat Lamone like I did last time?"

I nod. "Exactly that. Because we know Pat is behind this. Pat and Brittany. There's no way Doc Sheraton knows about those photos."

"Except we'd be cluing Doc Sheraton in," Callie says. "I'm not the one who's at risk here. You are."

Courage—at least I think it's courage—pulses through my veins.

I came close to having a baby on my own today. That takes guts.

You know what else takes guts? Calling Pat Lamone's bluff.

"It's time to take a few risks," I say. "Why should we let Lamone have the last say in this? Why should we let him ruin our lives?" I stand up, straight and tall. "Let's go into town."

"Are you sure?"

"I'm damned sure."

CHAPTER TWENTY-TWO

Brock

I kneel, Dale's flashlight still strapped to my hat. "I found something."

I pick it up. Shine my light on it.

"What is it?" Dale asks.

"It's another red fingernail. A fake plastic fingernail, like the one Donny found outside."

"Which means..." Dale scratches his head. "Whoever moved whatever was in this attic space was wearing plastic fingernails?"

"That's not what it means at all. It means that one of the bodies they moved was probably wearing plastic fingernails."

"Yeah," Donny says. "First of all, anyone coming to do heavy criminal work like moving decaying bodies wouldn't be wearing plastic fingernails."

"Women can do dirty work," I say.

"Sure they can, but would they really be wearing plastic fingernails to do it? They were probably wearing gloves, regardless of gender."

I nod. "Good point. Which means these fingernails are from one of the bodies they moved, or they've been planted."

"Damn," Donny says.

I clear my throat. "I don't know who's behind this. But

here's the thing. Maybe they were planted, but we don't know that. I think we have to go on the assumption that these are clues whether they were planted or not."

"I agree," Dale says.

"Have either of you found anything else suspicious up here?" I ask.

"I haven't," Donny says.

"Me neither." Dale shakes his head. "We're dealing with people who know what they're doing. Which means it's all the more likely that these fingernails have been planted. One outside the building and one up here."

"Could be," I say, "but what if they aren't? What if they came off one of the bodies that was up here?"

"We don't even know for sure that bodies were up here," Donny asserts.

Dale shakes his head again. "Don, we know. You *know* that we know."

"You're sure about the smell, then?" I say.

Dale nods. "As sure as I am about anything else in my life, Brock. That's not something you forget."

"So what now?" Donny asks. "It's not like we can search for some woman who might have eight red plastic fingernails. It won't work."

"No," I say, "but we can give these to Hardy. Get them dusted for fingerprints."

"They're awfully small," Dale says.

"True."

I'm out of ideas. My cousins know more about deranged people and how they think than I do.

"Here's what we have for now," Donny says. "Two fingernails and some bones."

"Let's get them all checked for DNA." I rub my chin against a suddenly uncontrollable itch.

"Agreed." Dale removes his Rockies cap and scratches the top of his head. "We'll get somebody to run fingerprints and DNA. But not Hardy."

"Got it," I agree. "We'll get our own people on this."

"In the meantime," Donny says, "what else do we do here?"

"I don't think there's anything else to do here," I say, "but we'd better go to those other GPS coordinates before someone moves all the evidence from there as well."

"How do you think they know we were here?" Donny asks.

"Probably something as simple as footprints," I say.

"But there's no mud, just solid ground. No prints. Except where I stepped in the dog shit that first time." Then his eyebrows fly up. "Dog shit! That's it!"

"What are you thinking, Don?" Dale asks.

"Whoever was here has a dog. I know that doesn't mean a lot. Lots of people have dogs. But whoever comes here brings a dog. Maybe two dogs."

"Or a couple of strays just hang out here," Dale says.

"No," I say. "Remember what we found last time? Dog shit *inside* the barn. If strays came here to seek shelter, they wouldn't be shitting *in* the barn."

"Exactly," Donny says.

"So they have a dog or dogs," Dale says. "How does that help us?"

I widen my eyes. "Oh my God."

"You see what I'm saying?" Donny smiles.

"Yeah. This is a clue. They use canines."

"They could just be bringing pets around." From Dale.

"Really? I doubt it," I say. "These dogs are trained. Otherwise they wouldn't bring them. Dogs would just get in the way. Especially around decaying bodies. They'd be going crazy."

"Okay, I see your point," Dale says. "But how exactly does this help us?"

"They're probably trained guard dogs," I say. "We may be able to trace these people that way."

Dale cocks his head. "Would guard dogs shit inside a barn?"

"Why wouldn't they?" I ask. "They don't live here. It's just like outside in here, ground and all."

"I think guard dogs have to be registered in most states," Donny says. "Except that whoever these people are, they aren't exactly law-abiding citizens."

"No," I say, "but they had to have their dogs trained somewhere. It's a long shot, but we might be able to trace them that way."

"Okay..." Dale puts his baseball cap back on his head. "The idea has merit, but still it's going to be like looking for a needle in a haystack."

"I agree," I say. "But that's all we've got, Dale. That, some old bones, and plastic red fingernails. What do you think is the most easily traced?"

"Dogs," Dale finally relents.

"I can look into it. Put Callie on it," Donny says. "We've got the databases at the office."

"Perfect," I say. "I know it's not much, but what else can we do?"

"We can get out to those other coordinates as soon as possible," Dale says.

"Problem is, we all have other things to do," I say. "We all have jobs. Jobs that don't wait."

"What about tomorrow?" Dale says. "Sunday."

"The winery may be closed on Sunday, but the beef ranch isn't, Dale," I say.

"The winery never closes. I always have to be watching fermentation. But if you can't make it tomorrow, maybe Donny and I can."

"Tomorrow won't work for me," Donny says. "Sorry."

Dale sighs. "All right. You've convinced me. We need some recovery time after today. In the meantime, we've done everything we can here for now."

I nod. Recovery time. Now my cousin is talking sense.

I need to get home. I need to shower this disgusting filth off my body.

And then I need to call Rory.

I should've called her before now, but I was giving her space.

Tonight? I need to see her. I'm not exactly sure why, but she is the one person I want to see right now after all of this.

"Let's take one more look around the perimeter," Dale says. "Then let's get the fuck out of here."

We climb down carefully, and I eye the hole we've left in the ceiling. "They're going to know we were here now."

"They already know we were here, Brock," Donny says. "These are not amateurs. The fingernails may have been plants. The bones too. But the dogs? They're using dogs for a reason, and it's not to throw us off track."

"I agree," I say. "The dogs are our best bet for now."

"Callie and I will get on that first thing Monday," Don says.

I nod.

The mention of Callie makes me think of Rory once more.

Damn.

I should've taken her into my bed.

Yeah, I wanted to try something new. Not do the patented Rake-a-teer system.

Right now, though, I need to fuck.

And I only want to fuck one person.

CHAPTER TWENTY-THREE

Rory

I'm standing on the sidewalk in front of Doc Sheraton's home when my nerves strike. My feet don't want to move.

"You okay?" Callie asks.

"Yeah."

"What happened to the *I'm damned sure I want to do this*?"

I clear my throat. "I'm good. Good. Just for a moment, I saw myself spread-eagled and naked coming across everyone's Twitter feed."

"We don't have to do this, Ror."

"No. We *do* have to do this. We need to put an end to this once and for all." I stride up the pathway to the front stoop, and before I can think better of it, I knock harshly on the door.

Callie stands next to me, her eyes on fire.

We're ready. Don't fuck with the Pike sisters.

Except that no one comes to the door.

I pound on it once more.

"Rory, they have a doorbell."

"I don't care. I feel like pounding on the door, and I'm going to pound on the door." I throw my fist against it a third time.

"You can hurt your hand," Callie says.

"You kidding me? I feel nothing. I'm angry right now, Callie. Really, really angry. I can't believe they think they can do this to us."

Finally the door opens in front of me.

"Of course," Callie says dryly. "Going to break a few windows over here as well?"

Pat Lamone stands in front of us, framed by the doorway. "The Pike sluts. Where's your criminal brother?"

"Filing a false police report carries a penalty of up to six months in jail," Callie says.

Pat ignores the comment. "What do the two of you want?"

"We want to see Doc Sheraton."

"He's out of town."

"Great, just great," I say.

"Where is he?" Callie demands. "We want his number."

"I'm not giving you his personal cell number." Pat's hands whip to his hips.

"Yeah, you are. We think he might be really interested in this email that came from his account." I shove a hard copy of the email under Pat's nose.

He grabs it from me. "Let me see that."

"We know Brittany sent this. Or maybe you did. Whoever did had access to the doc's computer."

"I didn't send it."

"Right. You expect us to believe that." Callie shakes her head. "You're even dumber than I thought."

"Actually, this is probably Brittany's work."

"So you're going to sell out your little girlfriend," I say. "Typical."

"Brittany and I broke up."

"Which explains why you're in her father's house." I roll my eyes.

"Okay… We didn't technically break up. But my plans are to break up with her."

"You better quiet down," Callie says. "She's going to hear you, Pat."

"Brittany's not here. She went to Wyoming with her dad. I'm house-sitting."

"Why'd they go to Wyoming?" I demand.

"How the hell should I know? Business, I guess."

"What the hell kind of business does a small-town veterinarian have?" Callie asks.

"Do I look like a freaking encyclopedia? I don't know. I'm just house-sitting."

I whisk past him then, walk right into the home. "You won't mind if we come in, then. Have a look around."

"I don't mind, but the doc might. You're trespassing."

"You a cop?"

He says nothing.

"Of course he's not a cop," Callie says. "And if you call the cops, we'll be happy to tell them what you've done."

"You don't have anything on me."

"Want to bet?" I say.

"Yeah, I'll take those odds."

Callie and I exchange a look. We're not going to tell him about the child porn charges. We'll keep that to ourselves.

"Go ahead, then," Callie says. "Call Hardy. Call the whole fucking force."

"You're bluffing."

"Try us," I say.

I'm well aware that my photos could still be plastered across social media. And in a disgusting way, I'm almost hoping he tries to post Callie's. Then we get him.

"Where are the photos?" Callie demands.

"Like I'd tell you."

"We found the ones you buried. Same place where you found our key." I scan the hallway. "Nice try."

"We're going to find all the photos," Callie says, "and when we do, you're going to be in a world of hurt."

"Yeah, I know, I know. You can send Donovan Steel after me. The whole fucking Steel family."

"The Steels have a lot of power," I say.

"You think I don't know that? I know more about the Steels than either one of you do."

Callie scoffs. Holds out her left hand. "I doubt that."

"Yeah, yeah. I heard the good news. You think because you're engaged to Donny Steel you know everything? There are things Donny himself doesn't even know."

"Like what?" I raise my eyebrows.

"Like . . . Steels are everywhere."

"They're a big family," I say.

"That's not what I mean. Now get the hell out of Doc Sheraton's house."

"I don't think so," Callie says. "I think we're going to have a look around while we're here."

"And you're not going to call the cops," I say, "because you don't want to know what's going to happen to you if you do."

His lips quiver. Just a touch, but I notice. I frightened him. Perhaps he does know that it's illegal for him to possess those photos of Callie. He doesn't need to even post them. Possession is all it takes.

But first, we have to *prove* that he possesses them.

"The photos probably aren't here," Callie says. "Not at Doc Sheraton's. They're probably in his room at Mrs. Mayer's house."

"I'll have you arrested if you break into that nice old lady's house," Pat says. "Her heart can't take it, especially after your brother and his cronies smashed it up."

"Jesse's innocent and you know it," I say. "Besides, we have no intention of breaking and entering anywhere."

"What the hell do you think you're doing right now?"

"Why, you invited us in," I say, giving him my best wide-eyed innocent look. "Didn't he, Callie?"

"He sure did. I'm an eyewitness."

Pat scoffs and shakes his head. "You two bitches are something else."

I smile then. My most sickeningly sweet smile I can come up with. "Oh, Pat, my darling. You have no idea."

He drops his gaze to my chest. "You're still hot."

Then he looks at Callie. "And you're still an ugly duckling."

"Shut the fuck up," I say.

Callie says nothing.

Good. He's not worth the response.

"I should've fucked you that night," Pat says. "That night in the van."

"You really think I would have let that happen?"

"I don't think you would've had a choice."

"So you want to add rapist to the rest of your criminal monikers," Callie says. "Nice."

"What did you mickey me with?" Pat asks.

"Nothing."

"Then why did I wake up somewhere else?"

"Don't know." I shrug. "You couldn't get a freaking boner either."

It's a low blow, and it's probably not true. We didn't get that far, and I didn't go near his crotch.

"Right," he says.

"It's a shame you don't remember, Pat. You had performance anxiety."

Callie chuckles next to me.

I can't help myself. This guy's an asshole. The asshole of assholes.

"You might want to watch what you say to me, Rory," Pat says. "I can still make your life pretty miserable."

"Not as miserable as I can make yours." I walk toward the kitchen. "Let's split up, Callie. Check each room. Anything a little out of the ordinary? Take a photo."

CHAPTER TWENTY-FOUR

Brock

As soon as Dale and Donny drop me off at my place, I call Rory.

"Hello."

"Hey, Rory. It's Brock."

Her throat clears. "Hey."

"Listen, I'm sorry I haven't called."

"I got your email. About renting out the cinema."

"Oh, good. So are you excited? About putting together a program?"

"I'm . . . kind of in the middle of something right now."

"Are you free tonight?"

A pause.

Then, "Seriously? You're calling me at the last minute to go out with you tonight?"

This time I pause. How do I respond to that? I tried to give her space, to help her to think that I wasn't just after one thing. Of course I *am* after that thing tonight. After the fucking day I had.

"It's been a busy week at work. I apologize. I should've called you sooner."

"I think I might be busy."

"You think?"

"I just told you. I'm kind of in the middle of something."

"What are you in the middle of? Maybe I can help." I look down at my watch. It's nearly five o'clock already.

"I'm . . . investigating."

"Then I definitely want to help."

"Forget about it. We're done."

"We?"

"Callie and me."

"Where are you?"

"We're at Doc Sheraton's house."

"The veterinarian? What are you doing there?"

"I told you. Investigating."

"Investigating . . . what?"

"Just investigating. But we're done. And about tonight . . ."

"Yeah?" My heart jumps as I wait for her reply.

"Yeah. I'd love to go out with you tonight."

Thank God. "Great. Where do you want me to pick you up? You want me to come to town and pick you up there?"

"No. I'll drive back home with Callie. Pick me up at our ranch house in about an hour and a half. Six thirty."

"Perfect. It's done. And Rory?"

"What?"

"I can't wait to see you."

Before she can respond, I end the call.

But I can't help but wonder—what is she doing at Doc Sheraton's house?

Then I call her back quickly.

"Yeah?" she says into the phone, her voice breathless.

"Hey, I need you to ask Doc Sheraton something for me."

"He's not here."

I wrinkle my forehead. He's not there? But Rory is? No, she so did not . . .

"Before you freak out on me," she says, "Pat is here. Pat Lamone."

"What the hell is he doing there?"

"He's Brittany's boyfriend. He's house-sitting. Doc and Brittany are in Wyoming."

"And he just let you in? To ... investigate?"

"Yeah. He didn't have a lot of choice."

"Rory, what's going on?"

"You wouldn't believe it if I told you."

"Try me."

"We'll see how things go tonight," she says. "Bye now."

This time she ends the call without waiting for my response.

So much for talking to Doc Sheraton. He would know all about guard dog registration. In fact ...

Oh my God.

Doc Sheraton trains guard dogs.

I knew that. He's a small-town vet. He takes care of horses, cattle, and house pets, but Snow Creek is a small town. He needed a side hustle.

He trains guard dogs.

In Wyoming.

Oh. My. God.

Why didn't I think of this? He'll know all about guard dogs. He may have trained the guard dogs that those degenerates are using.

But he's out of town. In Wyoming. Probably working at his guard-dog kennel.

I make a quick note on my phone. I don't have his cell number, only his office number in town. But he'll be back. He probably has appointments this week. I'll go talk to him.

Maybe take Rory with me.

Or . . . not.

Just because Dale and Donny brought their significant others in on this—one who happens to be Rory's sister—doesn't mean I should bring in Rory. Rory is hardly my significant other. She's a woman I've been on one date with. A woman I'm wildly attracted to.

I choke back a laugh.

A woman I turned down.

I'm still not sure I was myself Monday night.

Except I was.

Something inside me wants more with Rory Pike.

Tonight. Tonight has to go well. I can't piss her off again.

I shower, and boy, does that feel good. Getting the grime of that horrible tract of land off me.

Red fingernails. Guard dogs. Bones.

Dale has the bones. And it's time. It's time to have them analyzed. The experts will be able to tell how old they are, maybe even get some DNA. We just talked about all this, but something is niggling at the back of my neck. Time is of the essence.

"Dale," I say into the phone after punching in his number.

"Yeah, Brock?"

"We need to get those bones checked out right away. Like today if possible."

"I know that. We probably should've done it before now. But I just . . ."

"You don't have to explain. We don't really want to know who they belong to, but if they can help us . . ."

"Yeah. You're right," he says. "I get it. We do it ASAP."

"You got any contacts?"

"Not off the top of my head, but Aunt Ruby used to be a cop. She'll know who we can talk to about it."

"Dale... Don't tell her about the bones."

"God, no. I'll just get some names of people who can analyze them for us."

"How are you going to do that?"

"I'll think of something." He sighs. "Anything else?"

A lightbulb explodes in my head. I need help for tonight, and Dale is recently married to a beautiful woman.

"Yeah. Tell me how to..." God, am I really about to ask him this? "Woo a woman."

He laughs then. Dale laughs heartily, the kind of laugh I seldom hear from him.

"Seriously? You're asking *me*?"

"Yeah. I mean, I know how to get a woman in my bed. That's not what I'm asking."

"Hell, I may not have been a womanizer in my youth like you, but I don't know anything about wooing a woman. Ask Ashley. I was a mess. I didn't even know how to hold her hand at first."

I hold back a chuckle. Being laughed at is probably not what Dale needs right now. "Who would know, then? Not Donny. He was exactly like me."

"But he sure got Callie."

"That's true."

"What about your brother?" Dale asks.

"Brad? Yeah, maybe."

"He's been with Marie for what... Two, three years? Clearly he's kept her happy."

"Yeah. I'll call him. Thanks, man."

"Don't mention it. I'll let you know what I find out from Aunt Ruby."

Brad and I are close but not close, if that makes any sense. We're close because we're brothers. We love each other. We have each other's backs at all times.

But we're opposites in a lot of ways.

Which is why he may be able to help me. I punch in his number.

"Hey, Brock."

"Brad, bro. How's it going?"

"Okay. What do you want?"

"I'm shocked," I say in mock sincerity.

"You know I love you, man," Brad says, "but you never call me just to call me and ask how it's going."

"Touché. I have a question."

"Okay. What?"

"I have a date tonight, and I want to impress her."

"And you're talking to me? Just do what you always do."

"No. I don't want to bed her. I mean, I do"—*God, do I, after the day I had*—"but this woman means something to me. I want to impress her. I want to …"

Brad laughs. "Seriously? My little brother? Never thought I'd see this day. At least not for another ten years or so."

"Neither did I."

"Who is it?"

"That doesn't matter."

"Of course it matters. Do I know her?"

I sigh. Why not tell him? "It's Rory. Rory Pike."

Silence for a minute.

Then silence for two minutes.

Finally, "Wow. Rory Pike. Not only do you choose the most beautiful woman in town, but also the one where you have twice the competition of a straight woman."

"Yeah. So?"

"Hey, I like Rory Pike. Everyone does. The Pikes are good people."

"So tell me, then. What do I do?"

"Is it your first date?"

"Second, actually."

"What happened on the first?"

"Well . . . She basically invited me into her bed, and I . . . I turned her down."

Laughter then. Joyous and jovial laughter.

"I'm really glad my life is funny to you, bro."

"What can I say? This is hilarious."

"Thanks a lot. I can't believe I listened to Dale. He told me to call you."

"Hold on, hold on. So you're totally serious?"

I don't answer at first. What a stupid question. Of course I'm serious. Would I bare my soul like this to my only brother if I weren't?

Brad finally speaks, after clearing his throat. "All right. First, you need to get to know her. Ask her a lot of questions about herself."

"We talked a lot about that last time," I say. "About how she wanted to be a professional opera singer, but she didn't make it."

"Good. She already knows that you're interested in her, not just her awesome body."

"Except she thinks I'm not interested in sleeping with her, which I totally am."

"If she asks, explain it that way. Explain that you didn't want to rush into bed because you really like her."

"Man, this is so not me."

Brad chuckles. "Tell me about it."

"I offered to . . . I offered to produce a recital for her."

Silence another moment.

"Brad?"

"Man, do you have it bad."

I open my mouth to tell him he's wrong, but nothing comes out.

"Brock," he says. "If you really like this woman, don't screw it up."

"What do you think I'm calling you for? Tell me how to *not* screw it up."

"Just go against all your natural instincts, and you'll be fine."

"Thanks. Thanks a lot."

"Okay, I'm kidding." He sighs. "All right, only half kidding. You're a great guy, Brock. Everyone loves you, but you have a reputation as a womanizer. Everyone knows that, including Rory Pike. So . . . you have to go against your instinct."

"Dude, I went against my instinct last time. I didn't hop into bed with her when I had the chance."

"You just said you wanted this to be more."

"I do, but that doesn't mean it wasn't the hardest thing I've ever done not to hop into Rory Pike's bed. Have you seen her tits?"

"Everyone has seen her tits, Brock. Everyone knows she has the best rack this side of the Rockies."

A strange feeling settles in me. My brother has noticed Rory's tits. Hell, of course he has. He's a heterosexual male. Even the gay men I know love her tits.

And now? I don't want anyone looking at those amazing breasts but me.

God, what is happening to me?

"All right," I say to my brother. "Thanks for the help."

"Any time. Be yourself. You're a great guy. Just don't do what you normally do to get a woman into bed. Get to know her. Ask her about herself. Care, Brock. Just care."

"Got it. Bye."

Now ... to plan an amazing date with Rory Pike.

CHAPTER TWENTY-FIVE

Rory

"This is *your* place," I say.

Brock stops the car—a green BMW tonight, as opposed to the Tesla last time—in the garage to the guesthouse behind his parents' ranch house.

"It is."

"I thought we were going to have a date."

"We are. I'm going to cook for you."

I can't help myself. I laugh. I sound like a cackling chicken, but still I laugh.

"Something funny?" Brock says.

"No. I mean ... Do you cook?"

"I'm no Aunt Marjorie, but I do okay."

"You mean you don't have someone to do your cooking? Full time?"

"No. My parents do."

"You seriously cook for yourself every night?"

"Not every night. About half the time I eat with my parents at the main house."

"Okay, this is making more sense now."

"You know, there's more to me than just this gorgeous hunk of man you see before you."

I laugh again. He *is* charming. I'll give him that. He gets out of his car and comes around to the passenger side and opens the door for me, just like he did last time.

Yes, charming.

But I'm not unaware that this is all a perfectly scripted Brock Steel move. After all, last time he promised me the Brock Steel experience, and then he turned me down when I invited him to have his way with me. After telling me that lovemaking was an integral part of said experience.

So truly, I didn't get the Brock Steel experience.

A beautiful dog meets us at the door.

"Hey there, Sammy," Brock says.

Sammy looks to be some kind of German Shepherd mix with a lush brown-and-black coat and beautiful brown doggy eyes.

"Hey, gorgeous." I kneel and give him a pet on the head. "What kind of dog is he?"

"He's a she," Brock says. "I don't know. Obviously some German Shepherd is in the mix. I got her at Lifeline Rescue in Grand Junction."

"Really? That's where I got Zach."

"You have a dog?"

"Yeah. Callie and I went over and adopted dogs a couple of weeks ago. Zach and Dusty. They're awesome."

"I didn't know you liked dogs, Rory."

"Who doesn't love dogs? They're the best."

He gives Sammy some scratches behind her ears. "They are."

I follow Brock through the entryway around the formal living and dining room to a large country kitchen, where a vase of gorgeous red flowers sits as a centerpiece. He must see me gazing at them, because he says, "Dahlias. From Mom's greenhouse."

He lets Sammy out the back door, and then he turns to me. "You eat red meat, I hope."

I'm tempted to make another meat comment like I did Monday, but that got me nowhere fast. "Of course I do. Have you forgotten that my family owns some cattle? We don't just do wine, although that's the major enterprise."

Which has been shut down, but I don't need to remind him of that.

"Good. I have two amazing cuts of filet mignon wrapped in uncured bacon. Twice-baked sweet potatoes, and curried cauliflower."

"And you really made this all yourself?"

"Okay, okay. Grilling the filet mignon is no big deal. I can do that in my sleep. And curried cauliflower is easy. But Aunt Marjorie made the twice-baked sweet potatoes and brought them over to me. They just need to bake the second time." He inhales. "Can you smell them? They smell amazing."

I inhale. Sure enough, I smell their starchy sweetness. "I love sweet potatoes."

"Good. I kind of took a guess on that. Not everyone likes them."

"I do, especially baked. Heck, I even like that horribly cloying sweet potato marshmallow casserole everyone serves at Thanksgiving."

He laughs then. A deep bellied masculine laugh. And he looks . . . so gorgeous.

Brock Steel is the spitting image of his father, only prettier. Jonah Steel is ruggedly handsome, and Brock is Jonah with slightly finer features.

All the Steels are gorgeous—men and women. Yet I'm considered the most beautiful woman in Snow Creek?

Crazy stuff.

"What can I get you to drink?" Brock asks.

"Would you think less of me if I just wanted a nice cold beer?"

He laughs. "I love a cold brew myself." He pulls two Fat Tires out of the fridge and hands one to me.

"Thank you." I take a long drink. "How do you know I love Fat Tire?"

"Good guess. You seem like the ale type."

"So you know your beer," I say. "Ale, not lager."

"You don't grow up on the Steel ranch and not learn everything about different kinds of alcohol. Uncle Ryan is a beer drinker, believe it or not. Wine is of course his drink of choice, but he likes a good brew."

"Really?" I lift my eyebrows. "I don't think I've ever seen him with a beer."

"Like I said, his preferred drink is wine. But he and I have been known to drink beer together on occasion."

"There's a lot I don't know about you," I say.

"There's a lot I don't know about you too. Have you started working on your program for the recital?"

I take another sip of beer. "Yeah . . . About that."

"Oh, no. You're not backing out on me now. I already rented the cinema."

"Who the hell is going to come, Brock?"

"The whole town, of course."

"Snow Creek isn't exactly an opera town."

"Maybe not, but we talked about this last time. We're definitely lacking in culture here. You can bring some operatic pieces, some musical theater pieces."

"No one's heard me sing like that since I was in high

school. They hear me singing rock with Jesse."

"Yes, they do. And this will show them how multitalented you are."

My cheeks warm. Is it the beer? Or is it Brock Steel? Probably both.

"I'm going to get the steaks on the grill. Would you take the sweet potatoes out of the oven for me?"

"Sure thing."

"Oven mitts are in there." He points to a drawer.

I can't help but watch his tight ass as he walks out onto his deck.

This man is beyond gorgeous.

Perfect genetic material . . .

And I *am* ovulating . . .

As much as I want to wash this thought from my mind, I can't.

It permeated me the entire time Callie and I were searching Doc Sheraton's house . . . which we had no legal right to do. Pat didn't call the cops on us, though, and we knew he wouldn't.

Which means . . . he probably still has photos of us.

Does he realize it's illegal for him to even possess those photos of Callie?

Probably not.

We checked the main rooms of his house but didn't check his bedroom. We did, however, check the bedroom where Brittany was staying.

And we found absolutely nothing.

Of course, we're simply amateur sleuths. Neither of us knew exactly what we were doing, so we could've overlooked something important. Callie's going to talk to Donny about it and get back to me.

I want to wipe that from my mind and enjoy tonight, but the fact remains that we did it...and while we did it, I ruminated on my ovulation cycle that's most likely occurring right now.

An egg is descending from my ovary, through my fallopian tube, looking for fertilization.

It's not fair. It's not fair to get pregnant on purpose. I should talk to Brock first.

But if I do...

Then I let out a laughing scoff. How do I know he'll even take me to bed? He didn't the other night.

But if he does...I could tell him I'm on the pill. And clean.

That's a lie, of course. Plus, he's a known womanizer. How do I know *he's* clean? Sure, I want a baby, but I don't want anything else going on down there.

No. Hard no. I can't get pregnant without him knowing.

I have to tell him first.

And Callie's right. This isn't the way to do it.

About ten minutes later, Brock comes back in with the two filets on a plate.

"Rare," he says. "The only way to eat a filet."

"Rare's great."

I don't want to tell him that I'm not sure I've ever had a filet mignon. Beef tenderloin is the most expensive cut of steak, and we Pikes don't save the most expensive cuts for ourselves. The best cuts of our beef production are for profit.

"What can I do?" I ask.

"Nothing. Just sit your cute little ass down." He nods to the kitchen table.

So we're not eating in the formal dining room. No biggie.

There's only two of us.

Brock goes to a cupboard, pulls out two plates, and sets one in front of me and one at the empty space. He adds cloth napkins—yes, *cloth* napkins—steak knives, forks, and spoons. I can't help a smile at his charming contrariness—a kitchen table that isn't set, but cloth napkins and freshly cut dahlias. Adorable.

"Do you want wine with dinner?"

"Honestly? I'd like another beer as much as anything."

He smiles. "Your wish is my command." He pulls another Fat Tire out of the refrigerator and opens it for me. "Do you want a glass?"

I shake my head. "Tastes better out of the bottle."

"You know? I think you're right." He pulls out another beer, opens it, and sets it next to his own plate. He places a perfectly grilled filet mignon on my plate and then one of the twice-baked sweet potatoes. He puts the cauliflower in a bowl and sets it in the middle of the table, along with a basket of rolls. "These are from Ava's. Fresh baked."

"I love fresh-baked bread. My mom's an amazing baker too." I inhale, the yeasty aroma making my stomach growl.

"You're hungry," Brock says, smiling.

"That I am."

What he doesn't know is that I'm hungry for something more than food.

I'm hungry for the man sitting right next to me.

CHAPTER TWENTY-SIX

Brock

Rory Pike likes to eat. I noticed that Monday on our date. She eats heartily and enjoys her food. In fact, watching her savor each bite is kind of a sexual experience.

"How do you eat like this and not gain an ounce of weight?" I ask.

"Good metabolism. All of us Pikes have it. Good genes."

She lifts her eyebrows at the mention of her good genes.

"The best genes, I'd say. You're a great-looking bunch."

"As are the Steels," she says.

"Well, don't tell my cousins, but you're more beautiful than any of the Steel women."

"You think so? I think it's only because you don't think of your cousins that way."

"That's probably part of it, but surely you know you're the most beautiful woman in Snow Creek. Everyone knows."

"I don't know that, and don't call me Shirley."

It's an old joke, and her cheeks redden. From embarrassment or from actually knowing she's the most beautiful woman in Snow Creek? I'm not sure.

"Would it surprise you to know that I don't think of myself that way?" she continues.

"No. If you did, you'd probably be the most conceited

woman in Snow Creek as *well* as the most beautiful."

She blushes further. My God, she's so beautiful. Everything about her. From her long flowing dark hair, her big brown eyes, her perfect cheekbones, her full pink lips. That long, slender neck that I'm dying to kiss.

I want to bite her on that neck, leave my mark.

Damn. *Down, boy*, I say to my cock.

Time to get my head away from her beauty. Both heads, actually. Brad said to ask a lot of questions, so here goes.

"Tell me all about yourself, Rory. What is your biggest dream?"

She doesn't answer for a moment, which surprises me. Her biggest dream was to be an operatic mezzo, and I berate myself for asking the question because we already talked about that on Monday. The last thing I want is for her to get sad again and talk about how she didn't make it.

I open my mouth to change the subject, when she surprises me.

"A baby," she says. "My biggest dream is to be a mother."

I stop myself from dropping my jaw. Talk about a surprising answer.

"Are you going to say anything?" she asks.

"I'm just…"

"Surprised?"

"Well … yeah. A little."

"Why? Because I'm bisexual? Because I've had relationships with women, which can't lead to a biological child? There is adoption, you know." She clears her throat. "And insemination from a sperm donor."

"Rory, I'm not thinking any of that."

"What then? Why is it so surprising to you?"

"I just … I don't know. You don't seem like …"

"The type? The type to be a mother?"

Obviously I've offended her, and I didn't mean to.

"You'll be a great mother," I say.

"And how do you know that? You don't know anything about me, other than my failed foray into opera."

Okay. I need a save.

Damn you, Brad. Ask a lot of questions, you said. And look where it got me.

"Easy," I say.

"Easy? I'm twenty-eight years old, Brock. Did you forget that? Did you forget the fact that I'm older than you are?"

"No, I haven't forgotten that. Rory, you'll make a great mom. Having children is a noble calling. I'd like to have them myself someday."

The operative word being *someday.*

She sighs then, slathers butter on another of Ava's rolls, and takes a bite. She chews. And she chews.

When I'm convinced she's masticated it into complete mush, she finally swallows.

"I shouldn't have said that."

"I asked you what your biggest dream was. If that's the truth, then of course you should've said it."

"Now you're going to think I have baby fever."

"Rory, I don't think anything."

"Why are you looking at me like that?"

How am I looking at her?

"What do you mean?"

"You were staring at my mouth as I chewed."

Okay, she's right. I was. Why not be honest? "You chewed for a long time."

"Because you were watching me."

Oh my God. This date is not going well. My brother does *not* know how to woo a woman. Either that, or I just suck at it.

"Did you and Raine ever talk about kids?" I ask.

"She didn't want any."

"Oh. Was that part of the reason—"

"Part of it. I really don't want to talk about the breakup."

"I understand."

God, could I fuck this up any more?

"How's your steak?" I ask.

"Delicious."

"Good. I'm glad you like it. And the potatoes?"

"Delicious."

"I'll tell Aunt Marj how much you like them."

So this is what we've been reduced to. Talking about the food. I need to fix this, and I need to fix it fast. Except I have no idea how to.

"Have Donny and Callie talked to you about when they plan to have their wedding?" I ask.

"Nope."

Another one-word answer. What the hell is wrong with me?

We finish our dinner in silence.

CHAPTER TWENTY-SEVEN

Rory

What was I thinking? Telling Brock—who would make an excellent genetic father for my child—that it's my dream to be a mother.

What do I *really* want out of life?

Well, that's the truth. I want to be a mother. More than I want just about anything else.

But before I do that, I have to fix the whole Pat Lamone thing. I have to make sure my future child's mother's pictures are not splattered across social media.

We're not talking at all as we finish our delicious dinner. At least it *was* delicious before I wrecked everything.

Now what? I guess I ask him to take me home because the evening is effectively shot.

I open my mouth to do so, when—

"Dessert?" he asks.

I don't turn down dessert. Ever. But tonight, I'm not sure I have it in me to eat something sweet.

"Plus, I thought I could introduce you to my favorite cognac. An Armagnac from France."

"Okay," I say after a pause.

I did enjoy the cognac the other night. It warmed my throat, had a beautiful smoky taste and aroma.

"What's for dessert?" I ask.

"I decided to go simple. Aunt Marjorie's homemade vanilla bourbon ice cream."

"Vanilla bourbon? That doesn't sound so simple to me."

"It's simple when compared to something like baked Alaska or cherries jubilee."

"You can make baked Alaska and cherries jubilee?"

He laughs. "I didn't say that."

I smile then. Good. We seem to have gotten over the awkward part. Took long enough.

"Do you want coffee?"

"No, I think I'll try the Armagnac." It may be the only time I have the chance to sample something so expensive.

He smiles again. "Good. It's going to go great with this ice cream."

"What can I do to help?"

"Absolutely nothing. Just sit there and look pretty."

I roll my eyes.

"Did I say something wrong?"

"No. But if I had a nickel for every time someone told me to just sit there and look pretty, I'd be a rich woman. There's more to me than a pretty face, Brock. I already told you I don't think of myself that way."

"I know that. You're hella talented. You're caring and nurturing."

"Nurturing? Why would you say that?"

"It's pretty clear. You rescued a dog, and you want to be a mother."

I laugh. Finally. "Yeah, I guess I kind of do have *nurturing* tattooed across my forehead."

"Absolutely."

"Funny thing is, no one really knows that about me."

"They don't?"

"No. The only person I've talked to about my love of children and my desire to be a mother is Callie. The dogs... Well, I've always loved dogs."

"Rory, you're much more than a pretty face."

I smile, meeting his gaze.

"You have an amazing body and incredible rack too."

My jaw drops, but then I notice the twinkle in his eye. I rise then, walk to the freezer where he's standing, and give him a good-natured swat on his behind. "I'd be a rich woman if I had a nickel for all of those too."

"Look," Brock says. "I could pretend that you're not the most gorgeous thing walking, but we both know that's not true. Believe it or not, Rory, that's not why I asked you out tonight."

"Why did you, then?"

"I want to know you."

"No offense, Brock, but you're not known as that kind of guy. You're kind of known as a love 'em and leave 'em type."

"I know that."

"And you seriously think it's different with me?"

"I don't know yet. I'd like it to be."

Oh my God. His genetic material is looking better and better.

And I'm starting to think of him as more than just genetic material.

Which does not bode well for me.

I can't afford to fall in love with him. Not with a Rake-a-teer. I'm not in the market for heartbreak. Only in the market for a baby.

A sweet and beautiful baby who looks just like Brock Steel.

"I was hoping for a response to that," Brock says.

"A response to what?"

"That I'd like this to be more, Rory. If you don't share that feeling, let me know now."

"Brock..."

"Don't give me the *I'm too young for you* BS. We're only four years apart."

"That's not really an issue," I say.

"Then what *is* the issue?"

I don't reply right away.

"I know you just got out of a relationship. A relationship that meant something to you."

I nod. I did just get out of a relationship, and Raine and I were in love at one time. But we weren't for the last several months before we broke up, and I'm not looking for a new relationship at the moment. There's too much else on my mind. But I can't tell Brock about any of that.

Can I?

"Raine isn't the problem," I say.

"Then what is it? I'll help if I can."

"Can I trust you?"

He takes my hand then, and I tingle at his touch. His hand is so much bigger than mine—dwarfs mine—and I like that. This is why I like men. I like the differences between us. I like the fact that they're mostly hard to my soft, that they're bigger than I am.

I like all the things about women too.

But right now? Miss Universe herself could walk into the room, and I don't think I'd see her. All I see is Brock Steel. All six feet and three inches of him, gorgeous and muscled, that tight ass in those jeans, that beautiful dark hair, and those eyes that are the piercing black of a raven's. His jawline is sculpted, like all the Steel men, but there's something perfect about Brock. And that dark stubble that graces his cheeks and chin. It's all so masculine, and all so magnificent.

"Babe, you're scaring me a little. Is everything okay?"

"Actually, Brock, everything is *not* okay."

He sits with me, right at his kitchen table. We leave the dishes, and I talk to him.

I tell him everything.

The whole story about me and Callie and Pat Lamone. About what we did to him. And what he did to us.

The whole time, as I stammer and stutter and choke back tears, he never lets go of my hand.

When I'm finished—when there's not one more word to tell—he squeezes my hand, leans forward, and brushes his lips across mine.

"I swear to God, Rory, he will *not* harm you."

"Just don't offer him money. That's what he wants. Callie doesn't want Donny to pay him anything, and I don't want you to pay him anything. If we start paying him off, he'll never stop asking for it."

"I don't want to give him a damned red cent," Brock says. "But I will. To protect you."

"But that's not what I want. Sure, I'd love it if you could protect me, but this is my bed, and I must lie in it. I was the adult in the room back then, and this is on me."

"You were a kid, Rory."

"Maybe. But in the eyes of the law, I was an adult."

"I'll figure this out."

"No, Brock. That's not why I told you. I told you because... Well, you asked. And I... For some reason, I wanted to be honest with you."

"So we're on the same page, then?"

"What page might that be?" I ask coyly.

"Maybe you're hoping this could be something more also?"

I bite my lower lip. I keep myself from nodding, because if I nod, I have to go all in. I'm not quite ready to go all in. Relationship? With Brock Steel? A known womanizer?

So not ready for that.

But a baby?

That, I'm ready for.

I've always been in tune with my body, but I don't believe I can feel every little process inside. In this moment, though, I swear to God I feel my ovary rupture, the egg release.

Sure, it's probably my imagination, probably because we're talking about babies. Because I'm sitting next to the perfect genetic material for my child.

It's probably a lot of things, none of which has anything to do with my ovary actually releasing an egg.

But right now?

I know I'm right. And I know if I go to bed with Brock, I will end up pregnant.

So I meet his gaze. I look into those gorgeous dark-brown eyes.

Brock, would you consider fathering my child?

CHAPTER TWENTY-EIGHT

Brock

I freeze. Totally freeze, like a statue.

Did she really just ask me what I think she asked me?

After she just told me about the issues she's having with Pat Lamone?

Her cheeks redden. "What the hell is the matter with me? I honestly wasn't sure I said that aloud. Can you just forget it?"

I don't reply at first. Forget? Really? How can I possibly forget that she just asked me to father her child?

Finally, I find my voice. "I can't say anyone's ever asked me that before."

"I know. I'm not sure what I was thinking. It's just... You were being so understanding, and I want a baby so badly. And well, *look* at you."

"So you think I'm good-looking? That I'd make a good-looking child for you?"

"Well... yeah. We both have dark hair, brown eyes. But seriously. Forget it. I ..." She shakes her head. "Callie says I get too emotional. She's right. I have that emotional artist's brain, compared to her logical brain. I let my emotions get away from me, and I'm sorry."

"You don't have to be sorry." My tone comes out kind of robotic.

"Yeah, I do." She lets out a forced laugh. "Do you still want to get to know me?"

Do I?

It only takes me a millisecond to reply.

"Yeah. I do."

She smiles, sort of. It's forced again, but it's...not an unhappy smile. If such a thing even exists. It's more of an apologetic smile.

"Good."

I take her hand in mine. Even her hands are beautiful, perfectly formed, with pink polish on her nails.

"Listen," I say. "I can't just forget that you said that, but I have to tell you, I'm not ready to be a father."

"I get it. It was a stupid idea. I have no business thinking about babies with all the other stuff going on in my life right now anyway."

"You have every business to be thinking about babies, Rory. If it's a dream you have, you have every right to think about it."

"You did say you wanted children."

"Of course. Someday. I just haven't given it a thought in the present."

"You're young."

"So are you. Twenty-eight is hardly old."

She opens her mouth, closes it, but then opens it once more. "Reproductively speaking, twenty-eight is getting up there for a woman."

She pauses, and for a moment I think she's going to say something else, but she doesn't.

I get it.

It's just nothing I've ever considered before.

I was hoping tonight would lead to the bedroom. I suppose it still could, but I'm not sure how to approach it now.

Me. Brock Steel. I'm not sure how to get this woman into my bed.

My God, what is the world coming to?

And the even weirder thing? Her comment about making a baby should have sent my dick running for the hills, but it hasn't.

I'm still so hard for this woman that I'm not sure I'll be able to stand.

Why does the thought of making a baby with Rory Pike have me primed and ready to go like this?

This is some scary shit.

Maybe I just need to get laid. Maybe I need an escape from all the crap coming down on my family. From the fact that I spent the day searching for human decay on Steel property.

Whatever it is, I want her more than ever.

I finish my Armagnac, letting it soothe my throat and my stomach.

"Rory," I say.

"Yes?"

"You're so fucking beautiful, both inside and out, and I really want to go to bed with you."

I'm not sure I've ever uttered those words to a woman before. Usually I just kiss her until she melts.

I could kiss Rory right now. I could give her all the patented Brock Steel moves.

But I don't want to do that. She's different. She's worth more. I don't want this to be a quick fuck.

I want it to mean something.

I want it to mean something to her as well.

"Can you please just forget that I said what I said?" she asks softly.

"Sure."

I'll try, anyway.

She finishes her Armagnac and then taps the glass. "This is potent stuff. Seems I let my mouth run quite a bit tonight. First my old high school drama, and now ..."

I touch her then. Stroke my fingers over the side of her cheek and down her slender neck. I tingle at the softness of her skin. "I'm not sure what's going on in my head," I say. "I want to be honest with you."

"Please do."

"I like you. I like you a lot. Sure, at first I thought it would just be great to get busy with the most beautiful woman in Snow Creek, but for some reason, I wanted to get to know you. And what I know about you, I really like."

"Honestly?" she says. "Ditto for me. I figured you were just some gorgeous playboy with a hard-on. You're not."

"It is nice to be known as something more than just a pretty face," I can't help saying.

"Touché."

I rise then. To hell with my hard-on. She's going to find out about it soon enough.

I can't get a read on her, but she knows what my fathering a child would entail, so surely she was thinking the same thing.

I grip her shoulders, pull her into my body, and smash my mouth to hers.

She opens for me. Smoothly and liquidly, her lips part as her tongue flows into my mouth.

Yes, we've kissed before. A wonderful and exhilarating kiss behind her band's van at Uncle Talon's party. But I knew that wasn't leading to anything.

This kiss?

This will lead somewhere. At least I hope to God it will.

I'm not after a quickie with her, but I'll take what I can get.

I deepen the kiss, pull her as close to me as possible so our bodies are aligned. My God, we fit together so well, like two perfect jigsaw puzzle pieces.

She sighs into the kiss, a soft moan, and it makes me want her even more.

This kiss… It's so full of passion and desire. But there's something else too. Something I can't quite put my finger on.

So I let my thoughts wander. No need to figure out why the kiss is different. Just enjoy it. Just enjoy kissing Rory Pike.

I smooth my hands over her shoulders, down her back, squeeze one globe of her delectable ass.

Her amazing breasts are crushed against me, and though I want to cup them, touch them, I don't.

To do so would mean I have to pull back a little, and for the life of me, I don't want to do that. I want her touching me. Even through her clothes, she burns into me.

We kiss for a long time. I don't know how long, and I don't care. I will *not* be the one to break this kiss.

I'm good at breathing through my nose, kissing a woman deeply, but my heart is racing so quickly, and my breath… My breath…

I pull away quickly, angry that I broke my promise to myself. I gasp in a much-needed breath.

Her beautiful face, her swollen lips from our kiss. She's…

Something in my heart breaks just a little, looking at her. Those high and rosy cheeks, the full red lips, the slight tremble in her stance.

She's affected by this. By me.

I reach out then, twirl a strand of her long hair around my finger. Then I pull her close to me again.

I start more slowly this time, ease her into the kiss, but then she takes the lead. She parts her lips and forces her tongue between mine.

No gentle kissing for Rory Pike. Not this time.

And that suits me just fine.

Something explodes in me. I push my hard cock into her belly, grab her ass, and grind against her pubic bone.

My God, I could come right now. Fully clothed, just rubbing against Rory Pike. I feel like I'm fifteen again, jacking off in my room.

That's how turned on I am at this moment.

This time, Rory breaks the kiss. Gasps in a breath.

"Brock…"

"Yeah, sweetheart?"

Her cheeks are already red, but she blinks a little at the use of the term *sweetheart*. It's not a term I use. I'm more of a *babe* or *sugar* or *you hot little thing* guy.

I'm not sure where sweetheart came from.

I reach forward to touch her cheek, but she pushes my hand away.

"I… I'm not sure, Brock."

"Not sure? You initiated that last kiss, Rory. You're the one who wanted me to give you a child. You do know how babies are made, don't you?"

Her lips tremble.

"I'm sorry," I say quickly. "I didn't mean to—"

She taps two fingers against my lips to stop me. "It's okay. My God, you can kiss like no one I know."

"You're pretty good yourself, babe."

She looks down then, down at her feet. I place my finger under her chin and tip it upward so she meets my gaze.

"I won't lie to you, Rory. I'm horny as hell right now, hard as a rock for you. I want to take you to bed. But I won't. Not if you don't want to."

"I..."

"Take your time."

God, I'm so fucking hard. I close my hand over my cock, adjusting the bulge.

Her gaze drops to what I'm doing.

"You can see how much I want you," I say.

"I want you too. God, I never imagined."

"Never imagined what?"

"All this. This...passion. I thought I had passion before. I thought I wanted another person before. But right now... It's like I'd give everything up for you. Just to have you this once." She clamps her hand over her mouth.

"It's okay. I'm feeling that too. It's some scary shit." I pull her hand from her mouth. "This is more than chemistry, Rory. It's... To tell you the truth, I don't know what the hell it is because it's not anything I've ever experienced before. But it's not something I want to turn away from, even though part of me is yelling at me to do that."

She nods then. "I understand. Believe me, I understand."

I adjust my crotch once more. "So the question is... What do we do about it?"

CHAPTER TWENTY-NINE

Rory

There are certain times in my life that I'll always remember. The first time I starred in a musical in middle school. I played Annie. I remember getting a standing ovation from the entire town, and at that moment, it no longer mattered how much that stupid curly orange wig made my scalp itch or how much I hated that red minidress.

All that mattered was the applause.

Then there was the time when I was crowned homecoming queen.

I was the favorite going in, so it never really occurred to me that I might lose. Still, having the previous year's queen place that plastic and rhinestone tiara on my head gave me a high I'll never forget.

And then . . . the first time I sang with Jesse and the band. I had just gotten back from an audition trip to New York a couple of weeks before, and I hadn't gotten one single callback. In fact, I had gotten some pretty bad reviews from the judges. I didn't think I'd ever sing again, and I'm pretty sure Jesse only asked me to sing with the band because my mom asked him to. She thought it would be good for me.

Of course I told him no.

But my brother wouldn't take no for an answer. He had

written a few songs for female vocalists, and he asked me to rehearse with them.

When I stepped up on the stage at the venue in Grand Junction, clad in tight jeans and a black tank top, my hair flowing over my shoulders, black leather thigh-high boots hugging my legs, and sang into the mic, to thundering applause, I felt elated. Like stars were lifting me up to the heavens.

Of all those times that stand out, that made me feel as if I were walking on air, it had to do with applause, with the thrill of attention.

But this time?

A kiss. A kiss from Brock Steel.

I'm getting the feeling. That amazing feeling of endorphins pumping through my body, floating above everything, of feeling happy in the most amazing way.

I've kissed a lot of people, male and female. I love kissing, and I've been kissed by some really good kissers.

And yes, I've been turned on. I've gotten wet from kissing, super wet.

Right now, I'm wetter than I've ever been, and I swear to God, it's better than the best applause I've ever gotten. It's better than being on the stage, with people clapping, shouting *brava*.

Brock Steel's kiss is better than all that.

Which means...

If his kiss is that good? Damn, the actual act itself is going to blow my mind.

I'm not on the pill. And he doesn't want to father my child. Which means he's going to have to use a condom.

I'm not a big fan of condoms. That's another thing I like about being with a woman. No condoms. No worry about an unwanted pregnancy. Of course, right now I want a pregnancy.

But not like this. Not when Brock is unwilling.

Definitely need a condom. No worries. This is Brock Steel. He *will* have condoms.

"Are you going to answer me?" he says.

Take me to bed.

I part my lips, ready to say the words, but they don't come.

"All right," Brock says. "I can take a hint."

"No!" I shout.

He lifts his eyebrows.

"That's not what I mean. I can't believe how much I want you, Brock. This isn't like me. I don't move this quickly."

"Asking me to father your child is moving pretty quickly, Rory."

"Yeah, that's a new one for me. My last two relationships were with women, so I couldn't really ask them that."

"So you only move quickly with men?"

I shake my head vehemently. "Absolutely not. I probably move more slowly with men."

He lifts his eyebrows once more.

"I don't understand this," I say. "I don't understand this at all."

"We want each other." He strokes my cheek. "It's not so difficult to understand from where I'm standing."

"No, I don't deny that. It's just . . . very unlike me."

"Maybe," he says, "doing what isn't like you is a good thing."

"But—"

He kisses me then. Hard.

His tongue is in my mouth, tangling with my own, and I squirm against the tickle between my legs. I'm so hot, so bothered, so freaking wet. He could slide right into me now, no foreplay required.

And you know what? I feel okay with that. I want him inside me. I want his hard cock inside me, pumping and pumping and pumping, easing the emptiness and the ache.

I could kiss Brock Steel forever, I'm planning to, until—

He breaks the kiss and pulls me into his arms. I gasp as he carries me out of the kitchen.

"Where are we going?" I ask, my heart racing.

"To the bedroom."

CHAPTER THIRTY

Brock

She's like feathers in my arms. Or maybe my adrenaline has kicked in, and she's become weightless to me.

All I know is I can't get to my bed fast enough.

I power through, hoping against hope that she won't tell me to stop.

We reach the master bedroom.

And she hasn't told me to stop.

But I want this to go somewhere. I don't want this to be a fuck and nothing else. So I put her down gently, her feet touching my carpeted floor.

"This is my bedroom," I say.

She swallows. "I figured as much."

"If we go in there, we're going to m— have sex." I almost said *make love*, but I caught myself.

I don't make love. I fuck. I like to fuck women, and I'm good at it. But I'm not sure if I've ever made love to a woman.

The fact that those words occur to me...

I'm frightened out of my mind.

"I'll never force a woman. Not ever. I want this more than anything, and I'm hard as a rock for you, Rory. So tell me now if you're having even the slightest second thought."

Her lips tremble a bit, and then she runs her tongue over the lower one.

I think I just got harder.

I caress the doorknob, turn it, crack the door.

"Last chance," I say. "We go in there, we're going to . . ."

Again I want to say *make love*. God, what the hell is wrong with me?

Making love. It's just a euphemism, after all. A euphemism for having sex, fucking, screwing, hitting the hay. Whatever.

She takes my hand that still sits atop the doorknob. "I know, Brock. I know what we're going to do in there. I want it."

I can't help it. I groan. A long, slow groan. "Are you ready?"

"Even I don't believe how ready I am," she says. "I'm wet right now. I can feel it. Every part of my body is screaming for you. The tickle, the need, the urge, the desire. It's all there. I'm so ready right now."

Another groan. "Fuck, Rory." I swing the door open.

The master suite in the guesthouse is large, but it's all one big room. My king-size bed faces the east window. I like to watch the sunrise over the mountains—at least on those mornings when I'm not up before the sunrise, which are few.

On my bed, the gray satin comforter is slightly wrinkled. That means Sammy was napping in here earlier.

I'll keep her outside for now. Rory and I don't need any company in the bed.

It's funny. The bed seems larger than usual. My perspective is so different with Rory. It's like the bed has a heartbeat of its own.

A lot of sex has happened in this bed.

For a moment, a fleeting thought crosses my mind.

Rory's the last woman who will ever be in this bed.

That's nuts. Completely nuts. I'm not sure why I thought that.

Doesn't matter. I need to get inside her, and I need to get inside her quickly.

"I need you," she says. "Please."

She pulls off her shirt, and I get an up-close view of that amazing rack. She's wearing a simple white lace bra, and those beautiful Ds are spilling out of the cups.

She reaches around to the back to unclasp it—

"No, let me." I turn her around, unclasp the bra, and then slide my hands over her flesh and cup those gorgeous breasts as they fall out of her bra.

They're warm to my touch, and her nipples—those nipples are hard.

I turn her back toward me. I have to get a look.

And I can't help a gasp.

I've seen a lot of naked women, so not much surprises me.

But Rory's breasts? They're more beautiful than I ever imagined. Large, but with only a minimal amount of sag. The perfect amount, actually. And her nipples… Dark reddish brown. Her skin is fair, so I assumed she'd have pink or light-brown nipples. But not Rory Pike. Her beauty is unique. Her areolas are the perfect size as well—like a half-dollar, wrinkled and puckered, squeezing her nipples outward.

For a second, I just stare.

No, I gawk. I gawk as if these are the first breasts I've ever seen in my life.

Like a freaking teenager with his tongue hanging out.

That's what this woman does to me.

All my experience? It's gone with the wind. I'm a schoolboy, untried, horny as hell, and itching to get my dick inside its first pussy.

"My God, you're beautiful."

"So are you." She unbuckles her belt slowly, seductively. "You going to get undressed, Brock? Or do you want me to undress you?"

"I want it all. I want to get my clothes off quickly so I can get you on the bed. I also want to undress slowly. Better yet, I want you to undress me. I want to undress you. I want to do it all, Rory. I want to strip each other so quickly that our clothes turn to shreds. I want it all."

"Well, this is the night."

Damn. Is she insinuating that we'll only have this one night? I'll never have time to do everything I want to do to her. Fast, slow, fast, slow. Medium. Everything. I want to eat her, suck her, lick her until she's screaming. I want to fuck her. Fuck her hard, fuck her fast. Then I want to fuck her slowly and gently. I want to turn her around and slide my tongue along the cheeks of her ass, eat her. Finger her ass, get it ready for my dick. I want to kiss her all over. I want to suck those nipples. I want to feel those beautiful lips around my cock.

I. Want. It. All.

Within seconds, all my clothes are in a pile on the floor.

Her brown eyes are wide.

"I guess I'm in a hurry," I say.

"It appears you're ready for anything." She drops her gaze to my massive cock.

"See anything you like?"

"You're huge," she says. "Huge and magnificent."

I try not to let it go to my head as she continues to stare.

But this woman's gaze on my hard cock has me ready to explode.

"My God, it's been a long time since I've had a cock in my mouth," she says.

"No."

She lifts her eyebrows. "No?"

"Rory, if you suck me right now, I will totally explode down your throat."

"That's okay. I like to swallow."

Man, she's killing me! "Damn, you're hot. No. I mean, if you do that, it'll be over too soon. If I'm going to explode tonight, I'm going to explode inside that hot little cunt of yours."

A groan. It comes from her. She likes that idea. She likes it a lot.

"My God, every part of you is perfect." I cup her breasts again. Thumb her nipples.

She sighs softly. "Feels good."

"I need to be inside you, Rory. I promise, we'll do this again, and I'll do it right. But right now—"

"Do it," she says through gritted teeth. "Please. My God, please."

My body takes over then, and I lift her in my arms once more, this time flesh to flesh, set her down on the bed, hover over her, let my cock dangle between her legs.

"Fuck," I grit out.

"Now. Please, Brock. Please. I need you."

I thrust inside her.

My God. Sweet perfection. She's so tight, she squeezes my cock just right. And—

I pull out quickly.

She gasps. "Is something wrong?"

"God, no. That was the hardest thing I've ever done."

"Then why did you do it?"

"Condom. Fucking condom."

"Oh." Her voice is sad.

"You okay?"

"I hate condoms."

"So do I, sweetheart, but—"

She opens her mouth about to say something but then closes it.

"What is it, Rory?"

"Nothing. I have to be honest with you. I'm clean. I get tested every time I get into and out of any relationship. But…"

"But…you're not on the pill."

"No, I'm not."

"Shit."

She wants a kid. She wants *my* kid. I'm so damned tempted. But—

I walk to my dresser, open the top drawer, retrieve a condom, and quickly cover myself.

It's not going to feel nearly as good as it just did seconds ago, but it will still be amazing.

I'm still hard as a rock for her, still can't wait to get inside her.

She spreads her legs for me, and I drop my gaze to the treasures between them.

She's dazzling. Every part of her, even her pussy. It's perfectly plump and pink. So wet and glistening.

I want to taste it. I want to eat her and eat her and eat her. But my cock. It needs to be inside her.

And damn, we're going to need to do something about this condom situation. But not tonight.

I crawl on top of her once more, and then I plunge inside her heat.

She seats me so heavenly. Even with the condom, I'm more sensitive than I've ever been. I could stay embedded in her forever.

I feel like I've come home.

CHAPTER THIRTY-ONE

Rory

I remember a time when I was a kid. It was a particularly harsh winter in Colorado, and I was out sledding with Jesse and his friends. Callie was too little to go, and Maddie was just a baby. Jesse didn't want to take me along, but I pleaded with him until Mom made him.

I lost my gloves midway through our afternoon, and by the time we got home, I was a popsicle.

So cold that I couldn't stop my teeth from chattering.

Mom yelled at Jesse for not taking better care of me, and then she took off my wet clothes, put flannel pajamas on me, wrapped me in a sheepskin blanket, and then moved a rocking chair right by the fireplace and held me on her lap.

Once my teeth stopped chattering and warmth spread throughout me, I felt totally comforted.

Totally home.

Until now, that's the best feeling I can ever remember having.

To compare it to having Brock Steel's cock inside me seems ridiculous. I was a kid getting comforted by her mother. Becoming warm after a fun but freezing day in the snow with my brother.

But damn . . .

Sure, this is completely different. It's sexual in nature, not nurturing.

But my God, the comfort.

The comfort that goes along with Brock inside me.

This is something I've never experienced before—not with a man or woman.

Maybe it's because I've been thinking about having a baby. I've been thinking about nurturing my own offspring the way my mother nurtured me.

Or maybe it's because of a million other different things.

But I can't help but wonder . . .

Is it because this is Brock Steel? Is he the person I'm supposed to be with?

He stays inside me for a few timeless moments, and I relish the fullness. The completion.

He's massive, for sure. And yes, it burned at first. When he went into me without the condom and then left, I thought I might die an untimely death.

Now he's back inside.

And I don't ever want him to leave.

Finally he pulls out and then pushes back into me.

The friction—every bit of it—is nirvana. I'm not sure my pussy has ever been so sensitive to invasion. For a moment, I even doubt my bisexuality. No woman could make me feel like this.

But then I understand.

No other man could either.

This is crazy. Completely crazy.

"Please," I say. "Don't stop."

"Wasn't planning on it," Brock says, his voice wavering just a bit. "You feel amazing, Rory."

"God, yes. So do you."

"I could stay inside you all day and night."

"Please." This time I whisper.

He slides in and out of me slowly, sensually, so that I can feel every millimeter of every stroke.

Yes, I want him to go faster. But at the same time, I don't. I want to revel in this, savor each slow stroke.

"Fuck," he says through clenched teeth.

"What?"

"Want to … Need to …"

It happens. He rams into me. Pulls out and thrusts quickly.

And oh my God, sparks fly through me as he fucks me and hits my clit with each thrust.

And I know … I know …

"Brock!" I screech out as the orgasm shatters me.

I see stars. I seriously see stars. I climax easily. I always have, but this … This is something I've never experienced. Not with a man, and not with a woman.

My whole body quivers, expanding and then contracting, everything ending in perfect pulsations between my legs.

He continues ramming into me, fucking me hard and fast.

"God, Rory. Oh my God."

He pushes into me once more, and I feel him. I feel him come. Each shattering pulse of his cock.

And I want it. I want it all. I want everything Brock has to give.

He stays inside me for a few moments, and then he rolls over, closing his eyes and rubbing his forehead.

"Rory." His voice is a low rasp.

"Yeah."

"My God."

"It was . . ."

"Spectacular," he finishes for me.

"Yes. That was magnificent."

"You're magnificent," he says.

"So are you."

"You need anything?" he asks without opening his eyes. "Water?"

"How about a smoke?"

He chuckles.

"I'm good," I say.

"Excellent. Give me a few minutes, and then we're going to do that again."

I close my eyes, my body still reeling. My nipples are so hard, and my pussy is still quivering. My body is still awash in goose bumps. This is unreal. I'm living in unreality at this moment.

Tomorrow is Sunday, a day off for me. Probably not a day off for Brock.

I should probably leave. Ask him to take me home. Sure, he says he wants to go again, but it's crazy to stay here. This is our first date.

Except it's not. It's our second date. Third if you count our lunch. Fourth if you count the brief make-out session at the party last week.

But I don't count that. I'm kind of a traditional girl at heart. Making out at a party with a guy—even Brock Steel—isn't a date. It's glorified high school. I'm dealing with enough high school drama right now. I don't need to add any more.

Brock lets out a soft snore.

I smile. Brock is a normal man. Underneath that gorgeous exterior and that womanizing personality is a normal guy who snores.

I can't help myself. I crawl toward him, snuggle into his shoulder. I close my eyes, inhale his spicy masculine scent.

Men. So different from women, and no less intoxicating.

But this man ... This man stands alone.

These feelings I'm having are new to me. I'm not one to fall hard and fast. Relationships take time, and I like to let them evolve organically.

But this ...

This is something new.

Something new ... and a little bit scary.

But in some way, it's not scary at all.

CHAPTER THIRTY-TWO

Brock

I wake to Sammy barking outside. I don't usually leave her outside at night, but I was a bit distracted by a certain gorgeous brunette who's still in my arms.

Rory is sleeping soundly snuggled up to my shoulder. And damn, it feels good.

It feels right.

What the hell is happening to me?

I move, trying not to wake her, and leave the bed and pull on a pair of pajama pants. Then I pad through the hallway and out to the kitchen, where I let in a panting Sammy, who is very happy to see me.

"Hey, girl. I'm sorry. I fell asleep." I scratch her behind her ears.

After she's done getting love from me, she walks to her water bowl and drinks heartily. Her water outside must have been empty. I've totally neglected her this evening, the poor girl.

When she's done drinking, she comes back to me where I'm sitting down at the kitchen table. I scratch the top of her head. "I'm sorry. I've been a little distracted by a beautiful woman. It won't happen again, girl."

She forgives me, of course. She's a dog, after all. Her belly is full, and she's loved.

I rise then. "Come on," I say to my canine friend.

She comes with me into the bedroom and jumps right up onto her spot at the foot of the bed.

Rory moves slightly and then opens her eyes.

"Sorry," I say. "Sammy didn't mean to wake you."

"It's okay," she says, yawning. "What time is it?"

"It's about two a.m."

She jolts upward. "I should go."

"It's okay. Stay."

"But—"

"Really. I want you to stay."

She smiles. "Okay." She lies back down.

I shimmy out of my pajama pants. "Since we're both awake..." I lie down next to her, pull her toward me, and kiss her beautiful lips.

She tastes as sweet and succulent as she did before. This woman doesn't have morning breath. Of course, it's not morning yet.

But already I know she won't have morning breath. And if she does, it won't matter to me.

Already I know that I'll take every chance I can to be with her, to get inside her, to hold her close to me.

I'm hard again, and damn, I didn't think to put a condom on before we started this.

I don't want to stop kissing her. Her lips are so soft, her tongue so velvety and sweet.

I want to pull her on top of me, have her straddle me, ride me.

Fuck.

I break the kiss.

"You okay?" she asks.

"Condom," I grit out.

She nods.

I rise, walk to the dresser, and take care of things. Then I settle back in bed. Already, I know that if I start kissing her again, I'll be inside her within minutes.

"You know," she says, "maybe you don't need that condom."

"Yeah, I do."

"No, that's not what I mean."

She climbs on top of me, but instead of sliding down onto my cock, she turns and hovers above my face. Then she removes the condom and sucks the tip of my dick between her beautiful lips.

"Damn," I groan.

I pull her down by her hips, nearly smothering myself with her sweet pussy.

And I do mean sweet.

She tastes like crab-apple butter. Weird, I know, but that's the first thing that pops into my mind. Sweet and tart and creamy.

Her labia are slick beneath my tongue, and her clit is already hard. I suck on it gently . . . and then not so gently.

I move my head from side to side, covering my cheeks and chin with her juices. I want to drown in her, drown in her beauty and her sensuality and her nurturing goodness.

This woman . . .

She's more than just the beauty of Snow Creek.

She's something truly special.

And I'm not just saying that because I have my face in her pussy.

I want to give her more attention, but I'm distracted by what she's doing to my cock. For someone who hasn't been with a man for a while, she's an expert at giving head.

She licks softly, and then she sucks hard, seeming to instinctively know when to pull back, when to go forward.

And oh my God, she has me on edge. Several times, I'm sure I'm going to spew, but then she pinches me right at the root of my shaft to hold back my orgasm.

I'm not sure I've had a better blow job in my life.

I'm pretty sure she could suck a golf ball through a garden hose.

I suck her harder, eating her. She swells above me, her pussy so hot and delicious. She's going to pop soon. I know all the signals. I flick my tongue over her clit, gaining speed and strength.

And then I feel it—the pulsing of her pussy against my mouth.

She moans and groans, her mouth still full of my cock.

She's coming, and though I'd love to let her come again and again and again, I can't hold off.

I groan, the sound muffled by her pussy in my face. And I let go. I let go, pouring myself into Rory's mouth.

And with each contraction of my cock, I know, more and more, that this woman is different. This relationship—if I can even call it that yet—is different.

Is it forever? I don't know, and I don't yet want to know.

But it's something amazing, and I don't want it to end.

Not for a long time.

CHAPTER THIRTY-THREE

Rory

It's been a long time since I've had a man's cock in my mouth. Brock Steel may not be the easiest blow job to give—he's massive, after all—but this is the most satisfied I've felt in a long time. I'm talking about the satisfaction I gave him, not the mind-blowing orgasm he just gave me.

And yeah, I swallow. I always have. I've never understood women who don't. If you like someone enough to give them a blow job, why wouldn't you swallow?

I like this man. I like him a lot. More than I ever thought I would or could.

He says I'm more than just a pretty face. He's much more than a pretty face as well.

I move off him and lie down next to him.

"That was fantastic," he says.

"Amazing," I agree. "You sure know what you're doing."

"So do you, sweetheart. So do you."

"See? We don't need a condom."

"Oh, yeah, we do. Because I'm not letting you out of this bed until I'm back inside that pussy again."

I giggle. I giggle like a schoolgirl. What is wrong with me?

"Does that cute little chuckle mean you're on the same page as I am?"

"I'm on a page I never thought I'd be on," I say.

"What's that supposed to mean?"

"You and me," I say. "It doesn't make any sense."

"Sweetheart, it makes all kinds of sense from where I'm standing, or should I say lying."

I giggle again. And I hate myself for it. "This is crazy, Brock. Totally crazy. I'm too old for you."

"Sweetheart, I don't care if you're forty-five. You are exactly what I want right now."

His words warm me, make me feel all giddy inside. Giddy like I haven't felt in a long time. Not since I first discovered relationships and sex.

Which means I haven't had something like this in a long time, and that's kind of sad.

"Where do you see this going?" I ask.

Then of course I want to take back the words. So not the time.

"Where do you want it to go?" he shoots back at me.

I'd love it to lead to a baby.

I don't say that, of course. I already put that particular foot in my mouth earlier. Thankfully he didn't go running away screaming like a banshee.

"Honestly? I don't know."

"I don't know either. Maybe we just take it as it comes. See where it goes. And we have a lot of fun along the way."

God, his voice is so low and sexy.

"Sounds good," I say.

"Do you still want me to take you home?"

I snuggle into his shoulder. "No. I'm good here if you are."

"Sweetheart," he says, "I can't think of anything more wonderful than waking up with you in my arms."

I smile against him. I haven't felt this relaxed in a long time.

★ ★ ★

I don't know where I am at first. This bed is different, and the dog at the foot of it is not Zach.

But then... The hard body next to me. The spicy outdoorsy fragrance of Brock Steel.

And I remember. I'm in Brock's bed.

We made love. Scratch that. We fucked. But it was good. It was so very good.

My body is on high alert. I feel... ripe. Fertile. Man, I still want a baby. For the first time, I think this thing with Brock could lead to something. Something amazing. I'm not going to screw it up by asking him to father my child again. If it does lead to something, he *will* eventually father my child.

And it will happen the way it's supposed to. Because we fall in love.

I suppress a chuckle because I don't want to wake him up. But seriously? I'm thinking about falling in love with Brock Steel?

That's the strangest thought I've had in a long time.

But I'll go with it. It feels natural. It feels good.

And I absolutely will *not* bring up the baby thing again.

I jerk as Brock's alarm goes off. He groans, turns over, grabs his phone, and shuts it off.

Does he remember that I'm here? I'm not sure for a minute, because he closes his eyes once more. He must've put the alarm on snooze. If he didn't have to get up, why would his alarm be set?

I tiptoe out of bed, but my ruse is ruined when Sammy jumps off the bed, wagging her tail and panting.

"Shush," I say, petting her soft head. "You'll wake him up."

"Already awake," Brock groans.

"Hey," I say. "I'm going to let her out, okay?"

"Yeah, sure."

"Do you need to get up for something?"

"There aren't any days off on a ranch," he groans again.

"Okay. Go ahead and sleep for as long as you can. I've got the dog."

I think of Zach at home. Callie or my mom will care for him this morning. I feel a rush of guilt. I should've texted one of them.

I grab my jeans and shirt and wiggle into them quickly. Then I walk out to the kitchen to let the dog out. I have no idea where Brock keeps the dog food, so I look around and find a bag of kibble in the pantry. I pour some into Sammy's bowl, and then I spy the coffeemaker on the counter. Coffee. That, I can do. A minute later, it's brewing.

Now what? I could make breakfast.

Except I have no idea what Brock likes for breakfast.

I laugh out loud. He's a Steel man. A total bacon, egg, and potatoes breakfast type. Or maybe Steel beef. They seem to eat that at every meal. My God, they must be cholesterol nightmares. Or maybe not since they stay so active.

I look inside the refrigerator. Sure enough, bacon and eggs. I don't see any bread, which is odd. We had those great rolls from Ava's bakery last night.

I wonder if… Yes! A few of the leftover rolls lie in a plastic bag on the counter.

I set several strips of bacon to fry in a cast-iron skillet I found under the stove, and I set the rolls in the oven to warm. Once the coffee is done brewing, I pour myself a cup and take a sip. Perfect. When the bacon is done, I crack eggs into the bacon grease. I guess I'm not helping the Steel cholesterol problem this morning.

I'm plating the breakfast when Brock walks in, fully dressed already.

He doesn't look happy.

CHAPTER THIRTY-FOUR

Brock

The sight of Rory in my kitchen, placing bacon and eggs on a plate, makes my heart do a little jump. She looks happy. She looks like she belongs here in my home.

For a moment, I want to stay here. I want to enjoy the breakfast she prepared and then take her back to my bed.

The phone call I just got from my father makes that impossible. *Get over here. Now. It's important.* That's all he said, but it was his tone that has me on edge.

She meets my gaze, her eyes troubled. "Is there something wrong?"

"Smells great," I say.

"I'm glad, but you didn't answer my question."

I kiss her cheek. "Nothing you need to worry about." I take a seat.

"I assume you like bacon and eggs, since I found them in the fridge."

"Breakfast of champions." I take a bite off a slice of bacon with more force than I mean to.

"How do you take your coffee?" she asks.

"Black."

She pours me a cup and sets it in front of me, and then she sits down next to me, where a plateful of breakfast is already set for her.

I sigh. "I hate to do this. And I mean, I *really* hate to do this, but I have to take you home."

"Something *is* wrong," she says.

"Not with you. Or us. But something requires my attention this morning."

"*I* require your attention this morning," she says, smiling seductively.

"You're not making this any easier."

"I think that's the point."

"Believe me, I can't think of anything I'd rather be doing than going back to bed with you. But..."

"It's okay."

"It's not okay," I say, "but it is what it is. But I'd like to see you again. Soon."

She smiles. That radiant Rory Pike smile. "Just say when."

"This evening?"

"I don't know, I have a jam-packed schedule." Then she winks.

"Great. Tonight it is. I'll pick you up at... I don't know. As soon as I can?"

"When you know, just text me," she says.

I take another bite of bacon, chew, swallow. "Thanks for understanding. You'll hear from me as soon as possible. I promise."

I finish my breakfast quickly and take my plate to the sink while Rory goes back into the bedroom to gather the rest of her belongings. A few minutes later, she returns, dressed and looking beautiful, her cheeks slightly blushed.

"I'll make this up to you." I give her a searing kiss. Then we walk out to the car.

★ ★ ★

About a half hour later, I walk into my mom and dad's backyard. I don't go through the house. I go straight out back to the pool house. That's where Dad told me to meet him.

Dad is already in the pool, swimming laps, which means he's stressed. Dad loves to swim, and he swims all the time. But this early in the morning? These are most certainly stress laps.

Which doesn't bode well.

I wave to him, not sure if he sees me, and then I head to the pool house and change into my trunks. If Dad is doing stress laps, I'm going to need stress laps as well.

I dive in on the opposite side. After five laps of my own, I hoist myself out of the pool and sit on the concrete.

Dad swims up to me. "Thanks for coming, Brock."

"You said it was important."

"It is."

"I'd ask what could be so important on a Sunday morning, but I already know the answer."

"Do you?"

"Not specifically, no, but I'm assuming it has to do with Uncle Tal's shooting."

"Yes and no," Dad says. "I want to tell you about someone."

"Okay."

"I want to tell you about your great uncle. William Elijah Steel."

My heart drums.

Why now? What's going on? Does Dad know something that I don't?

I hold back a scoff. Of course he knows something I don't. He knows a lot of things that I don't. That's the whole problem here—beginning with the stuff Brendan Murphy found underneath the floorboards. A whole can of worms—make that serpents—has been opened for the Steel family.

That's the reason I told Dale and Donny we should keep my father out of our investigation into those GPS coordinates.

"All right," I say.

"I found out about my uncle—half uncle, actually—by accident," Dad says.

I don't reply. What is there to say?

"I don't think about him a lot. I only briefly mentioned his existence to my brothers, and that was years and years ago. I think I mentioned him to your mother also, when we were first dating."

"Why is he such a secret?"

"My father never knew him," Dad says. "Wait. That may not be true. Let's just say my father never mentioned him to me. But that doesn't mean anything, because my father was the biggest liar on the planet. I mean, the man faked his own death twice."

My eyes pop open.

"Yeah, there's a lot you guys don't know," Dad says. "None of it is that important now. At least I never thought it was. But with these new developments... Hell, I never even knew who this half uncle's mother was. And that's the weirdest thing with this birth certificate that Brendan Murphy uncovered. The father is on the birth certificate but not the mother? How does that even happen? The mother is there at the birth."

"Got me. Except that Dale said—" I stop.

"Dale said what?"

Shit. I've stepped in it now. What the hell? This is my father. "Dale says that the Steel family is good at doctoring documents."

Dad doesn't deny my statement. He merely nods.

"So you already know that."

"Like I said, there's a lot your uncles and I haven't told you."

"And why is that again?"

"We've been through that. We wanted to spare you and your cousins and brother all the headache and heartache we went through."

"What about Dale and Donny?"

"We couldn't spare them everything, but we could spare them some. We couldn't erase what happened to them, but we could make sure that nothing like that ever touched them again. My father's brother is deceased. But he had children. Grandchildren."

"Oh?"

"Yeah. And it looks like a couple of them are coming out of the woodwork. They believe they deserve a cut of the Steel fortune."

"So give it to them," I say. "It's probably theirs anyway. You always say we couldn't spend our total fortune among all of us in five lifetimes."

"It's not that simple, son."

"Why not?"

"Because it was my father—your grandfather—who built this company into what it has become. His half brother had nothing to do with it."

"You're saying his descendants deserve nothing?"

"All I'm saying is that it's not that simple."

I know the look on my father's face. I've been seeing it since I was a kid, since I can remember. It's that stern look that says the subject is closed for now. *I'm your father, and I have the last word.*

He is still my father, and I respect that. He's a good father. But I'm an adult now. A grown man.

So much is going on in my head. I can't get that young nurse out of my mind. Someone put a vial of atropine in her baby's diaper, for God's sake. What the hell is going on? Why have they targeted our family?

Dad doesn't even know about the nurse in Grand Junction. I can't tell him—not without checking with Dale and Donny first.

But again, I know my father. I see his mind churning. He knows there's something I'm not telling him.

My father has always been able to read me like a book. Now that I'm older? I can read him like a book just as well. It's creepy in a way.

Dad pulls his shoulders back, stands tall and strong. He's ready to face me, ask me what I know.

I don't wait for the question. I dive into the water and swim.

More laps. Lap after lap after lap, until my body feels numb.

Finally I stop at the edge of the pool, lift myself out. Dad hands me a towel.

"Nice form," he says.

"Thanks."

"Nice save too."

"Meaning?" I ask.

"You know exactly what the hell I mean."

I meet his gaze, forcing myself not to nod. "I'll tell you what you want to know if you tell me what I want to know."

"I think you're forgetting who the parent is here," Dad says.

"No, I'm not. Not at all. But I'm a grown man, and I no longer have to answer to you."

"You're living in my guesthouse."

"Fine. I'll move out. I'm entitled to a tract of land on this property, just as Dale and Donny are. Just like all the rest of us are."

"Don't move out," Dad says. "Your mother likes having you here."

"And you?"

He clears his throat. "You know I like having you here. It was especially helpful when Talon was in the hospital. Having you close by while your mother and I were occupied with him was a blessing. We knew things were taken care of here at the house. We appreciated that."

"Fine. I'm happy to stay in the guesthouse. I'm happy to help out when I'm needed. Don't throw that in my face again, Dad. It's not fair."

He doesn't reply. That's the Jonah Steel way of apologizing. My father is tough. Tough and hard and uncompromising. He's a good man at heart, though. A very good man. Even when he goes off half-cocked, it's always for what he perceives is a good reason. A just reason.

"Let me give Dale and Donny a call."

"Brock," Dad says, "this is my business. It's my business more than anyone else's in this family. I'm the oldest Steel. I'm the CEO of this company."

"What if this doesn't have anything to do with the company? What if it's personal?"

"It always is, son. When you have this kind of money, it's always personal."

I glance at the pool, the water still rippling from my

laps. I'm exhausted. To dive back in would be stupid. I'm an accomplished swimmer, and I know this. Would I drown? No. But I need to let my body rest.

Dad knows this, and so do I.

"Tell me, Brock. Just tell me."

I see so much of myself in my father, both the good and the bad.

"Quid pro quo," I say. "I'll tell you if you tell me. Level with me, Dad. We are *all* involved now."

CHAPTER THIRTY-FIVE

Rory

After a raucous rehearsal with Jesse and his band in our main garage, I pack up my equipment and head toward the door.

"Where are you off to?" Jesse asks.

"I'm starving. I'm going to make myself a sandwich."

"We're going into town for lunch. Why don't you come with us?"

"What the heck is open in Snow Creek on a Sunday?"

"That Taco Bell on the edge of town just opened. We're going to check it out."

"Yummy." I roll my eyes. "No thanks."

"Actually..." he says, frowning.

"What, Jess? What?"

"We're going to find Lamone."

My head thuds into my stomach. "No. Please. You said you wouldn't..." I subtly gesture toward the rest of the band.

"I didn't tell them," he says softly. "Not about the photos."

I grab him and drag him through the door into the house, closing it behind us. "What exactly did you tell them?"

"That he's been spreading lies about our family, and I've had enough of it. Plus, we all got dragged in and questioned by Hardy Solomon on that dumbass vandalizing case.

Dragon didn't have an alibi—he was alone at his place—but the rest of us did. Luckily Hardy let it drop for all of us."

His words are true enough, but Pat Lamone isn't the first person to lie about me, Jesse, or anyone else. This is a small town, after all.

He opens the door and heads back into the garage.

I follow him. "So you're not going to Taco Bell?"

"Hell yeah, we're going to Taco Bell. We can't pummel the dude without a full stomach."

"Please, Jess. You guys are only going to make things worse."

"Listen," Cage, my cousin, says, "he's not going to get away with this shit. Right, guys?"

The other two murmur in agreement. Dragon Locke, the drummer, looks especially menacing. Of course, Dragon looks menacing when he's watching a bluebird sing. It's just his thing.

"I appreciate the sentiment," I say. "Really, I do, but it's not going to help things. This man tried to have Callie arrested for spilling coffee on him. What do you think he's going to do with the four of you if you beat him to a pulp?"

"He'll think twice about spreading lies," Jesse says. "Sure, he could have us arrested. He could have us arrested a million times, and when we're released, we're going to go back and pummel him a million more times."

"He'll get a restraining order." This from Callie, who somehow made her way into the garage without me noticing.

"Where'd you come from?" Jesse asks.

"Donny just dropped me off."

Jesse goes rigid. He and Callie's fiancé still have a stupid high school rivalry going. It's really time for them to get over it.

"Yeah," I say. "He'll get a restraining order."

"He's not smart enough to get a restraining order," Jesse says.

I open my mouth to agree with him, but then I stop myself. Pat Lamone has already proved that he's not as stupid as we think he is.

"A restraining order costs money," I say. "Can he afford an attorney?"

"I don't know," Callie says. "The first thing he'll do is go to Hardy Solomon, the sheriff, who'll arrest you guys. We'll get you out on bail, and it will probably be a condition of bail that you can't go near Pat Lamone. So he may not even need to get a restraining order."

"And who's going to keep us away from him?" This from Dragon. His menacing gaze hasn't strayed from mine.

"You're going to keep yourselves away from him," I say, locking my gaze with Dragon's. "Because Callie and I are not going to let this happen. We've gone through enough, and we don't want any more that he can hold against us and our family."

"Rory's right," Callie says. "Please don't do this, guys."

Jesse's hands are curled into fists. So are Cage's and Jake's. And Dragon looks like he's about to commit murder.

This is not good.

"Fine," Jesse finally says through clenched teeth.

"Thank you." I squeeze my brother's forearm.

I'm not completely sure we've convinced him. He and the band just finished an awesome rehearsal, and they're high on the music. They need to release some steam.

"We've got a gig next weekend," Jess says to me. "You in?"

"Me?"

"Yeah, you. The rest of us are already in. We're the band."

"You don't need me."

"Sure we do."

"Jess, you know what's going on. My head may not be in the game."

"Your head was in the game at the party a week ago."

"Actually, no it wasn't. I was semi-dialing in. It was a Steel party. This is an actual gig, right? Where real people will see you? Where agents might be in the audience?"

"Well ... yeah. But Rory, you ... You're the selling point."

I roll my eyes.

"Having that face and body on stage with us is a good thing," Dragon says, his voice low.

Damn. Dragon is pretty sexy, but I'm all in with Brock at the moment. Besides, he's never given me a look before.

"Sure. I guess. I mean ... I've got some stuff going on." I glance at Jesse.

Jesse nods. "We get it. We'll make do without you if we have to."

"It depends on what this week brings," I say. "Right, Callie?"

She nods. "Yep."

"You want to come with us for lunch, Callie?" Jesse says. "We're heading to that new Taco Bell."

"You know? A taco sounds pretty good. Count me in." Callie smiles.

"Callie and I will drive separately," I say.

"We will?"

"Yeah. There's six of us, so it will be difficult to pile into one car."

"My van's empty," Cage says. "We can all fit in there."

Cage's van. It's a different van, of course, than the one we "borrowed" ten years ago, but still… Makes me remember things I don't really want to remember. Not that they're far from my mind anyway, with Jesse threatening to fight Pat mere moments ago.

"Callie and I will drive separately," I say again.

This time no one tries to talk me out of it.

★ ★ ★

After a quick lunch of tacos, which weren't bad at all, Jesse and the guys head back to the ranch.

I was looking over my shoulder the whole time at Taco Bell, wondering if Lamone would saunter in. If he had, Callie and I wouldn't have been able to stop Jesse and the others from doing whatever they pleased.

"That was close," Callie says, echoing my thoughts.

"I guess Pat isn't the taco type," I say. "It'll be interesting to see if this place survives on Sundays or ends up closing like every other place in town."

"It's a major chain. It will do all right. And honestly, it'll be nice to have somewhere to get some food on Sundays."

"Agreed." I rise, go to the soda fountain, and refill my Diet Coke.

"Rory," Callie says when I sit back down.

"What?"

"Spill it."

"Spill what?" I say, feigning innocence.

"I know you went out with Brock again last night. I also know you didn't get home until this morning."

"How the hell did you find out? You were with Donny."

"Gotcha."

"You bitch."

Callie laughs. "You fall for that every time."

She's right. I open my mouth before I think things through. Callie and I are so different in so many ways. She thinks about everything before she speaks. In fact, she overthinks.

"So how was it?" she asks.

"None of your business."

"Since when?"

She's got me there. We've always told each other everything. Mostly everything, anyway. "Since today."

She takes a sip of her drink. "But this is Brock Steel."

She's going to play that card? "How is that any different from Donny Steel?"

"I guess it's not. Except he's so young. I wish he had stayed away from you."

"Why? Am I not allowed to have some fun?"

"Sure, you are. But you just got out of a relationship, and we all know how Brock is."

"Just like we all knew how Donny was."

She stops talking then. Until— "Are you ready for this?"

I think for a moment about spilling the beans. About telling Callie that I asked Brock to be the father of my child. About how things went after that.

But I don't. It's new. New and wonderful, and I don't want to spoil it. Not that telling my sister would spoil it, but with everything else going on, I just want something that's mine. Mine to enjoy. I feel like if I start talking about it, it will go away.

And I need something positive in my life right now.

But there *is* something I do need to tell her.

"Cal..."

"Yeah?"

"I told Brock. About Pat Lamone, about what we did, about the photos ... everything."

She drops her jaw.

"Don't be angry with me. But you have Donny to talk it through with. I just needed to—"

She stops me with a hand gesture. "You don't have to give me a reason. I understand. Sometimes you have to just say something. To get it out. Even it's to a stranger."

"Thanks for understanding."

What I don't say is that Brock Steel seems like anything but a stranger to me. I'm feeling things I never expected to feel.

"Oh." Callie eyes the door.

I look over my shoulder.

In walks Brittany Sheraton.

And Pat Lamone.

CHAPTER THIRTY-SIX

Brock

I sit across from my father in his home office. He doesn't speak at first, but it's clear who's in charge here. He has an office in the business building on the property, and he works a lot outside, but here—in his home office—is where he does his most important work.

The work that centers not on the business but on his family.

I never doubted that family is the most important thing in my father's life. He's made it clear since I can remember, when Brad and I were little. He taught us ranch work, and he taught us how to protect ourselves. We're both crack shots, and we both know how to defend ourselves against an unarmed opponent as well.

He taught us the ins and outs of the business, the value of money, and how to be a leader.

Brad and I owe him everything.

While he taught us how to be men, our mother taught us compassion. How to care for other human beings. Our father may have taught us how to care for the animals on the ranch, but it was Mom who taught us how to care for each other.

Not that Dad doesn't care for us the way Mom does. He would take a bullet for either one of us. I know that without a doubt.

But Dad is tough. Hard on the exterior. Hard as a rock, and I'm not sure I've ever seen him look harder than he looks right now.

I wait. I know from experience that it won't do any good to pressure my father into speaking. We'll talk only when he is ready, and my impatience will have no bearing on anything.

So I keep my mouth firmly shut.

And I wait.

I could ask where Mom is, but I'm pretty sure she's working on her latest book. She seems to spend every free moment she has, even on Sundays, working on her research or her writing. That's been her focus since she retired from private practice.

Dad rakes his fingers through his black-and-silver hair. And I look at him. I gaze upon his face, and I notice that he's starting to look . . . not old, exactly, though he is sixty-three.

But his face has the slightest of wrinkles, and he's gray at his temples and on the stubble that graces his jawline.

So, no, he does not look old. But he does look . . . weary.

Not tired weary, but weary in a different way.

As if something is raining down on him—something he hoped was in the past forever. Buried.

Finally, he speaks.

"Your great uncle—*half* uncle—"

"Stop," I say.

"What do you mean?"

"You keep emphasizing that he's my *half* great uncle. Because he's not direct blood."

"So what?"

"Neither is Uncle Ryan, Dad. He has a different mother from the rest of you, but you don't call him my *half* uncle. Dale and Donny don't have any blood at all. You don't call them my *adopted* cousins."

He clears his throat. Gazes at the ceiling for a few minutes. Then, "You're absolutely right, Brock. But the truth is, I don't think of him as family. None of us knew him. We didn't even know of his existence until about twenty-five years ago."

"What difference does that make?"

"It makes all the difference. You grew up with Dale and Donny. They're family to you. I grew up with Ryan. He's family to me. Blood doesn't make family."

"I agree, Dad, but this guy does share our blood. His descendants want some of the Steel money, and they probably have a good claim."

"Your uncle Bryce and I have been looking into this. They don't have a good claim. I told you that it was *my* father who built this company into the enterprise that it is. He took it from a million-dollar company—a very small million-dollar company—to a billion-dollar company."

I narrow my eyes. "How, Dad? How exactly did my grandfather do that?"

Dad goes silent once more.

"Why won't you answer? I'm your son. You're my father."

"There are things . . . I wish I could change some of the things my father did," he finally says. "He was a good man at heart. I try hard to believe that. I try hard to believe that he loved my mother. But he made her life hell. She was ill, Brock. So very ill. We didn't know until we were older than you are now. This man—my father, your grandfather—faked his own death twice."

"Yes, you told me."

"He also faked his wife's death."

I try not to act surprised. I don't want to act surprised

at anything my father says. If I do, he may stop talking. In truth? I'm shaking on the inside. With fear. With anger. With shock.

"Just how ill was she?" I ask.

"Mentally ill, not physically. Apparently she suffered from dissociative identity disorder, and then she eventually broke with reality altogether. She was committed from the time Marjorie was about two years old."

"It couldn't have been easy on her. What happened to Uncle Talon." A lump forms in my throat. Those same things happened to Dale and Donny.

"No, it wasn't, of course," Dad says. "But her mental issues started long before then. She was ..." He closes his eyes, swallows audibly.

"Dad ... ?"

His eyes pop open then. "She was raped. Raped by three men when she was sixteen."

"Oh my God." I want to throw up. I want to throw up all over my lap. I swallow, swallow, swallow. In some ways, this is worse than the sickeningly sweet smell of decaying human flesh.

"One of them was her half brother, my half uncle." Dad closes his eyes, inhales, opens his eyes. "So now you see why I use the term half?"

"How could ... I don't understand ..."

"I've asked myself the same questions over and over," Dad says. "I don't have answers, Brock. And I've come to the conclusion that it's better that I don't. It's better *not* to be able to understand that kind of evil. Much better."

I gulp again. Swallow back the bile that threatens to slither up my throat. "I suppose you're right."

Bam! His fist comes down on the hardwood desk. "You're damned right I'm right. I've made a lot of mistakes in my life, Brock. I admit it. But I stopped trying to understand how people can be so evil long ago."

"But her brother? Her brother..."

"Her brother. And Uncle Bryce's father. And Aunt Ruby's father."

My jaw drops again.

"Yes. Have you ever noticed that you've never heard either Aunt Ruby or Uncle Bryce talk about their fathers?"

"I guess I... I guess I never thought about it. Our family is large, and Uncle Bryce..."

"Uncle Bryce's father's name was Tom Simpson, and he was friends with Larry Wade, your grandmother's half brother. They had another friend as well, whose name was Theodore Matthias—Aunt Ruby's biological father—but he went by many aliases."

"And those were the three..."

"Yes. The three who raped your grandmother and sent her into a tailspin when she was only sixteen. They were also the three men who abducted and tortured and abused your uncle Talon."

I stand then. I grip my hands into fists. "And Dale and Donny?"

"We don't know. It's possible, although they all died shortly after Dale and Donny were taken."

I pace around the office, and then—

"Motherfucker!" My fist goes through the drywall as if it had a mind of its own.

My father doesn't look even slightly surprised at my outburst. He shouldn't be. I well remember him spackling up the drywall from his own outbursts when I was a kid. He never laid a hand on Mom, Brad, or me, but the walls took a lot of his rage when he was in one of his red moods.

"Family. Family is always important. That's what you taught us, Dad. Family over everything. But your uncle, Uncle Bryce's father, Aunt Ruby's father. I don't understand. I don't understand how people can be so sick."

"I've said it before. It's better that you don't understand."

"Dad, I—"

"Stop. Stop right there. Where you're going, you have no business going. I've seen things. Uncle Talon has seen things in the military. I witnessed a man—Uncle Bryce's father—shoot himself. I saw his brains spewed all over his kitchen. I can still see it today. That's something you don't forget. He did it to avoid being arrested because I found out what he was doing."

I'm still pacing. Then I look at the hole in the drywall that my fist made. My knuckles are bleeding, but I feel no pain. Not even a slight twinge.

"Why?" I demand. "Why are you laying all of this on me?"

Dad stays calm, though stress is flowing off him in waves. It's almost visible in its thickness.

"Quid pro quo, Brock," Dad says. "You asked for this. And if you're man enough to ask, you're man enough to hear the answers."

Man enough to hear the answers.

A grown man.

I told Dad I was a grown man, to stop treating me like a child.

I stay quiet for what seems like an eternity but is only a few minutes. Finally, "Tell me, then. Tell me what all this has to do with our newfound great uncle." I close my eyes, open them.

"Our newfound *half* great uncle."

"I don't know yet, Brock. All I know is that it's tied together somehow. Uncle Bryce and I have discovered bits and pieces over the years, and we haven't shared everything with Uncle Talon, Uncle Ryan, and Aunt Marj. Not with your mother or Aunt Jade. Perhaps we were wrong in doing so, but as the two chief officers of the corporation, we just felt…" He sighs, grips his forehead, shoves his hair out of his eyes.

"Damn it, Dad." I'm ready to put my other fist through his damned skull. "You didn't want to burden our family because family trumps everything, right? You didn't want this touching us. Your motives may have been pure, but look at where we are now. All this shit is coming up right now. In the middle of—"

I punch the wall again with my right hand, bloodying my knuckles even more. Again I feel nothing.

"Damn it, Brock, you're going to fix that."

"Why don't you fix it, Dad? After all, you fixed everything else. You and Uncle Bryce unilaterally decided what was best for the rest of us."

"That's my job, Brock. I'm your father."

"Yes, you're my father. But as you just reminded me, I'm a grown man. It's not your job to keep important information from me. And it certainly wasn't your job to keep it from Uncle Talon and Uncle Ryan. Uncle Talon got shot, Dad. Fucking shot! Maybe this all could have been avoided if—"

"Shut your damned mouth, Brock Steel. I didn't raise you to talk to me that way."

"No, you raised me to stand up for what's right. To be a man. Well, I'm a man today, Dad, and I'm calling you out on this bullshit. Your brother was shot, for God's sake. Now, what the fuck are you going to do about it?"

CHAPTER THIRTY-SEVEN

Rory

"Oh, for God's sake," I mutter, silently thanking the universe that Jesse and the others already left.

"Just ignore them," Callie says.

"That's your advice? You've never ignored anything in your life, Callie."

"Of course I have. I'm the one who used to walk around under an invisibility cloak. Remember?"

"That invisibility cloak was always in your own head, and you know it."

"He called me an ugly duckling. He called me your ugly duckling sister."

"Seriously? That's where all this is coming from? That's what convinced you that you weren't as beautiful as I am?" I shake my head. "Callie, you're smarter than that."

"Yeah. I know. True enough."

"We can't let him get to us. We have to be strong."

She nods. Funny how my self-assured sister isn't nearly as self-assured as I always thought she was. Only recently, we discovered that we've each been envying the other.

I guess it's true that everyone is their own worst critic.

"Let's change the subject," Callie says. "Tell me more about Brock."

"There's nothing to tell."

"So he's okay with your bisexuality?"

"We've been on two dates, Callie. We haven't really discussed my bisexuality."

I hate lying to Callie. We actually discussed it in depth. Still, I want to keep this private. Special and private.

"Okay. Fair enough. But you've told me that your last three relationships have ended because your partner couldn't accept that part of you."

"That's true."

Two women and one man. All of whom I loved with all my heart. I see now that none of them were forever loves. Especially since they were all so insecure.

"I guess I don't understand," I say. "I've had three partners, and all of them were afraid that I would leave them for someone of the other gender. Does that even make sense? Do straight people constantly worry that their partners are going to leave them for someone else?"

"No. Not in a perfect world, anyway. I suppose there's an element of jealousy in every relationship."

"When I'm in a relationship, I'm committed," I say. "Why don't they ever understand?"

"Do you think Brock is different?"

"Callie, I'll repeat myself. We've had two dates. I don't know if Brock is any different. All I know is that he's twenty-four and he's probably not looking for anything serious, which works for me right now. Except for the whole *wanting to have a baby* thing."

She smiles.

"I've got to say, you and Brock would make a gorgeous kid. There's something about that rugged, dark bad-boy type."

"So you chose a blond nonrugged type?"

"I had a major crush on Dale when I was young," Callie admits. "Now there's a bad-boy type if there ever was one. Donny, not so much. A womanizer for sure, but not rugged like Dale. Or Brock."

"Just because he wears a suit and tie doesn't mean he's not rugged."

"I suppose. He's definitely not the Steel I thought I would fall for, but we have so much in common. Our love of the law, for one thing. And we just … We just fit, Rory. We really fit."

I smile. They do fit. I've seen it. They radiate happiness when they're together.

Then she stops smiling.

"Good job," she says. "For a few seconds there, I forgot that Pat and Brittany are here."

I glance to the side. They've sat down at a table not far from us.

Right within earshot. That can't be a coincidence.

"I suppose it's time to go," Callie says.

"Why? We have every right to be here."

"That's not the point," she says in a low whisper. "I don't want them to listen to us."

"You're right." I take the last sip of my Diet Coke and stand.

"Hey," Pat says, gesturing to me.

Really? "Well, hello, Pat," I say sweetly. "Brittany."

"How's it going?" Pat asks.

Callie rises then. "Go fuck yourself."

I can't help it. I burst into laughter. I was being sickeningly sweet, but my sister will have none of that.

Callie walks quickly to the wastebasket, disposes of her

trash, and walks outside.

I stand there a moment.

"So what's your game?" I ask the two of them.

"I have no idea what you're talking about," Brittany says.

"I think you do. I'm pretty sure we have all your evidence. But if we don't, just know . . . Anything that sees the light of day is not in your best interest."

I turn then and walk defiantly out of the restaurant.

I'm the only one they can hurt. They can try to hurt Callie, but they'll go to jail for child porn.

My nude photos could be on the internet within seconds if they still have copies. I need to stay strong.

I need to hold my head high.

If the world sees me naked, I can come back from that. Madonna did. Vanessa Williams did.

Of course, neither of them were photographed spread-eagled.

Stay strong, Rory. Stay strong. Never let them see you cry.

No, I won't cry over this. I'll concentrate on what's important.

"What took you so long?" Callie asks when I get into the car.

"Just saying goodbye."

"It's best not to give them the time of day."

"Maybe. I'm not going to let them get to me anymore, Cal. I can't. He may try to destroy me. They may try to destroy both of us. We can't take it lying down. We have to be strong. Or at least appear to be strong."

"I know that. I think I just told them to fuck off."

"You have your way, and I have mine."

"Okay. I trust you know what you're doing."

I don't reply.

The truth is, I have no idea what I'm doing. I only know one thing.

I have to stay focused. If I lose focus, everything will crumble.

CHAPTER THIRTY-EIGHT

Brock

"I'm going to take care of it," Dad says quietly. "And it will be a lot easier for me to take care of it if you tell me everything you know."

"Not without speaking to Dale and Donny," I say defiantly.

"So be it." He picks up his phone. "Let's get them over here."

★ ★ ★

Dad's face goes white.

Not much shocks my father. He has seen a lot in his life. More than I even know.

But after Donny and I—Dale couldn't make it—tell him that we suspect human remains were being kept on some of the north Steel property, my father turns pale as a ghost.

"We're going to try to check it out through the guard dogs," Donny says. "We don't really have any other leads other than the red fingernails."

"What about the bones?"

"They look to be really old. I called Aunt Ruby, and she gave me the name of a guy in Grand Junction who can run some tests on them for us."

"Why didn't you boys come to me?" Dad says.

H

"Because, Dad," I say, "you haven't been honest with us. Uncle Talon hasn't been honest with us. How are we supposed to find out who shot him if we don't know all the information?"

"Your mother and I really wanted to protect you boys."

"We get that," Donny says. "But you had to know this would come out at some point."

My father rakes his fingers through his unruly hair. "It doesn't seem to be related to the Steel relatives coming out of the woodwork, but why now? Why would this all be starting again? The people behind it are all dead and buried."

"What people behind it?"

"The people I told you about, Brock. My half uncle, Bryce's father. Aunt Ruby's birth father, Matthias. And then of course the brains behind it all. Wendy Madigan."

"That name sounds familiar," I say.

"Madigan. Jeremy Madigan," Donny says.

"Jeremy Madigan?" My father raises eyebrows.

Donny clears his throat. "Jeremy Madigan is the guy who sold the bar to the Murphys way back when."

Dad scrapes his fingernails over the stubble on his chin. "Okay. I think Jeremy Madigan was Warren Madigan's brother."

"Who was Warren Madigan?" I ask.

"Wendy Madigan's father," Dad says. "She was Uncle Ryan's birth mother."

"So Uncle Ryan's mother was behind everything?" Donny says.

"Yes. But it goes even further back than that. This goes back so far..."

"You're talking in riddles, Dad," I say.

Dad sighs. "It's a lot of information. But I don't understand.

All these people are dead. I saw Wendy Madigan die. I saw Theo Matthias die."

"Did you see your father die?" I ask.

Dad glares at me then. "I did."

"Both times?" I ask.

He nods.

"And the third time?"

Dad shakes his head. "No. He was in prison. But I did go to identify the body. And you can bet I made damn sure it was him and that he had no fucking pulse."

"What are the chances these other people faked their deaths as well?" I ask.

"The chances are pretty high," Dad says, "except that they're all ancient by now. Well into their eighties. It's unlikely they're still alive, even if they faked their deaths twenty-five years ago."

"Good point," I say.

"But the same thing seems to be happening," Dad says. "Dead bodies. Although as far as I know, they were never on our property. Not back then."

"What the hell are you talking about?" Donny asks.

"Human trafficking," Dad says. "The people who took your father. The people who may well have been involved in taking you and Dale. They're all dead now, and the FBI broke up that ring decades ago. My father... He wasn't involved. At least not directly. But I'm pretty sure he had knowledge of what was going on."

"My dad told me that our grandfather paid five million dollars, and that the money was used to abduct him, my father."

Dad nods. "That's correct."

"Still think good old Gramps didn't have anything to do

with this?" I say sarcastically.

"I don't know." Dad shakes his head, threads his fingers through his hair again. "I believe he loved our mother. I believe he loved us. I don't think he would've intentionally caused any harm to any of his children. But there are other circumstances at work here."

"It's time for you to level with us, Dad," I say. "We shared our information with you. We deserve the same in return."

"Yeah," Donny echoes, "and I also want to know why you originally thought that the attempt on my dad's life was meant for you."

"We're getting into some delicate areas," Dad says. "Your uncle Bryce and I... We've uncovered some things over the years. Things my father did. Things his father did. Things we tried to reverse. We haven't always been successful."

"Where does this new half brother come in?" I ask.

"I told you the basics. His descendants have come out of the woodwork, and they want a piece of the pie."

"Who are these people?"

"And what exactly are they asking for?" From Donny.

Dad takes a seat in his chair, faces us directly. "I have to talk to Uncle Bryce."

Anger heats my body. "You have to talk to us. Right now. Or I'm going to put another fist through your damned wall."

"Brock." Dad rises once more. "I am still your father, and you will not address me that way."

"We're on equal footing now, Dad. Our lives are being fucked with. Not just yours. Not just Uncle Bryce's. Mine. Donny's. Everyone else in this family."

"Now listen—"

Then a knock on the door.

"Damn it," I say under my breath.

"What is it?" Dad demands, his tone full of rage.

The door slides open, and Mom peeks her head into the room. "What are you so angry about, Jonah?"

"I'm sorry, Melanie. What do you need?"

"I just wanted to let you know I'm done for the day."

"Good, sweetie."

"What are the three of you doing in here?" she asks.

"Just family stuff."

"Well, last time I checked, I'm a member of this family. Fill me in."

"It's nothing, Melanie."

"Don't tell me it's nothing. I see the look on your face. I heard how harshly you spoke to me before you knew I was the one knocking. Although I'm not sure who else you thought it might be."

"Damn." Dad clears his throat. "The boys are here. Things are . . ."

"Does this have something to do with Talon's shooting?"

"We don't know yet. But probably."

"You can't keep this stuff from Mom," I say.

"Our son is right, Jonah. You will *not* keep this from me."

My mother is my father's true Achilles' heel. He'll do anything for her. Anything. She trumps all of us.

Dad says, "I suppose it's time for a family meeting."

"When you say family . . ." Donny says.

"We will include you, Brock, and Dale, since you already know a bit about what's going on. But the others . . ."

"Were children," Mom says. "Maybe it's time."

"Four of our nieces are still in college," Dad says. "We can't."

Mom sighs. "I suppose you're right."

"Damn it," I say. "You can't protect us forever. For God's sake, someone is storing human bodies in our—"

Mom shrieks. "What?"

"For God's sake, Brock." Dad walks to Mom, takes her in his arms. "It's okay, Melanie."

"No. This can't start again," Mom says. "Not again."

"It won't. I'm going to take care of this."

"Jonah, please. Whatever this is, stay out of it. Keep our sons out of it. Have you forgotten they tried to kill me?"

My jaw drops. "What the hell, Mom?"

"Quit using that language in front of your mother," Dad says.

"It's all right," Mom says. "I've been listening to you talk like that since we met."

"Who the hell tried to kill my mother?"

"It was a long time ago, way before you were born."

Donny and I look at each other. My God, what the hell is happening to our family?

CHAPTER THIRTY-NINE

Rory

The call comes around seven thirty p.m.

"I need you," Brock says. "Now."

His voice reeks of pain, of anguish, of something I can't quite pin down.

"Okay. What do you need?"

"You. Can you come over?"

"Your place?"

"Yeah."

"We're just getting ready to sit down to dinner. Sunday dinner."

Silence for a few seconds. Then, "*Please.*"

Something in his tone. It's different from anything I've ever heard. Anything I've ever experienced.

I can't say no to him. If I do, something terrible will happen.

"Okay. I'll be there as soon as I can." I end the call.

Then I rise from the table. "I'm sorry, Mom. I have to go."

"Why?" she asks.

"It's . . . a friend. He needs me."

Mom's eyes brighten when I say "he." Yeah, my mother loves me and accepts me, but she wants me to end up with a man. I hate it, but it's true.

Well, Brock Steel is a man. A man like no other. I don't know what's going on, but he needs me, and I'll be there.

I have to be there.

I feel it in the marrow of my bones. I must be there for Brock.

"I apologize," I say again.

"It's okay, Rory," Mom says, smiling. "We'll save you a plate."

"Thanks."

I give Zach a quick pet on the head as I leave the kitchen. Out of the corner of my eye, I see Callie feed him a piece of her pork chop.

Mom looks the other way. She's a sucker for dogs.

I get into my car, my nerves on edge. I'm worried. Worried for Brock. So much is going on with both of us.

About twenty minutes. That's how long it takes me to get to the driveway of the guesthouse where Brock lives. I stop the car, park, exit, and walk to the door. I walk, even though my instinct is to run to him. To fix whatever's wrong. To never let him go.

I lift my fist to knock when the door opens.

Brock stands there. His hair is wild, his dark eyes wide, and he's wearing no shirt. Only jeans, his feet are bare. His muscles are tense and rippled.

I stare, my lips parted. Before I can take in the beauty of his chest though—

He pulls me to him and crushes his mouth to mine.

So this is what he meant. *This* is what he needs.

He's stressed, on edge, panting and needy.

Is this what I want? Do I want to give him sex right now? When it's obviously an escape for him? An escape from something I know nothing about?

Yes.

I do.

I want to be here for him. And if that means I get used in the process, so be it.

The kiss is dark and angry. Full of rage, yet full of need. Full of desire and passion.

My God, it's wonderful.

I want to be used. I want to be taken. Whatever is bothering him, I want to be the one to erase it from his mind.

My thighs fit perfectly into the indentations of his hips as he walks quickly, with purpose, toward his bedroom.

I was hungry for dinner. Hungry for the first time in a long time. I've been forcing myself to eat, as I know I need my strength. But since Pat Lamone came back to town, my heart hasn't been into eating.

But Brock's filets tasted good last night. So did tacos this afternoon for lunch, and I was actually looking forward to my family's Sunday dinner for the first time in a while, despite the fact that Pat and Brittany showed up at Taco Bell after Callie and I were done eating.

Is it because of Brock? This man?

I don't know. I don't care.

I know only this. I'm feeling things I haven't ever felt.

Physical things. Physical things that are trying to intertwine with emotional things that I don't fully understand.

All wrapped up in this man. This beautiful, hungry man.

This man whose kisses are more powerful than any drug could be.

The bed. I'm on the bed now. My shirt is gone, and then my bra.

Brock's lips. Brock's lips around my nipples.

We skipped all that before. No foreplay. I'm not sure he wants foreplay now. The way he's sucking my nipple, it's like he's fucking me.

He's an animal, and I'm his prey.

And I wouldn't have it any other way.

He tugs on my nipple, bites it. Then sucks it hard. All the while he plays with the other one, twisting it, pulling it. Flaming arrows dart through me, straight into my pussy.

He's violating my nipples, and my God, the pleasure… It's so intense. I'm ready to climax from this alone.

"My clothes, Brock. My pants."

He groans, still sucking hard on my nipple.

He says nothing—at least nothing in words. My nipples are being sucked and prodded and pinched, and I'm adoring every minute of it.

Except I need more… I'm so wet, so ready, and I need him inside me.

He's so focused. Laser focused on my breasts. If this is what he needs, this is what I'll give him.

With every single touch, I become so much more sensitive. I lower my head and inhale the fragrance of his hair. It smells like the rest of him—clean and spicy and masculine. I stroke his head, sift my fingers through his thick hair. I almost feel like I'm comforting him, which is so strange, considering he's devouring my nipples.

I want to get out of my jeans, kick off my shoes, lie naked next to him.

He's still wearing his jeans. I smooth my hands over his bronze and hard shoulders. So beautiful. His muscles are taut, and I slide my hands down his back as far as I can go. He's warm, so warm. I want to kiss him all over. I want to feel the hardness of his muscles against my lips.

I have to get them off my boobs first.

"Brock," I say softly.

He groans again, the vibrations reverberating against my chest.

"Brock . . . I need you inside me."

Another groan, and then he pulls on the nipple between his teeth. Sparks shoot into me.

He finally drops the nipple. "You're so beautiful, and your nipples—they taste better than I even imagined."

My nipples have a taste? I'm not sure they do, but I'll go with it.

"You're beautiful too," I say. "Let me touch you. I want to touch every part of you, Brock. Please."

He moves his hand away from my other breast. Then he stands and removes his jeans.

No underwear. He was going commando. And his cock. It's so big, so hard, and so beautiful. The skin tone is slightly darker than the rest of him, and a couple of purple veins meander over and under and around it.

He pulls me up next to him, and his dick pokes me in the belly. Then, he pushes me back down on the bed. I lift my eyebrows.

And I understand.

He removes my shoes and socks, and then he slides my jeans and underwear off me quickly.

We're both naked now, both ready.

"What do you need?" I ask.

"You."

"What can I do for you? What do you need right now, Brock?"

He sits next to me. "Just touch me, Rory. Please. You're so beautiful. It's almost hard to imagine that you were created by mere human beings. You're an angel, Rory. Touch me. Please."

His words leave me breathless.

His face is so close to mine, and though I expect him to kiss me, he doesn't. So I do as he asks.

I touch him.

I begin with his nose, sliding my index finger over it—its perfection, its straightness. Then I trace his upper lip, his black stubble tickling my finger. I slide my other hand down his cheek to his neck and then to his tan shoulder. I rest on his shoulder for a second, reveling in its muscular shape and hardness. With my other hand, I touch his full lower lip. And then I slide it down his neck onto the other shoulder. I squeeze, gripping his shoulders, embracing the musculature.

I bring my hands together over his chest, his hard pectorals. A smattering of black hair—the perfect amount, in my opinion. His chest isn't bare, but it's not fuzzy either.

And my God, it's so warm and so hard. His abs are glorious, a perfect sixpack, and they lead to his black bush and his massive cock.

"My God," I sigh.

He doesn't reply. Simply cups both my cheeks, thumbing them, and then he traces one finger over my lips.

A big part of me is surprised. When he called, his voice was filled with so much anguish, I thought he'd want to fuck—a quick, hard, and dirty fuck.

But it seems what he needs right now, more than anything, is comfort.

Though I'm horny, and I really want his dick inside me,

I'm willing to give him what he needs.

What he seems to need is to touch me in return.

My breasts are rosy and swollen, my nipples still hard and slightly sore from his rough attention.

It's a good sore, though. A really *good* sore, and I want more of it.

Brock bends down, kisses the side of my neck, sending shivers through me. His lips travel over my shoulder all the way to my hand. He kisses my palm and then each finger, ending at the tip.

My jaw drops. This is so not what I believed Brock Steel to be like. I never expected anything slow and gentle. Especially not after our first time.

Comfort. I was right. He needs comfort.

I take his other hand in mine, rub his palm with my thumb.

"Rory," he says.

"Yes?"

"There's so much I want to say to you. So much I'm not ready to say to you. So much I'm afraid you're not ready to hear."

I swallow. Surely he's not thinking...

"So I'm going to leave words alone for now," Brock says, "and use my mouth for other things."

Then his lips meet mine. This kiss is so much different from the one we shared when I first got here. It's gentle. Gentle and sweet, until—

It becomes not so gentle.

His dark anger is back, and he's kissing me hard, with a fiery passion of a thousand flaming arrows.

My body erupts in a passionate explosion. What started as a simple smolder is growing, the embers inside me flaring.

In a flash, we're horizontal, and I'm not sure how we got here. Brock is on top of me, still kissing me hard, his smattering of chest hair abrading my sensitive nipples.

His cock dangles between my thighs, erect and ready.

And then—

CHAPTER FORTY

B r o c k

I'm inside her, balls deep.

She feels so … I can't even describe it because it's so new to me. I've had a lot of sex. I mean, a *lot* of sex. Every woman is different—the physical sensation, that is. It's no less true with Rory. She doesn't feel exactly the same as any other woman I've been inside.

What's different is that I'm feeling something more. Something beyond the physical.

Something I'm not ready to feel.

What I said to her—that I'm not ready to say the words and she's not ready to hear them.

I don't even know what those new words are. I just know that they exist somewhere in my mind, and I won't be able to keep them dormant forever.

My God, she gloves me like no other.

I could stay here forever, not moving, not fucking her at all. Just joined with her, this incredible feeling of completion.

For a moment, nothing else matters. I can forget the conversation with my father and Donny.

Forget that my mother's life was threatened all those years ago.

Forget—

I pull out and plunge back into Rory.

Such a perfect fit. Every ridge and crevice inside her, every part of her hugs every part of me.

She closes her eyes, sighs softly, parts her lips.

God, I want to kiss her. Kiss her and fuck her slowly, savoring every bit.

But I can't. Not now. I pull out and ram inside her again.

So much for staying gentle.

I knew what I needed when I called her, and this is it. Nothing can change that now. No amount of touching and feeling and kissing her beautiful neck. No amount of sucking and twisting those nipples, squeezing those beautiful breasts.

I'm back. I'm back where I was when she showed up. Where I was when I made a meal out of her nipples.

I'm here again, and I'm fucking her. Fucking her as hard as I can.

And with each sigh that spews from her lips, with each sigh and soft moan, I know she wants this as much as I do.

"Yes," she says softly. "Feels so good."

"God, yes," I groan.

And then, before I have a chance to stop it—

I plunge inside her, emptying into her.

I lie there for a moment, bracing my weight on my upper arms so I don't crush this beautiful woman.

But I can't leave her, can't bring myself to pull out.

Her thighs are perpendicular to me, her calves wrapped around me, pulling me close to her.

She doesn't want me to pull out either.

Can't pull out.

I'm ready, ready to go again.

I'm still hard. So—

"Oh my God! Brock!"

Rory scrambles beneath me, pushing me off her.

"The condom. We didn't use a condom!"

I drop my mouth open. No words come to me.

I forgot the condom.

And Rory's not on the pill.

No problem for her. She wants a kid.

I rise from the bed, stalk to the bathroom, stare at my reflection in the mirror above the sink. My face is shiny with sweat, my hair an unruly mess of sweating curls.

I look the way I feel. A jumbled mass of hormones and emotions that I don't understand.

What was I thinking?

Answer—I wasn't thinking at all. I was emoting. Totally emoting because of the conversation I had with my father, my cousin, my mother.

Emoting about all the horrible things our families are involved in and knowing that salvation lies within Rory Pike.

Salvation?

There's no salvation for me. No salvation for the Steel family. Not now. Perhaps not ever.

And now I might've gotten a woman pregnant.

I'm twenty-four years old, just a kid in so many ways. I scoff. Didn't I just tell my father that I'm a grown man? And now? I may really have to step up.

"Brock?"

Rory's voice. Rory's soft, sweet, comforting voice.

Hell, this won't bother her a bit. She wants to be a mother. She wants me to be the father.

Damn it all to hell.

I breathe in, out, and again, and hold it for a few seconds.

Then I return to the bedroom.

Rory is sitting up in bed, her knees clasped to her chest and her arms around them.

Her cheeks are red—and she looks beautiful. Despite the frightened look on her face, she has a gorgeous just-fucked aura that sheathes her in glamor.

"How could you?" I accused. "How could you let me do that?"

"What?"

"The condom, Rory. Why didn't you remind me?"

A flash of anger crosses her eyes. "Probably for the same reason you didn't remember it. I was into the moment, into it with you."

"Still … You're not on the pill."

"So this is my responsibility? You're kidding, right? I'm the one who remembered at the end. I'm the one who pushed you off me. That was *me*, not you."

"Yeah, after the deed was already done."

"Seriously? You're going to blame me for this?" She slides off the bed, reaches for her jeans, and pulls them on.

"You're the one who wants a kid. Not me."

"You know what? Fuck you, Brock. I shared something deep with you. And I thought … Christ, what was I thinking? You'd make a shitty father, Brock Steel, and I don't want your damned kid." She slides her socks on her feet and then her shoes. "Where the hell is my bra?" She darts her gaze around the room.

I spy it, on top of my dresser. After I got it off her, I threw it. I didn't realize I'd thrown it so far.

I grab it, take it to her. She rips it from my grasp and puts it on.

"I'll help you with that," I say as she struggles to snap it.

"Thanks, but no thanks." She finally gets it snapped and then grabs her shirt and dons it quickly. "I'm out of here." She stomps out of the room.

God. I'm a jerk. An absolute jerk.

Here's a woman—a beautiful woman who comforted me— and what am I offering her in return? Accusations and anger.

"Rory..." I follow her out, still naked.

She's at the door, petting Sammy. "Bye, baby girl. I'm not sure when I'll see you again."

"Rory, come on."

"Goodbye, Brock. Have a nice life."

She walks out the door, slamming it behind her.

Go after her. Damn it, Brock, go after her. I run back to my bedroom, slide my jeans on quickly, and nearly stumble getting back to the door.

Rory is already gone.

CHAPTER FORTY-ONE

Rory

I'm halfway home when the tears come.

It's a little after nine o'clock, and of course the pharmacy in Snow Creek isn't open on Sundays anyway. I could drive to a twenty-four-hour pharmacy in Grand Junction for a morning-after pill, but I know I won't.

If I'm pregnant, I will keep this baby. Brock doesn't have to be involved.

And it's just as likely that I'm not pregnant.

Okay, that's not exactly true. I know I'm ovulating, so there's a chance I'll conceive. Some couples try for years, track ovulation schedules diligently, and still don't conceive. No reason at all to worry.

Except that of course I'll worry.

I shake my head. Was it only forty-eight hours ago that this was what I wanted? I actually asked him to father my child?

I've gone completely insane.

I don't want to go home. It's Sunday evening, and I have a lesson at ten in the morning.

Ten a.m. isn't eight a.m. Going for a quick drink won't hurt.

I change my route and head to Murphy's.

Then I change my route again.

The bar isn't open on Sundays. And if I am pregnant? I can't drink anyway.

Damn.

Damn, damn, damn.

Now what?

No way am I going back to Brock's.

I don't want to go home. Callie's probably out with Donny, and Jesse is probably out with the guys.

I sure as heck don't want to talk to my mother and father.

What if I truly am pregnant?

Will Brock want me to . . .

I can't even go there. Absolutely not. My body, my choice, and if I'm pregnant, I *will* have this baby.

I have nowhere else to go. I have to go home.

It's getting late, so I'm surprised to see Jesse and the band in the garage.

"Mom was letting you practice this late?" I say.

"Believe it or not, she was, but we're packing up now." Jesse closes his guitar case.

Right. Jesse and the band have a gig coming up.

A gig without me. Except it doesn't have to be without me.

I'd like to get away. Even if it is just a road trip to dive bars on the western slope.

"I changed my mind," I say. "I'm totally in for the tour."

"It's a little late for that, Ror. We've already got the program all set up without you."

"So? I know your repertoire."

"It's too late. Besides, you have your lessons."

"The world is not going to stop if Janae Jefferson doesn't get her next piano lesson."

Jesse wrinkles his forehead. "This doesn't sound like you.

You love those kids."

I don't bother replying to my brother. Instead, I look over him to Dragon Locke, who's staring straight at me with smoldering hazel eyes, his long black hair unbound and hugging his shoulders, and his lips... full and luscious.

And you know what? I'm up for it.

"You're right," I tell my brother. "And I understand."

Then I sidle up to Dragon. I have no idea what I look like. Do I look pregnant? Do I look like I just got fucked? Most definitely the latter, maybe the former. I have no idea. I didn't even look at myself in the rearview mirror on the drive back here.

"Rory," Dragon says in his deep voice.

"Feel like getting out of here?"

"Sure."

"We're all having a beer, sis," Jesse says. "Out on the deck. I started the fire pit."

Okay, I wasn't thinking of my brother, cousin, and Jake Michaels coming along for the ride, but it'll have to do.

"That sounds great," I force myself to say with a fake smile plastered on my face.

I duck out. I don't dare go to my bedroom, or even to the bathroom. I don't want to know what I look like.

Jesse rolls his eyes at me. Once the guys are out on the deck, he pulls me aside.

"I don't know what you're thinking, Rory, but stop it right now."

"What? He's good-looking."

"Hey, Dragon's my buddy, my bandmate. That doesn't mean I want one of my sisters with him."

"I don't need your protection, Jess."

"No, you don't. Not when we're talking about any normal guy. Or woman, for that matter. Dragon's different. He's got a dark side, Ror. A really dark side."

"Maybe that's what I'm looking for."

"Look, you're on the rebound. I get that. And Dragon... Well, he doesn't do anything for me, but the chicks seem to dig him."

"I'm not Maddie, Jesse. I'm twenty-eight years old, and I know how to handle myself."

He holds his hands up in mock surrender. "Don't say I didn't warn you."

We join the others on the deck, where Cage has opened a sixpack of Fat Tires. He hands me one after opening it.

The condensation swirls up in a cloud of mist, as if a genie is magically rising from a bottle.

I take a deep sip.

Who the hell needs Brock Steel anyway?

Then...

"Shit," I say.

"What?" Jesse asks.

"I'll be right back."

I go inside, head to the bathroom this time, deliberately not looking in the mirror. I hastily pour the beer into the sink.

What the hell am I thinking?

I already thought of this before, when I was heading into town to Murphy's. If there's even a chance I might be pregnant, I can't drink.

And I can't be trying to seduce Dragon Locke either.

Brock Steel came inside me tonight. To try to go to bed with someone else within a couple of hours of that?

Pretty darned icky.

And it's not me. Not at all, no matter how angry I am at Brock.

Do I go back out? Get a Diet Coke and say I finished my beer inside?

Or do I just go to freaking bed?

I toss the empty bottle in the wastebasket, leave the bathroom, and head back into the hallway—

"Rory." Dragon's deep voice again.

"Hey."

"You're coming back out, I hope."

"Probably not. I finished my beer. I'm pretty exhausted."

"It's ten thirty."

"Yeah, but I just remembered I have an early piano lesson in the morning."

"Thought you wanted to get out of here." His gaze sears into mine, nearly weakening my knees. Not like Brock, but it's nice I can still respond to someone else.

I feign a yawn. "Change of heart. I'm just too tired. Maybe another time."

"Suit yourself," he says. "I'll miss you."

I lift my eyebrows. He'll miss me?

I smile. A big wide smile. "Well, I wouldn't want you distressed about it. Let me get a Diet Coke, and I'll be right back out."

Dragon gives me a half smile. The man is sexy, that's for sure.

"Sounds good." He saunters away.

CHAPTER FORTY-TWO

Brock

I lose count of how many shots of tequila I take. It's not like me to drink like this. I never do shots.

But here's the thing. I may have gotten a woman pregnant tonight, and when it comes right down to it, the thought doesn't make me angry or frightened.

The thought makes me feel . . . kind of good.

I'm not in love with Rory Pike. But I am feeling things. Things I don't understand. Things I don't really want to understand at this point in my life.

She's on the rebound, and I love helping a woman on the rebound. I just didn't expect it to be so . . . consuming. It never has been before.

And I certainly didn't expect to get a kid out of it.

I blamed her. I blamed her for not reminding me about the condom. But it's my fault. No one's fault but my own. I didn't think about the condom because I was so distraught and because I wanted her so badly.

My God, she is beautiful.

And giving and comforting.

She let me munch on her breasts tonight as if they were candy bars.

She let me take from her, and she was willing to give.

And now she's gone.

I should call her. Apologize. No, I'll go over there.

Except it's close to eleven o'clock, and I've had way too many shots to get behind a wheel.

Phone call it is, then.

"Hello," she says. Her tone is noncommittal.

"Rory, it's me."

I concentrate, try not to slur my words.

"What is it?"

"I'm..."

Sorry. I'm so sorry.

"...drunk," is the word that comes out.

"Great."

"I need you."

"What you need, Brock, is a time-out. Maybe a good old-fashioned spanking. You're acting like a child."

She's not wrong.

"I'm drinking. So much is going on."

"And you think I care about this because..."

"I don't think anything, Rory. I just wish I had handled things differently."

"Is this what passes as an apology in your mind?"

God, I'm fucking this up. Why did I call her? Why did I drink seven shots of tequila?

"I..."

I drop my phone as I puke into the kitchen sink.

"For God's sake," I say.

At least it all got in the sink, and I don't have to clean it up. That's what the garbage disposal is for.

Sammy pants at my heels, and I lean down to pet her. "I royally fucked this up, girl."

Her big brown eyes are wide as she seems to say to me, *yeah, you sure did.*

I pet her, thinking about how comfortable the kitchen floor looks.

I need a shower, but I'm way too drunk. I'd probably slip and give myself a concussion. My bed would be a lot softer, but this tile floor will be nice and cool. I stretch out on the floor, and Sammy curls up next to me.

★ ★ ★

I jerk awake at Sammy's bark.

"What is it, girl?"

Then I hear it. Pounding on the door.

What the hell?

Sammy follows me to the door, and I look through the peephole.

Rory.

Rory Pike standing on my stoop at my front door.

I draw in a deep breath and open it.

"My God, are you okay?"

"Uh...sure."

"You just stopped talking in the middle of our phone call, Brock. I thought you had fainted or something. Passed out, hit your head."

Shit. Right. I was on the phone with Rory when I threw up.

She wrinkles her nose. "My God, you smell like a skid row bum. With a side of tequila." She pushes me inside. "You need a shower."

"Only if you join me."

She scoffs. "You have *got* to be kidding me."

She pushes me through the foyer and down the hallway to my bedroom. Then into my bathroom.

"Take off your jeans. I'm going to start the shower." She turns the water on, and the whooshing sound is like thunder in my ears. Make that roaring thunder.

I fumble with my jeans, get them halfway down my thighs, and then sit down on the toilet. My legs don't want to stand anymore.

"Oh, no, you don't." She tugs my pants the rest of the way off, pulls me into a standing position, and pushes me into the shower.

"It'd be more fun if you came in here with me."

"Shower," she says. "And use soap, for God's sake. Where's your toothbrush?"

Where *is* my toothbrush? "In the drawer, the left-hand one."

I grab the side of my head as a hammer pounds into a wall. It's just Rory opening and closing the drawer. I swear she's being extra loud on purpose. Seconds later, her arm pokes through the shower door, her hand holding my toothbrush slathered with toothpaste.

"Brush," she commands. "Brush really well."

"I don't brush my teeth in the shower."

"You do tonight."

CHAPTER FORTY-THREE

Rory

The phone call from Brock was a sign.

I was ready. Ready to take my Diet Coke and join Dragon somewhere. Somewhere that was not my back deck. We were about ready to leave on a walk—despite my brother's glare—when my phone rang.

Brock.

Totally drunk.

I would've let him stew, except I heard his phone clatter to the floor, and I was afraid he'd harmed himself.

Turns out, he was just drunk.

Serves him right.

Still, the call was a sign. Doing anything with Dragon Locke tonight would have been a big mistake, especially if it turns out I'm carrying another man's child.

I'm not that woman. I don't want to be that woman.

The truth is . . . The only reason I was going after Dragon is because of my feelings for Brock. Feelings for Brock I don't want to have.

I'm probably not pregnant. But if I am, I'll be keeping this kid. Brock can be involved or not be involved. His choice. No sweat off my back.

Except a part of me wants him to be involved—really

involved—not just with our child but with me.

A big part of me wants to see where this could go.

I don't know. My little sister reformed the biggest Rake-a-teer of all. Can I reform another?

Do I want to?

"Damn," I say out loud. "I do want to."

"Want to what?" Brock steps out of the shower.

"I hope you scrubbed behind your ears," I say. "And you better have brushed those teeth really well. I'm talking gums as well."

"See?" He gives me a wide grin.

"I'm a little more concerned with your breath."

He towels his hair.

"Stay here. Get something on. I'm going to go make you a pot of coffee."

"No coffee. I'll be up all night."

"That'll serve you right. You need to sober up."

"I'm good. I'll be all right."

"Shut up. You're getting a cup of coffee, and you're going to drink it all."

He smiles. This time it's a real smile. "Yes, ma'am."

I head out of his bedroom and into his kitchen, where I start a pot of coffee. A pot of *strong* coffee. Wasn't I just here this morning? Seems like a lifetime ago.

It's after midnight now, and I have that ten a.m. lesson.

I sit down at the kitchen table and wait for the coffee to brew. What am I doing here? I absently touch my abdomen. *Are you in there?*

I won't know for two weeks.

I'm not sure if I'll ever have sex with Brock again. He was so angry with me. Of course, then he got drunk, and then he called me. That indicates that he's feeling something. Perhaps something similar to what I'm feeling.

It probably frightens him as much as it frightens me.

He's twenty-four. So young. Not ready to be a father. What was I thinking, saying those words to him? He was probably counting on another ten years of womanizing before he even thought about settling down.

The coffeepot gurgles, indicating that the brew is finished. I rise, grab a ceramic mug from the cupboard, pour Brock a steaming cup, and head back into his bedroom.

Only to find him passed out on his bed, buck naked.

I chuckle despite myself. He'll sleep it off. That five o'clock rancher alarm is going to chime at him early.

I turn to leave but then look over my shoulder.

A rush of feelings surge through me. Desire, yes, but also the yearning to comfort him. Lie down with him and take him in my arms, to keep him safe until morning.

Ridiculous, I know. He's perfectly safe, and Sammy won't leave his side. She's snuggled at the foot of the bed, her head up and cocked, as she watches me.

I walk toward her and scratch her behind her ears. "You're a good girl. You'll take care of your daddy."

She whimpers softly.

"I can't stay," I tell her. "I just can't."

She whimpers again.

"Such a good girl."

And . . . I'm talking to a dog.

I have my own dog at home, waiting for me. Zach sleeps on my bed with me now that we're sure that he's house-trained. He doesn't have to be in a kennel at night.

I need to go home. Be with my own dog. Be with my own

family. The people who will have my back no matter what.

Even if...

Even if those damned photos see the light of day.

I resist the urge to reach toward Brock as he sleeps. I resist the urge to stroke his tan skin, smooth his still-damp hair.

I rise again, try to drown out Sammy's whimper, and leave the bedroom.

In the kitchen, I turn off the coffeepot and dispose of the coffee that Brock didn't drink.

Then I leave.

★ ★ ★

My alarm rings at eight the next morning, and I yawn and stretch. Zach pushes his cold, wet nose against my shoulder.

"You need to go out?" I say sweetly.

Then I smile. Last night I thought I was being silly to talk to Sammy, but talking to dogs is something I've always done. I wonder if Zach and Sammy would like each other, whether they could play together, live together as a pack.

Already I'm thinking these thoughts. As if Brock and I have some kind of future. As if...

I lightly touch my abdomen again.

As if...

I just don't know. These feelings are scary. Scary and freaky. None of my other serious relationships have elicited such emotion in me, and this isn't even a relationship.

It's two dates and fucks, the last of which ended in an argument.

I jerk at a knock on my door.

"Rory?" Callie's voice.

"Yeah, come in."

She comes through our shared bathroom door. She's in her pajamas.

"You're here. I thought you'd be at Donny's."

"His bedroom furniture hasn't been delivered to the guesthouse yet," Callie says. "So unless I want to sleep on the couch with him, I needed to come home."

"Oh."

She lifts her eyebrows. "You okay?"

"Yeah. Except..."

"What? What is it?"

"Last night, I slept with Brock."

Her eyebrows go farther. "Is that a bad thing?"

"Are you kidding? It was amazing. Probably the best sex I've ever had, but there's an itsy-bitsy problem."

"Which is?"

"He didn't use a condom."

Her eyes widen. "Oh."

"I'm not on the pill. No reason to be, since my last relationship was with Raine."

"I doubt there's anything to worry about. I'm sure Brock Steel is as clean as they come."

"That's not what I'm concerned about." I nod toward my dresser where my purse sits. "Grab my purse and look inside."

Callie walks to the dresser, grabs my purse, and dumps its contents—

"Oh shit." She pulls out the tissue-covered ovulation stick. "You took the test."

"Yeah. I'm ovulating."

"Man."

"Right?"

HELEN HARDT

"Well…you won't know for sure until you miss your period. And even then it might be nothing. You'll have to take a test. No reason to worry."

"I'm actually not worried. You know I want a child. But I don't want it this way. Besides, I made some mistakes."

"Like what?"

"I did something really stupid, Cal. I asked Brock if he'd be willing to father my child."

"Oh, Rory. You didn't."

"I did. And he politely declined, which I understood. The problem is that when we went to bed last night, we were both so eager and into it that he forgot the condom."

"That's on him, then."

"Yes, partially. It's also on me. I could've reminded him."

"You didn't intentionally neglect to remind him, did you?"

"Of course not. I'm not manipulative like that."

"Good. I didn't think you were, but I had to ask. You know, after you asked him to father your child. Which, Rory, you shouldn't have done."

"Tell me about it. To be honest, I wasn't even sure I'd said it out loud. I guess it's just been on my brain."

"I don't know how you can think about that in the midst of everything else that's going on."

"Honestly? Neither can I. Except that it's just so important to me, and I feel like my clock is ticking."

"We've been through this before."

"I know. I feel like I'm being selfish. I'm putting my needs before everything else. Before yours. Before Brock's. Before our family's. I mean, Mom and Dad's livelihood just got destroyed in a fire, and I'm thinking about bringing another mouth to feed into the house."

Callie says nothing. I can't blame her. What can she say? Only that I'm right, and she knows it.

A few moments pass, and then Callie speaks.

"There's nothing we can do about it now. You may be pregnant, and if that's the case, we'll deal with it. No use worrying, so I'm going to change the subject."

"God, please do."

"I've been thinking. If Pat still has those photos of me in his possession, we can get him on child porn charges. He doesn't actually have to post them. Just to have them in his possession is illegal."

"Cal... We have them in *our* possession."

"I know. We need to destroy the ones of me."

"And we don't need to destroy the ones of me?"

"We'll destroy all of them. Obviously. But I think we should get them fingerprinted first. See if we can find anything."

"No. I don't want to do that."

"What if we find Lamone's fingerprints on them?"

"We'll also find yours, mine, and Jesse's."

"Yeah, but if we tell the fingerprint guy how we got them, that they're not ours—"

"Callie, for a would-be lawyer, you're missing an important point."

She sighs. "You're right, of course. We'll destroy them."

"Good. Let's do it today."

"I have to get to work," she says.

"Tonight, then."

She nods. "Tonight it is."

CHAPTER FORTY-FOUR

Brock

Jackhammer headache. I'm not unfamiliar with it.

Man, I know better than to drink tequila. That liquid fire gets me drunk to the point I don't give a shit about whatever was bothering me, but I also pay for it in the morning.

It didn't even work this time. Seven shots, and I still couldn't get Rory off my mind.

And God, am I paying for it now.

I have vague recollections of the evening after I drank the tequila. Calling Rory. Dropping the phone. Throwing up. Falling. Sleeping on the kitchen floor.

Then Rory. Sweet Rory coming to my rescue. Throwing me into the shower and forcing me to brush my teeth.

Because of Rory, I'm not going to retch this morning because of the way my mouth tastes.

It still tastes pretty bad, though.

Tequila is not friendly.

It's eight o'clock. I have another vague recollection of my alarm going off at five and then throwing my phone across the room.

Yup, sure enough, there it is next to the wall. Along with a dent. Between putting my fist through Dad's office wall and now this? I'll be doing chores around the house as soon as I can find the time.

Damn, damn, damn.

On top of that? Dad's going to have my ass for not showing up to work on time.

Normally I'd care, but I'm so damned pissed at him.

Our conversation goes through my head again.

Someone tried to kill my mother. When? I'm not sure. Twenty-five years ago, when all this other stuff went down.

And now ... It seems to be happening again.

Someone tried to kill Uncle Talon with the bullet that may have been meant for my father.

Tequila shots—despite the hammering in my brain—still look pretty good.

But I won't go there.

I need coffee. I need another shower. I need to brush my teeth again and again.

And then ...

I'm not sure. I guess I'm going to Wyoming to visit those other GPS sites. And I guess I'm going to take my father with me.

* * *

Turns out Dad didn't go out on the grounds today either. He's in his office when I hand him the GPS coordinates.

Then my phone buzzes.

My heart leaps. Rory.

Except it's not Rory. It's a number I don't recognize.

"Brock Steel," I say into the phone.

"Yeah, Mr. Steel. It's Janine. J-Janine Murray."

"Who?"

"The nurse. From Mr. Steel's case."

Right. Damn. The nurse who Donny and I met with a week ago. The one who poisoned Uncle Talon with atropine that was provided to her by way of her baby's diaper. Could this get any more fucked up?

"I'm sorry. Can I help you with something?"

"Yeah, I tried to call the other Mr. Steel, but he didn't answer."

"Donny?"

"Yeah, Donny. He didn't answer, so I called you. You gave me your number."

"Right." Man, is my mind fuzzy this morning.

"I'm frightened."

"Did you call Monarch? Get round-the-clock security?"

"I did. But that person. He contacted me again."

I nearly drop the phone. "What? When?"

"Sometime overnight. I found the voicemail this morning."

"Do you have security installed?"

"Yeah. It was installed late last week. Plus there's a guy in a car watching my mother and the baby at all times in the house, sent by Monarch."

"All right. Good. What did the person say in the voicemail?"

"The voicemail said this isn't over." Her voice cracks.

Damn. "All right. But he didn't ask you to do anything?"

"No. Not this time, I mean."

"All right. We know you're safe. You're being watched. By Monarch—" I stop abruptly.

Monarch Security clearly dropped the ball at the main house. Someone got into the house and left that safe-deposit key for Donny. Someone got into Uncle Talon's safe and stole the orange diamond ring and replaced it with a feather. Man, so much on my mind. Donny and I haven't even told Dad and Uncle Talon about that last fact.

Why are we still using Monarch Security?

"I'm going to find a different security company for you," I tell her. "In the meantime, keep using Monarch and wait to hear from me."

"Why do I need different security?"

I don't want to alarm her, so what the hell do I say? "We're just looking into expanding with a bigger company," I lie. "You'll hear from me when I have information."

She gulps audibly. "Yeah. Okay."

"In the meantime, your mother can't let the baby out of her sight. I'd prefer that you stay home. Or we'll find you a safe place to stay. All three of you."

"I have to work, Mr. Steel."

"You know what? You don't. Stay home. Call the hospital and tell them you're sick. I'll figure something out."

"That may work for a few days, but they're not going to believe me. I'll lose my job."

"Don't worry about that."

"How can I not worry about it? I have expenses."

"You'll be covered."

Truly? Did I really just offer to pay the expenses of the woman who poisoned my uncle?

"I can't allow you to—"

"You can. You came to us, and we appreciate it. It would've been great if you had come to us before you poisoned my uncle, but you didn't."

Silence on the other end of the line. Crap. I went too far.

"Look, I—"

"Don't," she says. "I understand. I shouldn't have done what I did. I was just so frightened for the baby." Her voice cracks again, and then she chokes into a sob.

Silence this time from me. The baby. Her child.

My mother and father would do anything to keep me safe. I'm not a father, so this is probably a feeling I don't quite understand.

It wasn't Janine the nurse who poisoned Uncle Talon. It was Janine the mother. The mother who thought she had no choice. The mother who would do anything to protect her child.

The lioness. Just like my own mother.

"I get it," I finally say. "I'm sure anyone else would've done the same thing."

"Thank God your uncle survived. If anything had happened, I wouldn't be able to live with myself. I'm finding it hard enough to live with myself as it is."

I'm not sure what to say to her then. Do I tell her she's forgiven? I'm not sure she is. Should I tell her she did the right thing? Hell, no. She poisoned my uncle.

"Are you there?" she asks.

"I'm here. Save that voicemail. Our experts will want to listen to it. Don't erase it from your phone, and don't block the number."

"I won't."

"Call in sick today. Do not go to work again until you hear from me."

"All right. If you think it's best."

"I do. Anything else I can do for you?"

"No. You've done enough. I can't thank you enough for the security."

"You're welcome. Goodbye." I end the call.

"Who was that?" Dad asks.

"What?" My head is pounding so hard I'm not sure I heard him right.

"On the phone, Brock. Who was it?"

"The nurse. The hospital."

"I ought to have her ass thrown in jail."

"But you won't. She was protecting her child. Just like you would protect me."

Dad glares at me for a moment but then nods. "Understood. Now let's take a look at those GPS coordinates."

CHAPTER FORTY-FIVE

Rory

"You can't be serious," I say over the phone to Callie after my ten o'clock lesson.

I hired someone to search Doc Sheraton's house and Pat Lamone's room.

That's what she just said to me.

"I am serious. Totally serious."

"And what do you suggest we pay for it with? Our good looks?"

"They're billing us."

"And again ... Bills eventually have to be paid."

"Don't worry. Donny will give me the money."

"You're seriously going to ask your fiancé to foot this bill?"

"He'll pay for it. It was his idea."

"It was?"

"Yeah, he gave me the name of the guy. Apparently this guy's the best, and he always gets in undetected."

"So he's going to search for the pictures?"

"Yeah."

"And you realize that if he finds them, they won't be admissible as evidence."

"Rory, do you think I was born yesterday? Of course I know that. I'm the one who's going to be the lawyer, remember?"

"Yeah, I remember. I just wasn't sure you did."

"I know you're freaked. I know you're nervous. We all are. But this is important. The Steels have used this guy before. If he finds evidence, he'll leave it where it is, and then we'll go to the police. We'll tell them there's probable cause that Pat Lamone and Brittany Sheraton have in their possession nude pictures of a minor. Me. Then they'll get a search warrant and do the search."

"Why not just get a search warrant in the first place?"

"We thought of that, but if we do that and they don't find anything, Pat and Brittany will be on alert that we're looking. If they do have the stuff, they'll either destroy it or move it."

"Okay. Fair point."

"We're skirting the system. I understand that. Donny is very careful about his ethics, but we both feel that this has to be done."

"What if the guy gets caught?"

"According to Donny, this guy never gets caught."

"Okay. I guess I have to take your word for it."

"Not mine. Donny's."

Still, my stomach feels like it's got a Ping-Pong ball ricocheting inside it. This will mean one more person knows about the photos. And only Callie is protected from publication. I'm not.

"You there, Ror?"

"Yeah."

"Are we still on for tonight?"

Tonight. When we destroy what we have. "Did you ask Donny about that? About maybe getting fingerprints?"

"I did, actually. He agrees. It's better to just destroy it. At least the stuff of me."

"You want to keep mine? Get fingerprints?"

"Well, we can't keep the thumb drive because it has both of us on it. But the individual photos . . ."

I sigh. I'm getting sold out. Just because I was a few days older than eighteen at the time. It's perfectly legal for Pat Lamone or anyone else to possess naked photos of me.

What is wrong with this world?

"It's an arbitrary line," Callie says. "I got lucky. I was underage. You weren't."

Again, I'm feeling self-absorbed and selfish. "You hardly got lucky, Callie. I agree with you in theory. We should have the photos of me checked out for fingerprints."

"We won't. We'll destroy it all like we already decided. I know you have a lot on your mind, especially now. Want to talk about anything else?"

I rub my forehead. "You already know everything. Plus, there's stuff going on with the Steel family. It's just . . . I never expected life to get so crazy."

"I know. Neither did I."

"If we can get Pat and Brittany taken care of," I say, "we can help Donny. We can help Brock."

I want to. I want to help Brock.

"I know. Their problems are much bigger than ours."

"Are they?"

"They are."

I take her at her word. She knows what's going on with the Steels, and I don't.

Which makes me feel even worse.

"You know me, Callie. You know I'm not a selfish person."

"Of course you're not."

"So I need to stop thinking about my own problems. Yeah,

I may have gotten pregnant. And yeah, I may have photos of my eighteen-year-old-self splattered across social media."

"First of all," she says, "a baby is something you want. So if that's the case, everything will work out. Second, you're beautiful, Rory. You have nothing to be ashamed of."

"Except my spread-eagled pose."

"Which you were unconscious for. Your eyes are closed. The truth will come out. I promise you. Besides, we don't even know if he has any more pictures. And if he does, whether he's going to splatter them anywhere."

I nod. True enough.

"So tonight," Callie says, "meet me in the parking lot at the courthouse."

No sooner do I end the call than my phone buzzes once more—a number I don't recognize.

"Hello," I say.

"Rory? Rory Pike?" The woman's voice sounds vaguely familiar.

"Yes, this is Rory."

"This is Davey—Davida Haines—from Western Slope Family Planning."

Hmm. Strange that she's calling me. I didn't leave the sperm bank under optimal circumstances.

"How can I help you?" I ask.

"I've been thinking about you since you left the clinic. I want to apologize."

"For what? I should be apologizing to you for walking out in a huff the way I did. It was immature, and I'm sorry."

"I appreciate that," she says, "but I was hard on you as well."

"It's okay, Davey. What you said rang a big bell, which

is why I left the way I did. I didn't want to hear it, but you're right. I haven't given this as much thought as I should."

Not that it matters at this point. I touch my abdomen absently. If Baby Steel is coming, I have to be ready.

"I'm glad there are no hard feelings," she says.

"Not at all."

A pause. Then, "Would you like to have dinner with me sometime?"

Yes, she's bisexual. My radar never fails. Another time? I'd be all over her offer. In fact, it would serve Brock Steel right if I went out with Davey.

"You still there?" Davey asks.

"Yeah. I'm sorry. I was just thinking."

"About what?"

"That I'm flattered," I say.

"Good. Then you're interested?"

"I am. Except…"

"Except what?"

"I'm kind of seeing someone else right now. It's not serious."

Even though I want it to be. Last night, I considered the drunken phone call from Brock a sign—a sign that I shouldn't go off with Dragon. Is it still a sign? I'm wildly attracted to both Dragon and Davey, but the idea of being with anyone other than Brock seems so … *wrong*.

Brock and I are in different places, though—such different places that I'm not sure anything will ever work between us, no matter how much I want it to.

Plus, there's a significant difference between last night and this morning—one I shouldn't ignore.

Dragon was looking for nothing more than a quickie.

Davey is asking me for a date.

And also…who says a date with Davey has to lead to anything? We don't have to end up in the sack—which is definitely where Dragon and I were headed.

"I understand," Davey says.

"You know what? I've only been on two real dates with this guy."

"Guy?"

"Yeah. I'm bisexual. Didn't I mention that at our interview?"

"You did. I'm bisexual as well."

Yup, the radar never fails.

Maybe this is what I've been looking for. Raine and my two significant others before her couldn't handle my bisexuality. If Davey is bisexual herself, she'll understand. She won't constantly be worrying that I'm attracted to men, because she's attracted to men as well.

I clear my throat. "Davey, like I said, I'm flattered. You're very attractive and obviously intelligent and caring, but… Can I think about it?"

"Sure. You have my number."

"I appreciate that. Part of me wants to say yes right now, but I guess…"

"You guess you should talk to this other person? This guy?"

"Yeah, I should."

I need to do some serious thinking, and not just about what I might want with Brock.

About the fact that I may very well be carrying his child, and that changes everything.

"Not a problem," Davey says. "It was nice talking to you again."

"You as well. Bye, Davey."

I end the call and then stroke my abdomen.

Until my phone buzzes yet again.

CHAPTER FORTY-SIX

Brock

I study my father's profile as I sit on the passenger seat of his pickup. Just the two of us, he and I, are driving across the Wyoming border. Donny and Dale were both unavailable, so it's Dad and me.

I wish my cousins were here for backup. I love my father—I do—but I feel like I don't know him anymore.

He's quiet. When my father's quiet, I begin to worry. It means his mind is working. He's thinking. He's thinking about things that I probably don't even know about. Sure, he came clean about some of the stuff, but it's clear.

There's a lot I still don't know.

Finally I speak.

"Tell me. Tell me who tried to kill Mom. And why."

He doesn't answer at first. Instead, he stares at the road in front of us. Driving to Wyoming is driving through a lot of nothing.

Finally, "Your mother had a patient. Her name was Gina. She was Aunt Ruby's cousin."

I widen my eyes.

"Your cousin Gina was named after her. Anyway, she was a patient of your mother's, and she committed suicide."

My jaw drops.

"Except she didn't actually commit suicide. That's what we were told, at first. But the person who took her wanted your mother to believe it, so he kidnapped her and left her to die in a garage, tied up, while a car was running."

I feel sick. My stomach's about to come out my mouth. How did she escape? I want to ask, but the words don't come.

"You know how smart your mother is. She managed to get her wrists untied, got into the car, and backed it through the garage door. She was treated for carbon monoxide poisoning."

Still, I say nothing. My beautiful mother. My brilliant mother. All this happened before I was born.

"Funny," Dad says. "I haven't thought about this in so long. But that's how your brother came to be."

"What?"

"Your mother was kept for several days, and she didn't have her birth control pills with her. So she missed a few days, and when she escaped, and she and I got back together, she got pregnant."

Pregnant.

Before they were married.

With this new knowledge, I feel a kinship with my father I never felt before. A different kind of kinship.

"So I guess you could say that if none of that had happened, we wouldn't have your brother."

Talk about a silver lining. "Look, I get that you love Brad. I do too. But for God's sake, someone tried to kill my mother."

"Yes. So much bad happened to our family during that time. So much we've all tried to bury. To keep it in the past. And when we do think of it, we try to think of something good that came out of it. The good that came out of your mother's kidnapping is your brother."

I pause for a moment. My father's philosophy is not a bad one. Will I look back on what I'm going through someday and see only the good that came out of it?

So far I'm not sure any good has come out of it.

The more we uncover, the more horror we seem to find.

"What you need to remember," Dad says, "is that your mother lived through it. She saved herself. Part of it was luck, of course, but part of it was her own intelligence and shrewdness. She's a clever woman. And I thank God every day that I have her and the two of you boys."

I nod.

"Brock, our family made it through the horror of those years, and we will make it through this. I promise you that."

"How can you make such a promise?"

"Because I will *will* it if I have to. That's how much I love you and your brother. That's how much I love your mother. That's how much I love this entire family. Everything we've done, we've done for family."

Then my father does something completely unexpected.

He laughs.

I turn to look at him, regard his profile once more.

"What the hell is so funny?"

"It's not funny, Brock. Just something that occurred to me, and it made me laugh. The absurdity of it all."

"Okay. You will have to clue me in here because I really don't understand what you're talking about."

"My own father," Dad says. "That was my own father's excuse for so long. For everything he did in his life. He did it for family. For my mother. For his children."

I say nothing. I don't like where this is going.

"And now here I am. Sixty-three years old, and I'm

making the same excuses. We buried all of this for you. For your brother, your cousins. So you wouldn't have to live with the darkness that our family had been through. And I'm laughing because... in the end, it didn't work for my father. Everything he tried to protect my mother from, us from, came barreling into our lives twenty-five years later."

And then I understand.

History is repeating itself.

Now.

The horrors of the past are resurfacing.

And I vow. I vow here and now as I stare at my father, his laughter finally subsiding, that I will never, *never* bury the past again.

"Tell me, then," I say. "Tell me about your father's half brother. The descendants who have come out of the woodwork. Do they have names?"

"Only one so far. The report came in late last night."

"What's the name, then?"

"It's a grandson, or so he says."

"Okay. Has he consented to a DNA test?"

"A DNA test may not be conclusive. We're talking about a half-sibling from two generations ago. Every family has second and third cousins floating around that have no claim to anything."

"It's a start, anyway."

Dad nods.

"What else do you have? Anything?" I ask.

"A last name," Dad says. "Lamone."

CONTINUE THE STEEL BROTHERS SAGA
WITH BOOK TWENTY-THREE

MESSAGE FROM HELEN HARDT

Dear Reader,

Thank you for reading *Smolder*. If you want to find out about my current backlist and future releases, please like my Facebook page and join my mailing list. I often do giveaways. If you're a fan and would like to join my street team to help spread the word about my books, please see the web addresses below. I regularly do awesome giveaways for my street team members.

If you enjoyed the story, please take the time to leave a review on a site like Amazon or Goodreads. I welcome all feedback. I wish you all the best!

Helen

Facebook
Facebook.com/HelenHardt

Newsletter
HelenHardt.com/SignUp

Street Team
Facebook.com/Groups/HardtAndSoul

ALSO BY HELEN HARDT

ACKNOWLEDGMENTS

Are Brock and Rory hot or what? I'm loving this pairing, and I hope you are as well. As I dig back into the original nine books of the series, I'm finding all kinds of loose ends that are making the next generation come alive with storylines! I hope you're enjoying the journey as much as I am.

Huge thanks to the always brilliant team at Waterhouse Press: Jennifer Becker, Audrey Bobak, Haley Boudreaux, Yvonne Ellis, Jesse Kench, Jon Mac, Amber Maxwell, Dave McInerney, Michele Hamner Moore, Chrissie Saunders, Scott Saunders, Kurt Vachon, and Meredith Wild.

Thanks also to the women and men of Hardt and Soul. Your endless and unwavering support keeps me going.

To my family and friends, thank you for your encouragement. Special shout out to Dean—aka Mr. Hardt—and to our amazing sons, Eric and Grant.

Thank you most of all to my readers. Without you, none of this would be possible. I am grateful every day that I'm able to do what I love—write stories for you!

Rory and Brock return in *Flare*, coming soon!

ABOUT THE AUTHOR

#1 *New York Times,* #1 *USA Today,* and #1 *Wall Street Journal* bestselling author Helen Hardt's passion for the written word began with the books her mother read to her at bedtime. She wrote her first story at age six and hasn't stopped since. In addition to being an award-winning author of romantic fiction, she's a mother, an attorney, a black belt in Taekwondo, a grammar geek, an appreciator of fine red wine, and a lover of Ben & Jerry's ice cream. She writes from her home in Colorado, where she lives with her family. Helen loves to hear from readers.

Visit her at HelenHardt.com